ACKNOWLEDGMENTS*

I offer a great many thanks to the following:

To Jesus Christ, God the Father, and the Holy Spirit, one-in-three, three-in-one, the fullness of all good and the absence of evil, the Truth and the Word, the Holiest Most High, in whom I trust for my eternal salvation. The Lord.

To my wife, Jamie, whose support, insight, and encouragement emboldened me during long nights and weekends, and whose faith in the Lord throughout this process has been an example to me and an invaluable asset to the completion of this work.

To those who directly contributed to this text through their feedback and encouragement: both of my parents, my sister Rebecca Shindel, and many brothers in Christ, specifically: Andrew Lindquist, Andrew Pitman,

David Caminiti, David Kibler, Dean McCarthy, Jim Ackermann, Matt Stanbery, and Phil Persing.

To Mark Joseph, for seeing unrefined, undisciplined talent in me as a youth and encouraging me to pursue the creative arts with integrity, discernment, and perseverance.

To the many pastors whose ministries the Lord has used to shape and mold my faith, specifically: Andrew Hudson, Bo Matthews, Bruxy Cavey, Craig Gross, Curt Shenenberger, Francis Chan, Gary W. Belk, Gayle Ryle, Dr. John Piper, Mark Driscoll, and Dr. Timothy Keller.

To storytellers, writers, and creative artists whose insights have given me an understanding of the craft, specifically: Aaron Alicea, Andy Siems, Jason Latshaw, Jeff Saylor, Jess Horsley, John Jansen, Dr. Michael Gonzales, Dr. Paul Buchanan, Scott Derrickson, Sean Gaffney, Dr. Thomas Parham, and Tom Koel.

*Does not imply endorsement of this text or author's worldview by the individuals herein named.

TABLE OF CONTENTS

*Please consult this section for a pronounciation key should any character names prove difficult.

PROLOGUE

The night is young. 10:13 PM. And I am alone at my computer, about to enter a free fall.

The free fall begins with a lie. Always. Every addict knows this, and every addict dreads it—that first lie—the lie that triggers the thought that leads to the action that ends in regret. A lie starts the process. Tonight that lie is simple.

This is your last chance.

What is "this," and what "chance" is the object? That too is simple. "This" is the present, the here and now, while I am alone with the means to sin. The "chance" is the occasion to use said means without fear of interruption or of discovery. The "last" implies that if this opening passes, I may not get another one. Such is the lie, and like any good deception, it is two parts truth and one part falsehood.

The truth is clear: this is a chance. I am in a position to pursue sinful pleasure—to get that thing that my body thinks it needs while my soul is certain that it does not. The falsehood and the crux of the persuasion is that this chance is indeed my "last." I do not accept this and dismiss it. Other occasions will present themselves. Of such a development I am certain, and the lie that this chance is my last is refuted. I have overcome.

Yet the truth lingers and, in so doing, gives the temptation a quarry in my mind. From there it will move its way into my soul and gnaw at my will for the rest of the night.

I have fought against Satan for this area of my life for more than a decade and often failed. Given my record of losses to victories, I must admit that he is relentless and cunning.

Feeble though this attempt may seem, the gauntlet has been tossed, and I have to answer. Refuting the lie was easy but ignoring the truth is not, and I am tired of fighting it. Perhaps this chance is not the last, but it is desirable. I have not fallen into my sin for some time, and this seems an advantageous evening to do so.

I should not have this problem. I am saved by grace, living in love, adoring Christ Jesus and seeking His glory. I should be beyond this, but I am not. Despite the prayers, sermons, and hope of freedom, I am ever accosted by this corrupt call. Once upon a time, it came every day at all waking hours without rest or mercy. Now it rises only at auspicious moments, when the door is closed and the time is ideal.

Over time, the nature of this ongoing fight has produced strategies to combat the challenge. Though I have nothing stopping me now, I have committed to others to whom I will confess later. Thus, while no interruption exists in the present, future discovery will occur; therefore, the option is less attractive than the lie makes it appear.

But the temptation is not gone. The truth and the idea linger, and I know why they remain. This sinful, addictive pleasure has a stronghold in my soul. I know this. Satan knows this. And he uses that knowledge to press his advantage. If he begins with a meager jab, he knows it can be reinforced. Years of embracing evil have scarred me; and in moments of weakness, old wounds can reopen.

I am mixing my metaphors. I need to stop analyzing this and say "no," get up, leave the room, and go to bed.

But it is so hard. Typing an address, pressing a button and letting the snowball roll is easier (until its imminent crash, that is). I am so close to decadence, and I will revel in it.

Yes, surrender is easy, but I do not want to. I cannot quit without a fight.

A fight. That is what this is—a conflict of wills and a test to endure—on the inside, anyway. Out here I am making a simple choice and living with the consequences.

But on nights like this, the fight feels visceral—as if more is at stake than defeating temptation. My soul is being assailed, and I am keeping the invaders at bay. Frankly, I wish I were in that reality rather than facing this internal strife. I wish I could face down my tempters as flesh and strike them with force by unleashing my fury. I wish I could face all the villains who taunt me and make them regret the war they have waged. If this was not a choice of restraint but, rather, open combat upon the field of battle, I would be strong, and they would not forget it.

But such is not the way of things.

This concept, however, may provide an escape—a distraction from the choice at hand. If even for an hour, it could delay the inevitable, and I would rather resist than surrender. Is undertaking such an action so foolish? Am I not at war in my soul? Is not the core of my heart under siege? Perhaps this construct is not so inaccurate. I cannot fight temptation on a tangible plain, but I can focus on how I might do so if I could. I can muse on it, get lost in it, pass time to it. If nothing else, such activity will allay the nagging—that clanging cymbal of the temptation in my mind.

I will envision this war as it may look in my soul, were that a stage and I, a player. How does it look there when I am here, when I feel strapped to this chair but have not fallen? I have a hope. I close my eyes; a breath leaves my lungs.

* * *

And I find myself in another land, standing atop a grassy knoll. In all directions are peaceful pastures, leading to streams of running waters. I can walk at peace, for Christ dwells here—in this "Solsland" that is his by claim, purchased with his blood on Calvary's cross. I am safe where he abides, and though I do not see him, I know he is present. The Holy Spirit is everywhere, in the sound of the brook and the wind on the air. I can breathe his comfort. Here, I am secure.

Where is my enemy? Where is the accuser? I have come to do battle, and he has declined. Perhaps the tempter shall not pursue—not while I am in this haven.

I bend down to the stream to drink, and something strikes the back of my head. My eyes grow dim, but before they close, I glimpse a vague figure in the distance across the stream. I believe it is a lion but cannot be sure. My vision is blurred. Fresh scent leaves my nose. The waters grow quiet. All goes black.

1 : THE OFFER

I awake in a room that feels familiar. A cone of light from overhead divides me from the surrounding darkness. No shackles bind me to my seat, an old and rickety wooden stool, but I consider myself a captive.

The click of a second light and I realize why. I am not alone.

The stout man sits behind a small silver table several feet in front of me. His rose-red lips form a sinister grin that is framed by his round and pale face. A glint of light from overhead reflects off the monocle at his left eye. His crimson suit hugs his obese body, but his matching top hat fits his head to perfection. Upon his belly rests a red tie, at the bottom of which is burning flame that simmers against his charcoal-gray shirt without devouring a single thread. He completes his ensemble with a pair of gloves that appear to have been dyed in blood from a deep wound.

Behind the short table under the shaft of light, he appears immense and overpowering.

As if his presence were not enough, more villains hide in the darkness behind him. At the edge of the light, I see pairs of shoes at the bottom of slacks that disappear above the ankle. Versus the sophisticate alone I stand a chance, versus the reinforcements, never.

But being outnumbered is not what troubles me. I am frightened that I am not surprised. I know this scenario more than I care to admit. And I know what is about to come.

The fat man speaks. "Here we are again. Playing our little game. Wasting our time. You say, 'no'; I say, 'yes.' Back and forth. Minutes spent; hours lost. Here we are. Here we play.

"Or do you think that your mind will escape to 'righteous thoughts'?" Leaning further across the table he asks, "Do you think that I'd let it?

"Face it." He screams, slapping his hand on the slab of metal. "You can resist for an hour, maybe two, but you and I both know how tonight will run its course. We have a history, you and I; and tonight, we have a date with them."

The funnel of light above him goes black, and at my right, an overhead ignites. Below it is a pedestal, lower than my stool. Upon it, *they* stand. Women. Pretty women. Women of various build and race. All are dressed to tease—neither scantily nor modest, and they smile at me with their eyes more than their lips. I look away (though, in part, I do not want to).

The fat man continues from the darkness to their right. "See anything you like?"

I do not respond.

He chuckles. "Thought so. You like them all. You *want* them all."

His small feet shuffle to the edge of the spotlight, and his belly appears within the beam while the rest of his body remains in shadow.

Now the real pitch begins. He speaks not as a cheat but an impeccable salesman—the kind to whom you give your attention and trust. I do not doubt that he has had many buyers (probably how he can afford that suit).

"This is easy," he tells me. "It's so easy. You have nothing to worry about. Anyone you tell will be quick to forgive you, and they won't remember it a week from now. You'll be forgiven. Get your kicks and get on with your life.

"What's worrying you? Wasting time? Is that it? This won't take hours of your life. Look at these faces. You recognize them. You know their names. Type one into that Internet and this whole thing will drive itself. Your evening won't be gone. A couple of minutes and you'll be done—and relieved. So relieved. You know where to look and how to get there. Cut yourself some slack and let it happen. Take ten, have your fun, get your fix, and move on.

"Of course, there's no need to rush. You can take as long as you like. You don't mind getting lost in the labyrinth—that's half the pleasure, after all. You know I'm not lying. I never lie."

I cannot see him, but I hear his deep breath. He savors the scent of my fear and my appetite. I know he has moved from the pedestal of sirens because I cannot see him when my eyes dart their way (despite my attempts to look anywhere else).

"You know I am right," the tempter continues. "I've been right before, and I am just as right now. I will always be right because the fight is not you. Not the *real* you. The real you wants this; the real you craves it, and the real you knows it to be true. Why are you putting yourself through this conflict? Only a fool starves himself when an endless buffet is presented before him. Take a bite.

"You've walked the straight and narrow long enough. No one can say otherwise. The many days when you stood your ground are not lost because of one night when you do not. You own your victories; reward yourself. This is victimless indulgence, nothing more—not hiring a prostitute or engaging another human. You are watching images in motion. No harm in that. None whatsoever. This is your getting a much-deserved release, as you've been thinking you would."

These last words tear through my heart. He is right. I have had such thoughts in the safety of the car or at night while lying awake in my bed. I considered this night an occasion for sin when I would let myself fall because I deserved it. I had said "no" a thousand times; I felt I had a right to say "yes." But this was a lie, a whisper of evil. The right to act wickedly cannot be earned. Since that time I had abandoned that notion and prayed for deliverance to this very day.

The tempter skulks in shadow and watches. The sirens on the podium gaze at me. I try to stare at the rusted floor and study the puddles of stagnant water, but my eyes shoot glances toward their direction, and they manage to catch me every time. Seeing my weakness the villain continues, no longer the salesman or the negotiator.

Now he has become the bully.

"Look at yourself. You are such a hypocrite. You're already in sin—already guilty. Consider whom you're seeing on the pedestal. You must be lusting in your heart. Quit lying to yourself; this fight is done. Might as well embrace the fall while you're here."

He is hidden in the darkness, and I cannot place his face. But his voice is everywhere—at my right ear and my left, at my neck and at my back. Eyes throughout the room are on me; all of them want my surrender. Sirens whisper gentle words that crave attention and response. I will not withstand them all—besides, the pimp is screaming now.

"If you had wanted to avoid this then you wouldn't be here now. Ready. Waiting. Wanting. No. You would've ensured you weren't alone and evicted yourself from solitude. But you didn't. You did not. You stayed here. Here—in private where you could be free, where it's just you and your desperate longings. You can still satisfy them all. Right here. You can do it. Be true to yourself and do it. Be who you are, not who you think you should be."

He has gone from seller to bully to preacher and now become a pleading beggar. The tone of the sad clown reveals his need for my succumbing to his words.

"Won't you be honest with yourself?" He asks me from the looming darkness. "No one else, just yourself. Be real. Tonight. For this one night. You can fight it everywhere else; but now, here, in this place be truthful. Be yourself. Be at peace."

The lone light in the room shines above his table. All has gone quiet. Everything is still. With his back to me, he moves below the beam, reaches into his jacket, and reveals a folded paper. I can see the old creases; it was thrown in the trash. I intended to forget it, but it has been retrieved. Held within the ray of light, the text on it is small but clear.

I can see the words—both names and addresses. They rush to the front of my mind in an instant, the sites where I have been and the names that I have searched. With his left hand the villain wipes a tear from his eye and with his right sets the list onto the stand.

He keeps his back to me and speaks. "You don't need to fight it, not in front of us. We want to give you what you want. No one will be hurt, and you'll forgive yourself. You've done it a thousand times; you can do it once more. And the next time you're alone, you can win. We'll let you have that one, but tonight belongs to us."

He slinks back into his seat, and those behind him step forward. None enter the light, but they establish their presence. The speaker's sweat-stained suit clings to his frame.

"You don't need to suffer," he tells me, "Christ suffered for you. You can live. Free."

These final words do not bode well for him. He invokes my Savior's holy name in order to get me to choose to sin. No. This villain has misplayed his cards. I am incensed at these remarks, and they raise my defenses like a reinforced wall. Years ago that excuse gave him traction, but these days I will have none of it. He has undervalued my love for my Savior and in so doing has sabotaged himself. The scent of my indignation must be odorous to him, for any look of concern on his face has shifted. With grotesque disgust, he stares in my direction.

The fixture above him goes black with a click. The red of his right eye is all I can see.

At the back of the room, his minions appear beneath another cone of light. Decked in their suits with their hats and their spats, I count eight of them, each with a weapon. One wields a knife, another a whip, and a third has a mace or something similar to it. Their boss saw his error and is changing the game.

I know what follows, for it has already happened. On countless evenings before tonight I have been in this same room on this same stool, heard this same pitch, and refused—only to be beaten until I break and accept their generous offer. Latent guilt will return with each punch, and the sum of their blows will destroy my defenses.

Before they reach me and cast the first strike, the gambit of their master works. Though I was resolute at first, his words now fill my mind with shame. Truth be told, he was not wrong. On many nights in the past, I gave myself a license to sin because I felt that grace would increase. Such an admission fills me with guilt for believing the lie and then acting on it. This is the gnawing, deeper guilt—the guilt of the thought plus the act plus the encore (the endless encore, the full addiction). They can see my mind at work, and they know they have an opening. I am too ashamed to fight, and I accept that I will falter.

The light above the tempter ignites. I see his grin. He knows how this works. He has made me an offer, and I will take it to escape the reality of what I feel—shame that drills to the core of my heart and also disables my will to resist.

"No."

I said nothing. Neither did the swine. Nor did the men in the shadows moving toward me. The deep voice came from someone at my back.

"This shall not pass as it once did."

I feel a hand upon my shoulder.

"Not this time," the speaker states.

The light above me illuminates and reveals the new agent to all. He stands behind me and to my right. His dark-skinned face is old and weathered, but his clean-shaven head bears no signs of age. He stares at my accusers and moves ahead to shield my view of the pedestal. His layered robes of golden hues match and complement his eyes. Armored plates of pearl white protect his chest, his back, and limbs. The soldier raises a sword in his hand, and the blade extends for two full yards. The point of it stares the tempter in the face, and the threat of attack holds his gang at bay.

That same look of hatred once cast upon me now grows in animosity toward my aid. The sophisticated mask of the villain is gone, and the visage of a demon emerges before us. His skin is less white but more gray, and fangs protrude from his crimson lips. The monocle falls from his eye to reveal a hole from which worms drop to the table.

I shudder, but the soldier remains unmoved.

"Do you not know, demon, of what has passed?"

"I know but care not."

"You should care, Mokmah. Vile deceiver. For this one is not alone in his struggle. Take account, traitor, of what has occurred: a prayer from a desperate son to his Father for deliverance in these days of temptation."

"Ah yes, the prayer. I am aware of the prayer, but was it heard, messenger? Has the king sent his army?"

"He has. A strong and sturdy battalion, armed for their task and ready for reckoning."

"Then bring it to us."

"We shall, Mokmah. In good time, we shall." As he speaks, the messenger moves in front of me and shifts his hand from my shoulder down my arm. He walks us backward away from my captors but keeps his sword pointed at their leader. Mokmah's eye stays fixed on it, and his minions skulk around him toward us.

"And what until then? Hm?" Mokmah asks. "Should I be afraid of this little one?"

"You shall fear who you have always feared, and he shall rain down upon you all that he sees fit for his glory."

"Well, that may be; but you, dear messenger, will not be alive to see it."

"I disagree."

I hear one of the thugs unsheathe a blade, and the messenger pushes me onto the floor. I can see little, for the room is pitch black less the spotlights that shine over my stool and the table. This messenger sent to my aid moves with speed and wields his sword as an extension of his body. His graceful movement and cunning strikes attest that this mission is not his first. He has performed this dance before now, many times against many enemies.

The goons move in and out of the light, but they are a different breed than their master. Though their bodies possess human form, their featureless faces do not look organic. Their skin bears the look of a dusty, old mirror—filthy, abandoned, unpolished, and useless. If their faces were cleaned and maintained, a beautiful sheen might reflect off of them. As they stand now, they are off-putting ghouls, animated mannequins dressed in fine clothing.

A spray of green blood erupts into the air when the messenger decapitates one of the villains. The headless body drops limp to the floor as another of his comrades is cut down beside him. Despite their numbers and constant assault, the villains cannot land a blow on the messenger. In contrast he strikes with precision and force, and each attack is a killing stroke.

The clash ends in a matter of moments, and the messenger stands within the light. Surrounded by a sea of dead bodies, with his sword held ready and dripping with blood, the warrior appears as a golden statue—a monument to skill and bravery. A few feet away in the middle of the room the blasphemer trembles behind his table.

"Thi—"

Mokmah's final words go unsaid as the warrior slices the demon in two. Cutting from the villain's head to the floor, the length of the blade also chops through the table. The messenger turns from the scene toward me, and both entities he cut crumble in a heap behind him. Across the floor the green blood spreads, and the lights go black without a warning.

Dark fills the room, and time seems to stop.

When the light returns a moment later, I see the layout of the cell. All that remains is my ally and me, plus a strange and heavy emptiness. The table, the bodies, and pedestal are gone, and a lighted ceiling replaces the lamps. A copper-colored metal floor accompanies rusted walls of brown, and the room feels like an old storage locker left to the elements.

I feel ugly being here and search for a door around the room. Embarrassment hits when I find it behind us. What is worse is that it is locked from this side. Had I tried to escape, I would have succeeded; however, I chose to stay in this peril. The messenger says nothing but opens the door, and we move into a narrow hallway.

The surroundings are similar to those in the room. The walls are rusted; the ceiling is low, and the floor is a path of corroded metal. The corridor stretches in the direction opposite us, for our door was at the end of the passage. We walk down the hall but find no exit. The door from which we came waits behind us, but other than it, no entries exist. This environment makes me feel uneasy, and I intend to say so, but the swordsman speaks.

"Are you familiar with this place?"

"I want to say 'no,' but I feel that's a lie."

"Why?"

"Because I feel I've been here countless times, in that room, fighting a fate I couldn't escape."

"Or one you *felt* you could not escape."

"Well, yes."

We reach the dead end of the hallway, but no exit presents itself. The messenger runs his hand along the wall and continues to speak as he inspects it.

"In a way, you are not wrong. You know yourself, and this environ you have formed echoes that which you have experienced—though you have never actually experienced it as such."

"Uh-huh." I can think of nothing else to say.

I am grateful that I have this ally at my side. In this hopeless place, I no longer feel lost, but I remain confused on a particular matter.

"How did you get in here?" I ask the messenger. "How did any one of us get in here? And can we get out the same way we came?"

"No, we cannot."

"Why not?" I ask.

"Because this hallway was not closed before now. The door I entered, the same one we exited, was at the end of a tunnel into which I cut an opening."

"And now it's blocked?"

"Or repaired. Or hidden. This is a place you felt you could not escape, remember?"

I muse on this for a moment when a banging noise begins, first lightly, then loudly and closer to us. I cannot place it, but I think it is coming from the other side of the walls of this passage, from someone (or something) trying to enter.

2 : THE ESCAPE

I see a curved blade cut through the corroded ceiling, carving a circle around one of the fixtures. Once the shape is complete the lamp falls to the ground, and a stream of natural light beams through the opening to the floor. After it an arm appears from the hole and waves to us while a voice from the outside calls, "All glory and praise to him who is worthy."

"For to him is due honor from the first to the last." This response from the messenger is said as a code between them.

An old but spritely white man peeks into the hall and looks at us before releasing a hearty laugh.

"Made it this long, have we?" he asks. "Well then, let our charge be renewed."

"Indeed, old friend," the messenger replies.

"Come, we shall lift you from this wretched dungeon."

"Him first," demands the messenger as he pulls me into the circle of light. "Raise your hands," he tells me, and I comply. Two arms grab mine and pull me from the corridor.

My eyes need a moment to adjust, but once they do, I am overwhelmed. We are in a pasture, and the air is cool. The dwelling in which I was kept was underground, hidden and undetectable from the surface. Unlike the pasture in which I arrived, this one boasts taller blades of grass and overlooks fields of grain. Under the rule and care of Christ, my soul proves a most inviting place, less the villains that I let linger and dark corners in which they hide. I fear that more will show themselves, and the shame within me arises anew.

Storm clouds approach in the sky above us.

This train of thought is interrupted, as one member of a pair of men grabs my shoulder. He is the bearded older one who cut through the ceiling and called to us. His clothing matches the messenger's—layered golden robes under plates of white. In addition, he wears a blue shawl about his neck and a matching sash around his waist. A thin blue band wraps around his head and ties in a knot at the back.

To his right is a younger looking warrior with olive skin and a full, dark beard. He wears three layered, hooded cloaks, one white and one gold underneath the outer purple. His beard is longer than that of the others. They both bear calm, inviting faces and nod at me before lifting their companion.

Once he joins us, the reunion is short. The messenger thanks them, and they give praise to the ruler of this land.

The three turn to me, and the youngest says, "Come, we must go."

Before I take a step, they are ten yards ahead. They squat when they enter the fields of grain and disappear among the stalks. Although I thought we were out of danger, I follow their lead and try to stay low.

The overcast sky grows darker above us, and wisps of wind howl on the air. A storm is coming; my fear returns.

Am I not out of danger? Will worse villains come? What have I not been told? At the edge of the grain we reach rolling hills, covered in giant boulders of gray.

The youngest of the three scouts up the hill while the rest of us wait and I catch my breath. The white elder hands me a canteen of water, and as I drink, the youth returns.

"No enemies on these hills," he tells us. "They may be near but hidden from sight. We should not stop, lest they find and surround us."

"Agreed," says the elder, as he glances to the third. "And once we reach the higher ground, perhaps we can see where the enemy moves."

I still do not know who our enemy is and continue to feel like the weak link in this chain. The bold, black messenger turns and smiles, "Worry not, heir of the kingdom. Though they are many, we are shrewd; and if the king wills it, you will reach The Tabernacle."

"'The Tabernacle'?" I ask.

"That is the name of our quarters."

"A bit on the nose, don't you think?" I say with a chuckle. "Who named it that?"

"You did," he responds.

Of course I did.

By now, the two others have begun their hike, and we follow at a distance a few yards behind them.

"Why do I need to get there?" I ask the messenger.

"That is where your army awaits you."

"Ah, I see." I feign understanding, but they see through it, and the bearded youth turns and presses me on the matter.

"Are you unaware of why you are here?"

I had not thought of it since the cell. Of course I came here for a purpose, and with a moment's thought I renew it.

"To evade temptation."

"See," he responds. "You need not think you do not understand."

"Pause," the white elder begins. "Consider the question. Know the answer and speak."

"And speak in truth," the messenger adds.

I suppose lying to oneself is the same as lying to anyone else, and they are right—a reflective breath and the truth becomes clear: I am here to battle Satan and to avoid falling into sin.

We climb around the mounds of stone until we reach the top of the hill and look out over an arid plain that separates us from a sprawling wood.

"The mountains to the south will not offer passage," says the youth as he views the landscape. "Crossing through the open is perilous, but I fear that it is still the best path."

"Our options are few, and all roads will bring danger," the elder responds as he watches the plain. "If we are not found by a patrol, those in the sky may yet see and reveal us."

"We may make the forest before they arrive."

"They are already here," the elder replies, pointing at bird-like demons circling over the wood. "Our mission is to bring our charge to his lair. If the south is blocked, we will run west until we can turn to a more direct road. If we are seen then a fray might ensue, but that should not keep us from taking the path."

I assume I am the charge about whom they speak, but I am unsure of what that implies. The elder must see the confusion on my face, for he steps toward me and touches my shoulder.

"Why do you wear such a skeptical look? Do you doubt that the Lord has heard and responded?"

"As I told Mokmah," the messenger chimes, "we are here because of your cry."

With a hint of revelation in my voice, I reply with confidence of new understanding. "Psalm 91. The prayer."

"*Your* prayer," The elder confirms.

My prayer.

I remember my prayer.

* * *

A few days ago, I was home and alone, and the oppressive temptation for that evening began. I sat on my bed full of both fear and doubt. How would I make it through the night without failure? I fell prostrate before God and read aloud from multiple Psalms as a prayer for deliverance.

> Have mercy on me, O Lord, for I am weak, O Lord, heal me, for my bones are troubled. … To You, O Lord, I lift up my soul. O my God, I trust in You. Let me not be ashamed; let not my enemies triumph over me. … Turn Yourself to me, and have mercy on me, for I am desolate and afflicted. … Lord, all my desire is before You; and my sighing is not hidden from You. My heart pants, my strength fails me; as for the light of my eyes, it has gone from me. … For I am ready to fall, and my sorrow is continually before me. For I will declare my iniquity; I will be in anguish over my sin. … Deliver me, O Lord, from my enemies; in You I take shelter. Teach me to do Your will, for you are my God; Your Spirit is good. Lead me in the land of uprightness. Revive me, O Lord, for Your name's sake! For Your righteousness' sake bring my soul out of trouble. … For a day in Your courts is better than a thousand. I would rather be a doorkeeper in the house of my God than dwell in the tents of wickedness. … In the multitude of my anxieties within me, Your comforts delight my soul. … I will set nothing wicked before my eyes; I will hate the work of those who fall away; it shall not cling to me.

I then came to Psalm 91. I had copied the text from beginning to end and had received solace from its wonderful words. I read it aloud, changing the 'you's' to 'I's' and 'me's' to 'my's,' transforming the pronouns to make it my own. After the first time, the temptation grew stronger; therefore, I begged again with more zeal:

> He who dwells in the shelter of the Most High will abide in the shadow of the Almighty. I will say to the Lord, 'My refuge and my fortress, my God, in whom I trust!' For it is you who delivers me from the snare of the trapper and from the deadly pestilence. You will cover me with Your pinions, and under Your wings I may seek refuge; Your faithfulness is a shield and bulwark. I will not be afraid of the terror by night, or the arrow that flies by day; of the pestilence that stalks in darkness, or of the destruction that lays waste at noon. A thousand may fall at my side and ten thousand at my right hand, but it shall not approach me. I will only look on with my eyes and see the recompense of the wicked. For I have made the Lord, my refuge, even the Most High, my dwelling place. No evil will befall me, nor will any plague come near my tent. For you will give your angels charge concerning me, to guard me in all my ways. They will bear me up in their hands, that I do not strike my foot against the stone. I will tread upon the lion and cobra, the young lion and the serpent I will trample down. Because I have loved You, therefore You will deliver me; You will set me securely on high, because I have known Your name. I will call upon You, and You will answer me; you will be with me in trouble; you will rescue me and honor me.

> With a long life you will satisfy me and let me see Your salvation.

I questioned my prayer. Should I be changing these words of Holy Scripture? Do I dare taint it with this self-centered turn? I could not answer, but I read it aloud again. I declared before the Lord, "You will charge your angels concerning me, to guard me in all my ways." I was at my breaking point, fragile before the throne of God, pleading, begging, and yearning for deliverance. Throughout that night he granted it. Having been rescued from my sinful desires, I slept in peace with my soul at rest. Such victories are medicine for the addicted. Such deliverance is proof of the Lord's saving work.

* * *

I prayed, and he answered. Now he answers anew. Here, during another desperate evening, the Lord is carrying me through temptation—through the wasteland of my soul, through the hidden rooms and darkened spaces, through unkempt lands awaiting harvest and quarries I have never known. These are his angels, charged for tonight, to see me through to the light of dawn.

The sky is blue again.

This momentary relief is interrupted with a jolt. I am pulled to the ground and hidden behind a stone as the messenger peers at the plain below us.

He points and says, "Our enemies move. See, they are hunting you."

He passes me a telescope, and I hold it to my eye to find a group of soldiers of varying sizes. Adorned in dark armor of shards and spikes, they are eight in number and glare in all directions.

At the front of their party is a mechanized creature, an orb-shaped head full of numerous eyes, red at the iris and pitch at the pupil. They have shutters rather than lids when they blink, and they look as though they are taking photos. This orb is carried on two stilted legs that take slow methodic steps as they walk. Six limp tendrils extend from the orb, dragging along the ground through the soil. Whether this is a means of looking for clues or tracking steps I do not know, but I hate the sight of that first probing thing.

"It is a sycoma," the youngest tells me, "and a cron follows at its heels."

Behind the sycoma, one-third its height, marches an armored, goblin-like being. The features of the cron are hidden beneath his armor, and he skulks unarmed, looking for someone to hurt.

A large and gothic cannon moves after the cron, and two other soldiers—one on each side—ride upon it. Neither appears to be driving the weapon; its own treads propel it forward. Two additional sentries, each wielding a great musket, flank the parade and keep pace with the cannon.

The olive skinned, youngest angel continues. "The four footmen are ra'shrogs, infantry of the fallen legions. You will cross many before your time here ends."

Behind the cannon a mechanical suit strides at twice the height of the soldiers. I cannot discern the driver's facial features through the canopy, but I see his arms making the machinery work. The suit is built for one thing: capture. Its left arm bears a grappling hook and a claw, and each is attached to a spool of wire above and below the shoulder, respectively. The right arm is longer and ends with a vice, but at its shoulders sit multiple muzzles, each one holding a compacted net.

The caboose in this walking train is a different sentry who is larger than the others and carries a spear.

"That tall one is a nefqahan—a demon giant. He guards the machine when it hunts and captures. He will prove formidable, I assure you."

His added assurance is unnecessary. I doubt nothing they have said. The movements of the hunters are crude but powerful, and their armor is discolored, disjointed, and odd. They appear far less disciplined or skilled than my guardians but also more vicious and more unrelenting. Their lack of sophistication makes them no less terrifying, especially when they outnumber us two-to-one—not to mention their possessing a mechanized suit, an enormous cannon, and a giant.

"And these are not the worst of them," the messenger tells me with a solemn pause. "Some other thing moves in search of you. Something worse."

This news does not help. We are outmatched. If today is but a taste of the enemy's presence, how shall I ever hope to overcome? Will he not always find and destroy me? My fear must be evidenced on my face, for the elder member interjects.

"The Lord has purposed to deliver you," he tells me, "and he shall do it."

"Despite knowing he's in power, I am afraid."

"We know," says the youngest. "You wear your anxiety like a crushing weight."

"Don't you see how armed they are?" I ask. "How am I to overcome that? I have no great skill with which to fight them."

"Seeing them weighs heavily, yes; but take courage, man. Do you not see the great joy in your weakness?"

"Joy?"

"Of course. In your weakness, the Lord's glory shines brighter, repelling the darkness from all about you. Or would you prefer to keep it at bay by your own strength? You are as a flickering candle in the crisp air of autumn, but your king, your deliverer, he is the roaring, eternal flame. In your frailty, his power rises, and it can banish the dark from your side."

"Then where is he?"

"He is ever-present by his seal," the youth says, pointing to my chest. I look in my shirt and see a tattoo—no, a brand, a scar—over my heart. A bold emblazoned cross, pointed at the bottom and wreathed with vines, is engraved into my skin. I do not have this mark outside of Solsland, but I am glad to have it here. The sight of it lifts my attitude.

The sun beats overhead, and I feel the heat as we move down the stony hill toward its base. As we do this, the youngest continues to inspire me.

"You should be encouraged, peacemaker. Satan knows the importance of your endeavor. You came to this point expecting to fail but instead you turned to the Lord your God. You sought his deliverance not only to survive but also to minister in the name of Christ. Oh, the joy in the kingdom at the sound of your cry. We are honored to be your charge."

I am proud to hear this—not proud but grateful (okay, maybe a little proud). The Lord heard my cry and moved on my behalf. They are right. I know that if I can survive this darkness, I should have less fear of it in the future. These past few days leading up to the present, I knew I would fail—it was obvious to me. But I did not. Now, if I can rally, if I go through this gauntlet without falling into sin, I will know that I can persevere and also *how* to persevere. This latter notion is powerful in the broken heart of a sinner.

We reach the bottom of the hill after the patrol has passed. Across the plain toward distant trees, they take off like Olympians. The others stay fifty yards ahead of the gracious messenger at my side. I am convinced that my sprint is his jog, and I am embarrassed for both of us.

When we enter the grove, I stumble into a tree and cough while attempting to catch my breath. They freeze and look back to the plain. I could not have been loud enough to expose us, but they must know something that I do not. Perhaps the enemy is not so distant.

The elder nods, and we travel again. In the forest I am louder than I had expected. My difficulty is compounded for this wood is not flat. The angels and I are climbing uphill. Each of my steps rustles through fallen leaves and reveals our position to anyone hunting us. My companions move with stealth and speed, but I have the strides of a lumbering troll.

We exit the tree line and reach a river that runs from the base of a waterfall to the right. Fifty yards to our left the water runs over a ledge. The drop could be forgiving—a height of twenty feet. Of course, it could also be two hundred. Judging by the speed of the current, I would guess the plunge is perilous.

We have to cross by jumping the stones that jut above the water's surface. In search of a path, I survey the rocks and find a few that I believe will work. I look at my companions and direct them to it. Each nods his approval, but the messenger insists that he cross first to ensure it is safe. He prepares to lunge at the first stone but ducks at the sound of a cannon's blast.

The rock is now pebbles at the bottom of the river, and the second shot sends two trees falling toward us. How far the patrol is from our location and how long they have followed, I do not know. Nonetheless, they have us now. The third shot blazes past my head. I look to my companions, who have ducked to the riverbank.

I must have frozen in shock, for I failed to dive for cover. I should be dead.

They motion to me to drop, and I do so. The world moves faster underneath cannon-fire. Blasts of heat and energy fly overhead decimating trees on the opposite bank. The messenger grabs my hand.

"We cannot pass across the river. You must flee over the falls."

My stunned expression must convey my fear, but nonetheless I voice my objection. "No. No. I can't. I—"

"You must. They are here for you. The falls will carry you downriver, and should we fail, you will have escaped. They cannot follow you by water, and climbing down the cliff will take time. You will evade them if you go. Now."

"No. It's too high." I hear footsteps in the trees and piercing calls from overhead.

The intensity in my companion's eyes drowns out everything around us. His grip becomes an iron vice, and he minces no words as he commands, "Trust in your King. He will deliver you. Go."

He releases my hand, rolls away, and signals the others to move. They rise in unison. I spring from the ground. They unsheathe their swords. I sprint to the cliff. Shots fire from the wood. I am at the edge; my eyes look down, and I see the pool below—several stories below. I have already leaped. Falling now.

3 : THE LAMB

The sun sets as I dive from the cliff, and the valley before me lays painted in light. Oranges and yellows of autumn trees augment the hue of the golden dusk. Hypnotized, I forget to fear. I know not how far the pool sits below me, for my attention is fixed on the landscape ahead. The warming orb creeps low in the distance, and the mighty river turns southeast downstream. At both of its banks, deciduous woodland spreads across the valley floor and climbs toward towering mountain walls. I know I am falling, but I feel I am flying, the majesty before me stalling gravity's push.

My toes impact water—a surface hard as marble. My whole body crashes through it. A sharpened cold hits my spine. A surge of pain strikes my limbs. The water is too deep. My ears pop from sudden pressure. I want to be limp, but my shattered arms clamor upward. They are useless. The current fights. I am pulled into the rapids. I forget about needing air. I am tugged, rolled, and crushed. The dark fills my eyes. Heat runs from my frame. Blood leaks from my head.

The river pulls me to its depths, but my face crests its surface. A single thought comes to my mind: feet forward. More follow: grab your wound, stiffen straight, and try to float. I obey. A human plank now on the surface, I gulp at air and feel the wind. A bitter cold rides upon its back. This biting chill cuts at my nose, and the twilight sky does not give warmth. The tide continues ever strong and pulls me over smaller falls. The rush ebbs, and the rapids cease. I have endured, but I dare not move. The calm of the current soothes my form. Finally, I float.

I know not how much time has passed when I feel a stutter in the water. Rings of tide flow away from me—an echo of impact from the shore. Something is coming, and that something is large. What was it that the angels said? 'Something' was in Solsland seeking me. 'Something worse,' they said. I tilt my head to the left and find nothing then shift it right and see a creature.

He skulks within the tree line several yards ahead of me. In the coming night and dense verdure, I can mine some small details. He has a long body that stands firm on four legs, and I recall the vague beast I saw when I arrived. He is closer now and larger than I remember. His unblinking eyes are bright crimson bulbs, and his large jagged teeth resemble shards of dirty glass. A low grumble comes from his gritted mouth as he stands and waits and watches me. His step sent the ripple through the river, and he takes another toward the bank as I float.

His gaze is broken. His eyes dart right, and he turns his head toward the opposite bank. A moment passes before he roars, turns the other direction, and dashes away. His steps are faster and lighter as he leaves. 'Something worse' has fled, but from what?

I turn left to survey the eastern banks and find myself closer to them than I had thought. I must have drifted this way unawares. The air seems warmer, and a light glows on the shore. The current carries me past it, but I grab hold of a root to keep myself from floating further. I look to the illumination, and my heart skips a beat.

On the riverbank in front of the trees, stands a young, unblemished, and radiant lamb. I pull myself from the water's surface and rest upon a heated landing. In the presence of The Lamb, the autumn air has disappeared. I feel the warmth of summer now—calm heat that lingers on the soil as the sun sets in the west. The temperature does not dry me, but it keeps me from the chill. The nearer I step to this magnificent being, the more comfortable I become. Truth be told, the climate change is not in the air but at my core, warming me from my center outward all the way to my fingertips.

I feel compelled to bow to this being, but I know it is a silly thought. Of course, before I can think to do otherwise, I have knelt and lowered my head. I glance upward, and The Lamb takes notice. Our eyes meet, and I cannot look away. His are deep and true and piercing, and I consider a surprising notion: I hope never to part from this being. His presence is a soothing balm; my injuries and dank clothes are but a memory in the glow of his light. I feel I have arrived at my destination and think this journey is complete.

The Lamb, however, disagrees, for he has stepped from the bank and into the forest. Though scarce moonlight makes its way into the wood, The Lamb's wool has a soft luminescence. I can find him easily among the trees. I do not wait for his invitation. I rise to follow. He stops and turns to acknowledge me before continuing on his path.

I use the terms "his path" specifically, for no trodden trails are available to us. This is dense and wild terrain, and while I trip on root and rock, he is sure-footed with every step. Though I make noise that could signal my enemies, I have no fear of attack at the present. While The Lamb leads the way and I abide in his wake, no foe will assail us (of this I am certain).

With this sense of security I forget my plight and muse on my own adoration of this being. I want to grab The Lamb and hold him in my arms. I want to carry him to open pastures, sit under the sun and lose sense of time. I want to bring him food and watch him eat and watch him sleep and wait for his waking. I have an overflowing desire to keep The Lamb forever. I want to speak, to ask him to sing or tell me his name, yet I will never dare do it. These are embarrassing meditations. How foolish am I to think I could feed him, as if he would need anything from me. I feel like a child when thinking these things, but I cannot help but consider them good. I should want to be ever close to this being. I should want to cling to him for my life's sake. I should want to rest in him, cherish and adore him. Certain beauty demands attention, and certain goodness deserves our longing.

This sense of attachment keeps my mind busy as we traverse the forest floor. The land is untamed, but The Lamb moves with grace. For me, however, the trip takes its toll. After some time, I am bruised and short of breath. The exhaustion from all that occurred in the day catches up to me as the night hours pass. I hope for a respite that does not come. This, of course, is my body talking; my spirit wants to follow wherever The Lamb leads.

Thus, I keep my eyes upon him, and my feet find the strength to take their next step. The strides are hard, but The Lamb seems to skip. He does not pause. He does not falter. He leads—and leads with concern. Every few steps he turns his head round to look at me. He does not do this to ensure I follow; I am certain he knows that I do. He turns for me, to remind me of his caring, to meet my eyes with his and reaffirm my confidence.

The steep climb reaches a plateau, and we are much higher than I had anticipated. I can see the falls from where I leaped, and they are lower than where we stand now. Fear at this altitude is palpable, and my knees begin to buckle beneath me. The landing we have reached feels small—more of a ledge than a secure stopping point. Though I hug the side of the mountain, I believe I will slip at any moment. The Lamb stands and waits for me, but I huddle into a fetal position.

I am cold—cold and tired. How did I get here? Why am I doing this? My body is hit by the blowing wind, and I feel it could carry me over the precipice. My head is buried in my hands. My eyes are closed. I do not want to be here.

Now it rains.

It pours.

I open my eyes and glance toward The Lamb through the small slits between my fingers. He looks right into me—neither at me nor through me. His stare is sharp, and it pierces my heart, telling me to keep moving despite my dread. He knows that the fear of the present did not send me to the ground; rather, it was the fear of what is next. I do not know what it is, but I am sure it will challenge me, and I do not want to face it.

I am embarrassed and keep my face covered long after I have come to grips with this breakdown. The Lamb stands in the rain under the darkened sky, knowing that I will rise and follow anew. Were this rain warm and more akin to a shower, I would give it a more symbolic meaning, perhaps like a cleansing or a baptism, but as it falls, the downpour is chilling. Cold streams leak through my clothes to my skin. I am aware this has been a coward's collapse, and I do not feel clean about it at all.

Once I accept this, I breathe and sit upright. The Lamb approaches. He is warm in the torrent. His eyes speak to mine, and I know I am forgiven, but my shame lingers. Refusing my resignation, The Lamb walks to my back and nudges me to rise. I obey.

While the rain continues, we hike a series of switchbacks that overlook the forest from whence we came. The Lamb walks before me to my right side, a barrier between the ledge and my lumbering steps. This course is not long, and this system of trails ends a few hundred yards above the plateau. I find myself standing at another ledge, before a chasm that separates me from a cliff face of stone.

The distance between the drop and the wall is two yards, but the point to which I would leap is sharp rock. Jumping to this surface when dry in daylight would be difficult; jumping to it while wet in darkness is impossible.

The Lamb is on the other side waiting for me.

I look downward into the abyss, and it extends forever into darkness. If I leap and find a grip, my hand will be sliced, and I will have a wound to accompany my climb. If I fail to grasp, I will fall to my death after several collisions on each side of the chasm. Of course, I could turn back and flee from The Lamb, but then my plight would become far worse. This is a no-win scenario, so I focus on my leader.

He pads his foot upon the stone on which he stands and nods to me. I shuffle backward about a yard to get a momentum before I leap. Three strides toward the precipice and I leap into the air, my outstretched arm aiming for The Lamb's foot.

My right hand finds a hold on the rock, and the rest of my body collides with the cliff. Relief from this success lasts a fraction of a second as I search for my footing and a grip for my other hand. I find it, but my victory has come at a cost. I am bleeding from the impact, as I knew I would, and pain shoots into my palm and side. The water continues to flow from the sky. I pause and make myself a promise: I will neither look down nor search for the end; I will look to The Lamb and follow him.

I blink and shake my head side-to-side to clear the raindrops from my eyes. Above me to my left, The Lamb awaits. I extend my arm toward the rock where he stands, keeping a firm grip as I pull myself toward him. The movement is simple, but it taxes my muscles. I will not be able to do this for long (which makes me expect that I will have to).

This process repeats itself. The Lamb takes a leap to a nearby ledge—one that I could not have discovered myself. He looks to me, and I reach toward him, find a grip near his foot, and move beneath it. I take a deep breath to get my bearings, and by the time I exhale, he has reached the next shelf. As much as we climb vertically, we move horizontally, and my arms begin to numb over the course of our journey.

My wounds have bled throughout the ascent and made me both light-headed and weak. I attempt to fix my eyes on The Lamb and fight the urge to glance into the darkness. Desperation seizes me, and I tighten my grip on the jagged stones. They drive into my wounded hands, compounding the pain for the rest of our climb. At least the rain has finally stopped.

The Lamb takes another step upward, and I follow. He moves left, and I do the same. He leaps up, and he is gone. I can see neither his foot nor the ledge to which he moved. Above me are the stars and below me is the abyss. My grip begins to slide, and I suck in a gulp of air.

A few feet above me, The Lamb's head appears. He leans over the edge and puts his hoof on my hand. Illuminated by his light, the ledge is fully visible, and I find a firm grip and pull myself toward it.

I roll away from the cliff and lay my back on solid ground. Blood forms in puddles at my sides. I turn my neck to the left, and I can see the whole valley. The trees have shed their autumn leaves, and a winter forest sits beneath the starlight. Turning to the right, I see a different canyon, shrouded in mist under furious clouds that hang in the air but refuse to rain. Distant beacons lie in the fog. I turn my eyes from the foreboding place before I can grasp any further details. I stare straight upward at a gentle moon that appears larger and closer than I have seen before now. A short smile forms on my face, and I feel a tugging at my collar.

I am being dragged, and I do not fight back. In fact, I do not think I can. I cannot move my legs or arms. I feel their cuts, their bruises, and abrasions, but I cannot move to address any of them. The extent of my wounds, I do not know, but The Lamb has taken hold of my shirt, and he is pulling me away from the ledge.

After he stops and releases me, I look for him to my left then my right. The valleys are now on opposite sides, and I realize I have been turned round. I see him at a puddle formed by the rain, his head tilted toward the water.

Now that I think of it, I am thirsty—and tired. My eyes lose the battle to stay open, and I feel rewarded for letting them close. The pitch black is soothing, and my mind starts to fade. I am forgetting the temptation, the fight, and the journey. I can let my mind wander into deep sleep.

A small, cold splash ignites my senses. My eyes open. My nose sniffs. My lips smack, and my tongue licks. Water—clean water—is in my mouth. From where did it come?

I look to my right where The Lamb last stood, and he is there again, leaning toward the puddle. He scoops a drink and holds it in his mouth, then walks toward me without spilling a drop. I know what is coming before it happens. I lay my head back and open my mouth, trying to be still despite my discomfort. His face over mine, he lets the water drip. Every ounce is sweet medicine. He moves back to the puddle and brings more refreshment, again and again, until I can speak.

"Thank you," is all I can say.

I feel my limbs. I roll onto my side but stop due to the pain and return to my back. My bruises are fresh, and my wounds are many. The Lamb licks a gash on my hand then my arm. His simple gestures clot these cuts, and he moves onto the other injuries. When he finishes, I rise to my knees, face-to-face with my healer. I put my weakened arms around him; he accepts my embrace and shuffles closer. He is warm in the cool of night.

This precious creature came to my aid when the current carried me toward a monster. He stayed before me and directed my path, showing me the way to walk. Because of him, I survived a journey to a place I could not have reached on my own. He saw to my deliverance at the end of my strength and healed me in my brokenness. He is Christ my Savior, and he is the king. I am ashamed I did not realize it until now.

This whole dominion belongs to him, and yet he is here accepting my embrace. The sting of my injuries subsides; the pain of my bruises feels less severe. While clinging to him, I am healed. I lay my head upon his back and savor this experience. Overwhelmed and overjoyed, I pull away to look at him. The journey and all its obstacles have been a small price to pay for this moment.

He directs his eyes upward past my shoulder. I turn toward the same direction. Behind a wall that I had assumed was a cliff, I see a man standing and staring at us. The moonlight silhouettes his form as well as that of the taller man next to him. I rotate as I rise in order to face the two men and find five others alongside them.

The first man lowers a ladder over the wall. I look behind me for The Lamb's approval, but he has vanished. The choice is mine. I know not what to do and fear that they sense my ignorance. The tallest one puts his hand on the wall and calls to me, "All glory and praise to him who is worthy."

As if it were a reflex, I echo the response, "For to him is due honor from the first to the last."

4 : THE TABERNACLE

I climb over the wall and find myself on a balcony. The landing extends the length of the plateau, similar to a porch across the full front of a house. The rock face opposite the short wall over which I climbed is flat until about a dozen feet, at which point it slopes as it ascends. The space is empty, and I see neither a door nor a path leading elsewhere.

The seven wait. Each is dressed in layered robes of white and gold with green stitching at the seams. The first man I saw boasts a bushy, red beard that frames his broad, inviting smile. The taller man carries a more reserved expression, and the moonlight glints off his golden eyes. His white mustache and beard contrast his weathered, slightly darkened skin, and his cropped haircut makes him look like a veteran who has not lost his edge. Given his aura, I assume he is the leader. His whole unit is looking at me, and I feel I should say something, anything.

"You can speak any time," a voice tells me, though none of these angels moved their lips. "Up here, young one."

I look toward the peak of the mountain and see another older gentleman, looking down at me from behind a wall about twenty feet high.

He opens his arms as he continues. "Welcome to The Tabernacle, your haven in this peril. We have been awaiting your arrival, for we are your multitude."

"My multitude?"

"You asked the Father for aid, and he has given it. We are those he has charged to you. Your forty-nine. Seven units of seven servants—here to fight at your side in this effort, to the glory of your Father Most High in heaven."

I glance away from the speaker to the robed men before me. They nod in a simple way that serves as both a greeting and an affirmation of their mission. I understand what he has said, but I do not believe it. My skepticism must show on my face.

"Why do you doubt the answer to your cry?" the speaker asks, pulling my attention back to the peak. "Your Father longs to grant you victory, and he will see you through it if you seek his face and purpose to love him. We are here to aid you in that quest, if you bear it still."

"I do." After all I have experienced thus far, I do not intend to quit this journey.

How I wish The Lamb were here. His presence is soothing when I am overwhelmed, and I certainly feel that way now. He could prod me forward to trust these beings, but instead I am full of anxiety. They can read it on me, and the speaker decides to rescue me from embarrassment.

"Fear not, little child. All will be clear."

He disappears behind the rocks, and I look at the seven warriors. I offer a stupid smirk.

The redhead puts his hand on my shoulder. "You will be fine, son of the Most High. Remember who you are in Christ and what he has called you to do. The rest will fall into place."

By the time he finishes speaking, an opening appears in the cliff. A portion of the rock is pulled aside like the thin front cover to a tent, and I realize that at least part of the rock wall is a facade. The older angel appears from the opening and embraces me, but I am too disheveled to return his kindness. I accept his hug with my arms at my sides.

He pulls away before saying, "Hello, little child. I am Manuel, and these are your humble soldiers, sent by him who delivers you from the snare and sets your foot upon the mountain. We are here in his service, that he may grant you victory. You are his, and you are not alone."

"Thank you," is all I can muster.

Manuel nods. He wears a white robe over linens of the same color with a gold tassel around his waist. Without hesitation, he begins the business of which he spoke.

"The elders and smiths were the first to arrive, and we established this camp upon the mountain. Once we had prepared it, additional allies came, each boasting unique skills for your desperate hour. They are many in number, and in time you may know them all. For the present, however, your meetings shall be brief, for much is to be done."

Much is to be done, but I am exhausted. I hope Manuel remembers this and offers me a break. I doubt he will.

"You are standing in the low lookout, the sole entrance into our lair. From this deck you can view the west from whence you came and examine the east where your enemy lies. As you can see, we keep a unit on watch to assure our foes do not fly upon us."

"Can they do that?" I ask.

"Fly? Oh yes, some of them can. 'Vhulraks' and 'stradains' we call them. You will meet them soon enough. For now, however, let us focus on more pleasant introductions."

"Wait, what about you?"

"About us?"

"Yes. Can you fly?"

"When the mission calls for it, of course, but we were not granted such attributes for this battle. I know not why. Do you?"

"Maybe it would have made things too easy," I jest.

"That may be precisely the reason." Manuel then directs my attention to the others, "These are the exharts. Though they are on watch at present, they will be your trainers here. They are commissioned to draw from you your best and as such will remind you of the cross that you bear. When you feel you cannot take one step further, they will demand that you take two. Their orders are to encourage you as The Comforter does. This is Deron, the head of their unit."

The tall man with a white goatee walks toward me. "I look forward to our time together, son of the Most High."

"Me too."

Manuel tells them we will return later, and I assume full introductions will take place at that time. We move through the doorway from the lookout to the interior, and I find myself in an enormous tent, the center of which is the peak of the mountain. From this pinnacle, the tarp extends, sloping downward in every direction from above a windowed upper room hollowed into the mountain. The tent is not a single open space, however, for we have entered a semi-closed room. The slope of the mountain provides some of the partition, and the rest, including the walls facing outward, is built of logs and clay. The interior walls extend fifteen feet high, after which the room opens toward the vaulted ceiling. This allows those in the upper room to overlook the entire enclave.

The current area in which we stand appears to be a forge. To my left are racks of finished swords above a row of barrels. At the wall ahead lies the door that leads to the next room, and along this wall stand three anvils and several shelves of tools. In the northeast corner, on the slope of the mountain, sit piles of metals, wood, and leather. Several kiln fires line another wall, and their makeshift chimneys extend through the floor; these send the smoke to another part of the mountain, though I know not where. On two tables at the last wall finer elements wait to be used. Several angels with sleeveless shirts work throughout the space.

Manuel gestures to the smiths to speak with us. Unlike the regal angels that I have met, these are covered in filth and soot and have no airs of rank or standing. They do not seem to mind their appearance, and neither do I (but it makes them intimidating in a different way).

Once they form a complete circle around us, they begin taking measurements and gauging my build while Manuel begins his introduction.

"These are the char'rashas, your craftsman, who put up this shelter and craft our arms and armor. They bring great care with the skills they possess. You must be mindful of all they craft for you."

"Kind words, Manuel," says a friendly face, "but we can detail such things to the youth.

"We will fashion you a strong suit and a fine sword to match, but Manuel is correct. We form here what we must. If the blade has extra folds, they are for a purpose. If the hilt bears text, it is to remind. If the bow has two strings, each has a use. When you receive your arms, be assured: they are fit to your task."

"Yes, Arif, thank you," Manuel says before looking at one of the angels who sketches on a tablet. "Cutler, seeing as *you* are in charge of this unit, would you please take a moment and introduce yourself to the charge?"

"Of course," the oldest man of the group says. "But I need another moment here." After taking it, he looks me in the eyes and extends his hand, saying, "'Cutler' you can call me. I am foreman of the forge and its artists. Have you any questions for us?"

"Yes," I reply, not realizing that I had. "Will you let me forge my own sword?"

Cutler looks at me then turns to Manuel, who seems to ask the same question with a raise of his eyebrow. The foreman strokes his chin in thought before looking to an anvil beyond the circle.

"I may, once the arayil and exharts have dealt with you. If they can confirm you are capable, I see no reason to deny your request."

Three members of the team shoot glances at each other, and I see the need to interject.

"Of course, I have neither skill nor knowledge in this field. I'll need the finest smiths of the legion to guide me." All three turn and look at me, and I add, "If they are willing."

They nod, and Manuel smiles at the development.

He and I move north into the next room, and the area is much smaller than the last. A single chair rests next to a table on which a large book and lantern sit. A torch hangs above each of the two entrances—the one that we used and one across from us. The walls are the same height as those of the forge, and the entire eastern wall is the slope of the mountain. I do not hear sound from the other rooms.

"Typically, the new arrivals would be fitted then wait here. The elders would discuss the newcomer's skills and assign his post in the current war. You see, with each new charge comes a different set of obstacles, and countless personalities lead to endless variations. While one may envision a mountainous land, another may find himself in the clouds, and a third may imagine herself in the sea. We are forced to adjust to each setting and the forms that the enemy takes there. Time is needed to determine the manner in which each soldier can best serve. We should not be long when considering your role. Do you mind waiting?"

"No. Of course not." This is an odd development. I would think that the angels would know my place in this, but what do I know of their processes. "May I read?" I ask.

"Yes of course. The book is yours, after all."

Manuel leaves, and I grab the text that waits. A Holy Bible. I am not surprised. If I were trapped on a desert island, this is the one book I would want. I open it hoping to find the Psalms, but most of the pages are blank. I flip a few in either direction and find a random verse here and there, but for the most part the book is empty.

"Shocking, is it not?" a voice asks.

I look up to find three angels, each dressed in a cobalt jumpsuit with white and gold stitching at the seams. They also wear gloves and shin-high shoes, all a dark blue that is distinct from that of the uniforms. Around each man's waist is a brown belt with several pouches attached to it. The angel in the middle is caramel skinned and the men at each of his sides are white. Torchlight bounces off their suits, and these three appear more like superheroes than soldiers.

"Do you like the uniform?" the centered one asks.

"Yeah." I tell him with a smirk (he must have caught me eyeing it).

"As do I," he says with a huge smile. "I am Abdalla of the diakonae. Beside me are Laszlo and Ivan; we are at your service."

"Thank you," I say to him, thinking about the empty Bible as well as how to pronounce that word he just said.

"Vexing you, is it?"

"Yes. How do you say it, 'Dee-oak—'"

"I was speaking of the book."

"Oh. Yeah. I don't get it."

"Yes you do. Take a moment, consider it, and the truth will come to you."

The three pass me and walk toward the forge, when I blurt, "What do the 'dee-oak-and-eye' do?"

"'Dee-ahk-own-eye,'" he says with a smile, "Similar to 'deacon'; and as such, we serve where we are needed. We spent much of the last two days in the wild, gathering details of your enemy's lair to report to the zaquenan. Perhaps we will see you there."

"'The zok-uh-nun'?"

"'Zaw-kweh-non.' The elders. Your war council. Those who have you waiting here with a near-empty Bible in your hands."

"The zaquenan," I say, repeating it correctly for him as well as myself. I then return my attention to the book and raise it. "Abdalla, is this a test?"

"Now if it were and I told you, I would not be doing you a real favor, would I?"

Abdalla and others leave, and I sit alone with the book. I open it once more, and scroll for Psalm 23. It is there:

> The Lord is my shepherd; I shall not want. He maketh me to lie down in green pastures: he leadeth me beside the still waters. He restoreth my soul: he leadeth me in the paths of righteousness for his name's sake. Yea, though I walk through the valley of the shadow of death, I will fear no evil: for thou art with me; thy rod and thy staff they comfort me. Thou preparest a table before me in the presence of mine enemies: thou anointest my head with oil; my cup runneth over. Surely goodness and mercy shall follow me all the days of my life: and I will dwell in the house of the Lord forever.

Psalms 22 and 24 are missing. I flip backward a few pages. Psalm 15 is there, albeit in a different version.

> Lord, who may dwell in your sanctuary? Who may live on your holy hill? He whose walk is blameless and who does what is righteous, who speaks the truth from his heart and has no slander on his tongue, who does his neighbor no wrong and casts no slur on his fellow man, who despises a vile man but honors those who fear the Lord, who keeps his oath even when it hurts, who lends his money without usury and does not accept a bribe against the innocent. He who does these things shall never be shaken.

Of course. Manuel said the book was mine. Abdalla said to think a moment, and the meaning of it would come to me. This was not a test but a testament. This is my Bible—my heart's Bible—the verses I have committed to memory and written on my soul.

This is discouraging.

Flipping through the text, I go through dozens of blank pages in between sparse verses written without context: Proverbs 3:5-6, Isaiah 1:17, Jeremiah 29:11, and a handful of others. This is a lifetime's worth of memorization. I look for Proverbs 6:6. Not there, but I know it. It starts with—um. Um. I snap my fingers for it to come to me, but it does not. I feel ridiculous not knowing.

"Excuse me, little child."

I look up to see a man who has a strong but kind face and skin red as clay. He is dressed like Manuel, in white with a gold tassel at his waist.

"The other zaquenan and I thought you might want this. They may be deliberating for more time than expected." He hands me a pencil and a knife with which to sharpen it.

"Thank you," I respond. "Please, sit for a moment."

"Do you not want to be alone?"

"No. I am ashamed of myself at present, and I don't like to be alone at such times."

"Yes, but those are the times in which we are forced to be honest. I do not think my staying would be in your best interest."

"No, I guess it wouldn't. Before you go, though, may I have your name?"

"You are delaying my exit for the wrong reason, little child, but I shall oblige you nonetheless. I am Viho of the zaquenan, and I must return to session."

With that Viho leaves me with the near-empty text, and I take the pencil to the page. Proverbs 6:6. This is stupid. I should know this. "Do … thou shalt … not … foolish." Ugh. I let out a deep sigh. I close my eyes. This cannot be that hard. I know this verse. We memorized it in high school because—because of the sluggard. Yes, as any other high school boy might have done, we memorized this verse for one simple reason: "sluggard" is a funny word. Proverbs 6:6.

> Go to the ant, O Sluggard, Observe her ways
> and be wise,

Ha. I remember. I knew it. I knew it the whole time, and I know others. I can go back to the beginning. Genesis 1:1-2, two of the most poetic verses in all of Scripture. They are there:

> In the beginning God created the heavens and the earth. The earth was formless and void, and darkness was over the surface of the deep, and the Spirit of God was moving over the surface of the waters.

I cut to the end. Revelation. I do not recall the exact reference, but I know the text:

> Surely I come quickly. Amen.
> Even so, come, Lord Jesus.

I know more. Somewhere buried deep down I know more—the Beatitudes of Matthew 5, the so-called "love chapter" in First Corinthians. They are in me, beneath the surface. I need to find them. I must remember.

Time passes; I write, jumping from one book to another—Romans 3:23 and 6:23, Psalm 9:10 and 34:15, Exodus 14:4, Ephesians 4:32, Micah 6:8, and John 11:35 (though I feel that one is a cheat). I dig for passages I forgot I knew—I start with a phrase and the rest follows thereafter.

> In the beginning was the Word … And the Word was with God, and the Word was God. He was in the beginning with God. All things were made through him, and without him

> was not any thing made that was made. In him was life, and the life was the light of men. The light shines in the darkness, and the darkness has not overcome it.

I stop writing the references and let the lead run. As time passes, the tip dulls, but I use the knife to sharpen it anew. A dozen translations from different eras of my life get mixed in a blender, but Scripture finds its way onto the page. Phrases ignite passages that raise context that points to content. The mind at work is a beautiful thing, and the verses etched within my heart weave an elegant, flowing tapestry of gospel.

I have buried these truths under song lyrics and jokes. I have displaced them from my mind with a pop culture encyclopedia. These vibrant, living words have been lost below the clutter of numbing trivialities—like a love letter forgotten under a stack of newspaper advertisements.

New shame hits now, and it cuts deeper than the addiction, for it is the idolatry I did not know existed. Regardless of this night's course, I have one new task ahead—getting this book filled and positioned with honor, its contents readily available and easy to access.

"It is time," Manuel says.

Startled, I look up and find him at the door. He smiles and gestures to walk with him.

"You have been busy," he observes.

"Not busy enough."

The next room is not the chamber of the elders. This is a wide area, and the mountain slope sits to my right and covers a great amount of the room. The remaining walls are lined with cots. Bodies occupy three of the beds, but sheets are over two of them. Over the third stand several angels in purple, and all turn to us. Manuel nods, and they resume their attention on the one in the bed as we move across the room through the other door.

"Medical ward?"

"Yes, little child. We will return here soon."

We are now in the first hallway of The Tabernacle, and it is intimidating, narrow, and short. The walls extend to the top of the lair and create a jarring, enclosed effect. A single torch is hung on the northern wall, and opposite it, steps built into the mountain's slope lead up to a doorway.

"A moment, before we enter," Manuel says.

I pause, and I can feel the beads of sweat form on my forehead.

"The elders do not reach their decisions lightly. We assign tasks in the manner we deem most appropriate. You may feel this unfair or unwise, but you must be mindful and able to listen. A time may come to protest, but it is not now. Do you understand?"

"Yes."

"Then follow me."

We walk up the stairs into a hollowed cave in the mountain. Windows are cut into the rock, allowing one to overlook each room of the lair. The elder's space is full of clutter, and a ladder stands in the southwestern corner. Above it is an opening that I assume leads to the deck on which Manuel first appeared. Below the windows along the walls are shelves of scrolls and sheets of parchment. A large wooden table sits at the center, covered in maps, drawings, and notes. Around it are seven wooden chairs, six of which are taken by elders in discussion. Their activity comes to a halt when we enter, and each of them looks at me.

"Ah, here he is," an aged and pale angel observes from the furthest side of the table. "So, little child, how do we wage this war?"

The question catches me off guard, and I look to Manuel to confirm I should answer. He touches my arm and addresses the elder, "We will discuss such things, in time, Alden. First, I will introduce him to his other forces and, of course, take him to visit our brother in the ward. Strategies will have to wait."

"Strategies?" I interject. "I'll be planning our strategies?"

All six stare at me, and pale Alden leans toward us, "Are you not fit to such a task?"

"I—" Pause. I take a moment and know the answer. "Perhaps in time."

"Well, that is your assignment. Be mindful of it on your tour." He returns to his maps on the table before closing, "That will be all for now. We shall see you soon."

And that is that. My introduction to the elders, and they made me our key strategist—I do not know who does that in a real army, let alone how I should do it here.

"Come," Manuel says, "you have more to see."

We descend the stairs and pass through the small hallway into a room larger than the medical ward. Six angels await us, and each wears a white top that is sleeveless and matches their loose-fitting pants. At their wrists are gauntlets of unpolished gold with pearl trimming and rounded edges. Five of them hold a wooden sword in hand, and the sixth stands with a bow and quiver of arrows. He wears a blue sash and carries himself in a different manner than the other five.

They look at Manuel, who gestures in return. They nod, and the first five walk toward the room's northeast corner. The archer however moves to the southwest side and climbs the slope of the mountain that extends into the space.

In moments they begin. The five men charge the archer who fires his arrows, that I now realize are blunted. His speed is extraordinary, but the attackers block his shots, using their wooden blades to parry the shafts away. Two of them are hit, but the other three move closer. Using his bow as a staff, the archer fends off an attacker and escapes from the slope onto the floor. In a single movement he lands and rolls toward one of his fired arrows, picks it up, and fires it again. Another of the attackers is too slow to block it, and their number goes to two. The archer darts toward another shaft, grabs it and fires, but it is deflected. A ready attacker stands over the bowman, but the shooter rolls toward a fallen arrow. He lets it fly—and then there was one. The final swordsman, who wears a black patch over his eye, gets behind the archer and hits him with the wooden blade. The noble defender closes his eyes, defeated.

He then speaks to the one who struck him, "Well played, Klahan."

"You did not mind your sides, Tarak. You dash forward and forget that all beside you moves to your back."

Tarak, the archer, nods.

"Shall we go again?" Klahan asks.

"In a moment," Manuel says, drawing their attention. "My friends, this is our charge."

I make that stupid smirk again.

"And these are your offensive warriors, the arayil. Oh, except for the archer, he is not of their number—he is an amunamai, one of your guards."

"Oh," I blurt, somewhat disoriented by the two words I have heard and cannot pronounce. Knowing these angels will be at my side adds a sense of security. My thoughts shift, however, when I realize something—only five offensive warriors are here. Seven should have been assigned, according to what I was told.

"Manuel, where are the other two warriors? Shouldn't there be seven?"

"Yes," the one named Klahan says, "there should. Yet two of our number are not among us but lay fallen in the medical ward, for you." He tosses his training blade to the ground.

"That is not your concern at present," Manuel assures me. "Typically, the arayil would run you through a gauntlet and report back to the exharts of your skill, but we are pressed for time; therefore, we will keep moving."

Manuel leads me out of the room toward the doorway in the south wall, but before we exit I turn round and address the warriors.

"I'm sorry for all that has happened to your brothers on my account. You should know that they were a source of not only liberation but also comfort. You're right to question my worth. I hope that in time I'll give you an answer."

Tarak follows behind me as we leave, and I hear them talking amongst themselves.

Manuel sees my anxiety and comforts me. "Pay them no undue stress, little child. They will come to know your value."

I do not respond.

We are in the next room, and the walls of lumber are covered from floor to ceiling with shelves of helmets, armor, robes, and belts. The slope of the mountain at the corner to my right is sanded to create intermittent decks, on which sit unlabeled barrels. An elevated landing sits in the middle of the room, surrounded by racks of swords and scabbards. Upon it are barrels of arrows and bows.

Six angels in golden robes take inventory. They pull blades that need sharpening, record the contents in barrels, and make a count of supplies, parts of armor, and arrows.

Manuel calls to them, "Child in peril."

Without a moment's hesitation, each of them rushes to us. Tarak joins their ranks, and they are grouped in an arch cresting away from me.

"You should see them move in battle," Manuel says, before clearing his throat and addressing the soldiers.

"Amunamai, what is your purpose?"

In unison they respond, "To keep safe him whom the King has chosen."

"To what end?"

"To the glory of him who is worthy and true."

"And by what means?"

"By all that are necessary, even unto exile."

"Meet your charge, that you may defend him well."

Their eyes focus on me alone, and they each bear the same pair of golden irises.

A tall, bold member of their ranks steps forward. He has dreadlocks held together by a thick gold band and places his large hand on my shoulder as he speaks.

"I am Alexavier of the amunamai, and I speak for all. We are as your shield, child of God, as you fight for the Lord's glory to the praise of his holy name. Be strong and of most excellent courage, for he can deliver you."

"Thank you, Alexavier," Manuel says. "Amunamai dismissed."

Manuel guides me through a doorway into the forge, and we exit through the covering by which we first entered. The chill of night hits me and sends a shiver down my spine.

In this quiet moment, a pressing question stirs in me, and I ask it before considering its timing or tone. "Where are the rest of the angels, Manuel?"

"You are astute, little child; a few are missing from our number. They are on task. Four of the diakonae departed two nights prior to gain intelligence regarding the foe, yet they have been delayed past their appointed return. Thus, we sent three healers at this time yesterday to find them, but they too have not returned to us. Seven now have been lost without answer, and the final three of your scouts left this night to search."

Manuel looks to the east where the mist hangs low in the valley. The beacons in the distance tease of life at work.

"Come," he says, "a small bit of refreshment may do you a great deal of good."

"May I return to the ward to see the survivor?"

"Soon. Oblige me first, then I shall take you."

I obey and follow him back to the room of waiting, wherein Klahan and two other arayil stand huddled around my heart's Holy Bible. A table has been prepared for me in the corner. Manuel leaves, but the soldiers do not look up from the book. I sit in silence, left to my thoughts, when I realize how convicting this situation has become.

Is it really this way? Are so many necessary that one might not sin?

I get lost in these types of questions for a period of time I do not track. My eyes grow heavy, and I consider how long it has been since I slept. Or ate.

Manuel returns with a plate of bread, various cheeses, fruits, and nuts. They know me well, for all my favorites are provided, along with a brimming pitcher of water.

I do not take long eating, and after I finish, a refreshed and content look must be on my face, for Manuel walks toward me with a smile.

"See," he says, taking the empty plate, "a great deal of good. Now, let us visit the ward."

5 : THE SURVIVOR

Returning to the medical ward proves difficult for me. Here lay the martyrs of my war. These warriors experienced pain on my account, and such truth fills me with a new level of unease. I am humbled by their actions but grieved by the loss. When I enter, three physicians in purple approach us with honest but forced smiles, and the first puts his hands on my shoulder before speaking.

"To lose two brothers in a single eve is not the hope of any healer, but they were glad in their sacrifice. Take heart, peacemaker. Casualties are the imminent children of war. Should you win the day, they will yet rejoice.

"I am Clement, head of the rahfaad, who are your healers. Behind me are Gakuto, most knowledgeable of our kin, and Evan, the most compassionate. The others of our number you shall meet at a later time, less our seventh, who awaits you at his bed. We look forward to further serving you and your legion, but we shall now retire to the room of waiting. We must rest until we are needed anew, for I am assured our task will be great."

I move toward the bed, and the youngest of my rescuers looks to me. He has a white patch over his left eye, and the cut behind it reaches from his forehead to his chin. His once regal robes are intact but shredded, and he wears numerous bandages beneath them. When he rises to greet me, I urge him to stay seated. His name is Jadon.

I ask him about the pain, but he downplays it.

He takes my hand in his and looks into my eyes, "You were right to flee at our behest, peacemaker. Make no mistake on that. Having you there may have hindered us, as your safety would have been our goal. In your absence, our minds were focused on the fray. We excelled in this manner, and in the end, there was little you might have done had you stayed."

"I could have fought with you."

"We brought you neither blade nor bow. How would you have waged war on them?"

"I—I don't know."

"Nor should you."

I take a moment to reflect on his words, and I ask the painful question, "Tell me, Jadon, who were the two that fought at your side—the bald one who came to my aid in the cellar and the aged one who also crossed the plains?"

"Your original messenger was Adofo, and the other with us was Gavrill. Both were assigned as arayil, and both were fit to the task. Adofo is known throughout our ranks as one who brings about the ruin of evil. The devils fear him, and his fall will be celebrated in the their halls tonight."

"I am sorry for it."

"As am I, but it was no fool's errand for which he fell, and he was not alone in his banishment from this world. Many of hell's minions were exiled in his time here. And I understand that you will soon be telling us how to slay more. Perhaps all." He grips my hand and smiles. "Since you are not yet called elsewhere and we have a moment to speak, allow me to tell you of what passed at the river. It may be of assistance in planning your attack."

I can sense Jadon's grief as he continues speaking. "After the third cannon blast, we knew your time to fight had not come, thus we exhorted you to flee. To our relief you did so, and our need to rise was at hand. As you leaped over the falls we made our way into the wood.

"Simple was our first attack, for the sycoma led in front. He looked about with his great red eyes, trying to find you through the trees, but Adofo cut the machine's stilted legs, dropping the eye to the floor. The tendrils stemming from the sycoma's hind reached for my brother to no avail, for behind Adofo came Gavrill, who took his blade to the largest eye of the villain. In an instant all its pupils turned to black, and the first of our enemies was dead.

"The second to fall was the cron, the small one who seemed to lead their march, and it was I who wrought his undoing. I came upon him, and he jumped at me, but I moved from his path and struck him at his head with the hilt of my blade. When he fell to the ground, I severed his skull. Two were dead, and six remained.

"Our blades were now set against larger villains. Do you recall the armored ra'shrogs? Two were on the cannon, and two were at its sides. The odds were fair at four to three, and the others wasted no time when attacking them. Adofo leaped left upon the first rider while

Gavrill dodged fire from the sentry walking at the right. I saw the second rider, who Adofo had yet to reach, aiming his own rifle at Gavrill. I threw my blade toward the shooter and watched it pierce him at the shoulder. As he fell, Adofo appeared from atop the cannon, having killed his challenger. He picked up my blade and threw it into the back of the sentry who had stalled Gavrill. Adofo then tossed his sword to me, as I was reaching the ra'shrog at the left. Once I had Adofo's blade in hand, I ducked beneath the enemy's fire, and with a swift stroke I severed my foe's body. Gavrill tossed his own blade to Adofo and grabbed mine from the back of the fallen sentry. We moved toward the back of the patrol, Adofo slashing the cannon to pieces on his way. And now the number of fallen villains was six, and three of us outnumbered their two.

"But alas, their leader sat inside that suit—such a cowardly means of fighting they use—and now before him stood his largest minion, the nefqahan, lesser giant of the demons. The spear he held was no mere staff but a rifle, for at its end was a muzzle from which he fired darts. One of these met Adofo at his side and cast my brother to the floor of the wood. Gavrill came upon the nefqahan and thrust his blade thrice at the giant. No hit rang true, and with his vicious weapon the demon dealt his own strike upon the sword in Gavrill's hands, shattering it.

By this time, I had arrived at the fray and used the blade of Adofo to cut the rifle in two. In response, the nefqahan kicked me backward into a tree, and I dropped Adofo's blade when he struck. Taking up the fallen sword, Gavrill cut the giant's leg at his knee. Dropping the demon to the ground, my brother grabbed him by the head, and wrung it in a full circle, snapping the giant's spine at the neck.

"Gavrill stood breathless when the patrol's leader fired. But the target was missed, for I had regained myself and pushed Gavrill away as the weapon cut past my face and through my right arm. I dropped, and the leg of the mechanized suit rose to crush me, but Adofo, refusing to surrender to death, grabbed my cloak and pulled me from the path of the falling foot. Gavrill now re-appeared and dragged us both along the forest floor around to the cannon's front, to hide us from the foe.

"'Can you rise and run?' he asked us.

"We both claimed to be able, and Gavrill led our flight. We fled from the cannon back toward the river. The suit pursued.

"When we exited the tree line Gavrill tossed us our blades—to Adofo his original sword and to me a shortened, broken blade. Gavrill then raised his scimitar and nodded to us to reform the line. We did so at the river's edge, and awaited our enemy's emergence from the wood.

"Before seeing him, his javelins, nets and a bola shot toward us from the trees. It was not until these were passed that he emerged. Seeing that Gavrill was uninjured, the driver focused his first assault on him and extended his right arm with the vice closed, creating a metallic fist. Gavrill dodged the first attack, but the second knocked him backward against a stone by the riverbed. Adofo stood in utter horror as the driver then used his left-armed claw to grab Gavrill's body as a trophy. Filled with rage, Adofo charged the suit with all his remaining strength. He ran to the back of it and climbed toward the top while the driver turned his attention toward me.

"His focus set on making my end, the driver was unaware of the wounded Adofo, who had since begun to slash at the suit's gear-made organs. In time the machine failed its driver and merely stood as a statue. Adofo then came to its canopy and smashed it until cracks covered its surface. The driver opened the hatch in hopes of retreat, but instead met Gavrill's scimitar, which I had since grabbed and thrown from afar.

"Adofo was unsatisfied, however, and kicked through the opened canopy window to strike the back of the driver's head, knocking him from the cockpit onto the riverbank. Adofo then leaped from the enemy's machine and grabbed the villain at his collar. The demon had a head of soiled silver with two red embers for his eyes. He wore a daunting red crimson tunic as if he were regal or of high rank.

"Adofo stood over him and yelled, 'Shame of the host. You have chosen most ill in all your ways. Now I send you back to the pit from whence you climbed, assuring you thus: your stronghold will fall.'

"The demon laughed and taunted in response, 'but your hand shall not be its undoing.'

"It was here Adofo fell, for The Beast appeared from an unseen shadow and thrust his entire form on the messenger. He tore at my brother with savage teeth, even as the driver gave out its last breath.

"This left The Beast and I alone. The villain stared at me, and I feared him. He then grabbed Adofo's head in his teeth, and twisted his neck as Gavrill had done to the giant. I flinched, and the moment I allowed was too much, for he was then upon me with his paw poised to strike. I noticed blood fell from his talons, having sliced me from my head to my neck.

"A strange thing happened then that I did not expect. The Beast fled. No roar, no attack—as if Adofo's end was a warning to me. The Beast simply sped away."

"Who is he?" I ask.

"The Beast?"

"Yes."

"Do you not know? He is your adversary. He moves without rest and seeks to destroy. Though he cannot have the elect, he yearns for their failure, for they are the hands of the Lord on earth. He seeks to break you and end your work, that no others would be rescued from his grip. He has entered this war to hunt you, for he knows that if he can break you tonight, the fall will wound you for years to come."

"Satan is The Beast?"

"Yes, Satan himself. He takes many forms in his attempts to devour, and in your plight he bears the guise of a lion. But being as he is, fallen and shiftless, he is not the beautiful creature known by men. No, the evil one has crimson eyes and skin of gray; his mane is peppered with embers and ash. He bears long scars along both his sides, revealing to all where his wings once sat. His teeth have come to shards of glass, and his paws have grown to sharpened talons. His tail is gone, but his speed is swift, and his assaults are cruel and vicious. Strange it is, that he allowed me to live, and I must tell you, peacemaker, that you cannot defeat him—not on your strongest day and on his weakest. He is far too great an adversary for any man.

"Now where was I? Oh yes. Bereft of strength, I fell to my knees over the body of my fallen comrades. I sat for a few moments considering the fray before hoisting their bodies upon my shoulders, one on either side. Such was my journey to The Tabernacle until the exharts saw me in the distance and came to my aid.

“That was several hours ago.

“When we arrived, I was well exhausted but not in harm of death; thus, Clement turned his mind to Gavrill, whom my fellow healers believed might live. Gakuto and Clem spent much time on Gavrill, but the valiant arayil knew his end was at hand. Thus, Evan sat and comforted him before he passed from life in this place. I was then attended and have since been on the mend.”

Jadon sits upon the bed and rests his head upon his hand. I sit in silence beside him for a moment, watching as his lips move without releasing a hint of sound. He finishes his musing and looks at me with a smile at his lips and a tear in his eye.

“I have lived and they have passed—two warriors of greater stature than I.”

“No, Jadon. No.” It is all I can say at first, but my mind catches up to my heart as I continue. “You remain because God ordained that you remain. If the others have died, it is because the—”

“Clear the beds!” Clement commands.

Jadon and I rise from our seats to find the head rahfaad and Gakuto carrying in a body of an angel I have not seen until now. Evan and the exhart leader Deron follow with another unknown to me. Behind them are four more exharts, each pair carrying another body—the last I recognize, Laszlo of the diakonae. Abdalla and another angel I do not know enter last.

Clement looks at the first of the fallen, a diakonae based on his outfit. “Toby. Toby.” The rahfaad begs. “Come now, you cannot have passed so soon? Answer,

Toby." He puts his hand on the angel's eyes and pauses. "He is gone."

Abdalla slams his fist into the threshold.

Evan turns to the three at the door, "Makaio, please, tend to him."

Makaio, the large but fit diakonae who entered with Abdalla, touches the other's arm and ushers him from the ward into the room of waiting.

"Curse this evil," Clement says as he moves from the body in the second bed. Gakuto looks down at it, but Clement stops him, "Bother not, my friend, he too is fallen. Come, help me here."

Gakuto obliges and the two now stand over the third bed and body thereon.

"Here is hope at last. Dashawn, Hear me. Noble diakonae, stay with us." Clement turns to the other rahfaad. "Evan, see to Laszlo."

Evan moves beside the fourth bed and places his hand on the closed eyes of Laszlo. After a moment the compassionate rahfaad shakes his head.

"Then to Dashawn falls our full attention," Clement replies.

Evan covers Laszlo's body with a sheet and looks to the rest of us. "Now, please, brothers, allow us to work."

The exharts who helped carry the bodies leave the room with their heads held low.

Jadon grabs me by the arm. "You also should leave. I will aid my kin in this hour but such is not your task. Wait with the others."

I go into the room of waiting and find it packed with many soldiers. Abdalla's eyes meet my own as he rushes toward me.

With a hug he holds me saying, "Servant of Christ Jesus, do not fear. Not all are fallen in this fray." He pulls away, his eyes drenched with tears. "We will stand together, firm in our resolve to keep you from the evil one."

He pulls away from me and looks to Makaio. "Come," he tells him, "we have reports to prepare."

"Wait." I beg them. "What has happened?"

"Much there is to tell. But later."

"No." I command, then softening I ask, "Please, Abdalla, tell me now."

"I cannot. For the tale is too grim in this present sorrow."

"I have heard much that is grim."

"Not this. Not yet."

With such words Abdalla and Makaio leave, and I stand with an assembly of five exharts. The angel with the red beard is among them, but his prior smile has been shattered to numbness.

"Did he tell you anything?" I ask.

"He did," he replies, staring to nowhere, before turning to face me so that our eyes meet. "He told us The Beast saw them flee from the shadowed valley toward the mountain."

"What does that mean?"

"It means he knows where The Tabernacle rests. And he will come for you."

6 : THE STRONGHOLD

The exhart stops speaking when Manuel enters. The elder's expression is resolute despite the recent, gruesome events.

"Come, little child, your council awaits."

The Beast could be here at any moment, and I am en route to a committee meeting.

Manuel leads me from the room of waiting back to the elders' chamber, but once we enter he passes the others and moves to the ladder in the southwest corner. We ascend it, and in moments I am overlooking the plains of Solsland. The wintered valley lies in the west, and the moon sits overhead. The east remains shrouded in mystery and haze, and many lights dance in the distance.

Manuel gives me a telescope and asks, "What do you see, little child?"

"I see life moving within a dark cloud."

"You do not see life but living death. Raise the tool to your eye."

I oblige him.

"Now, what do you see?"

"A most frightening thing."

"Tell me."

"I see a statue of burning ember, lighting and dimming at its chest as if it breathes. It is enormous, and all around it sits scaffolding, upon which climb many foul things. The statue extends from a citadel, a thick rock fortress of jagged stone. Flying creatures hover all around it."

"Look to the north and tell me more."

"The haze is thick. Full. At its surface I see the top of a globe and near it a great building extending north to south; it seems to extend forever, Manuel, and upon it moves a horde of men."

"Demons, little child, not men. Sentries. What else in the north?"

"I see ruins. A fallen city. Ravaged rooftops jutting through a sea of fog."

"Excellent," he says. "You know where the enemy lies, just as he knows where you do. You can now attend to the council at ease."

"Don't you think he will come for me?"

"Yes, but he has many forces yet to spare, and who knows what pawns he will send before coming. For the moment, however, you must put such fear behind you and focus on the task at hand."

Manuel leads me back into the war room. The zaquenan sit around the table, their fingers interlaced as though we have kept them waiting.

"I believe that full introductions are now in order."

Around the table, in clockwise order, sit six elders: Agyei, who has a weathered body but a zealous spirit; Alden, who addressed me when we entered earlier; Cato, Gyan and Si, all of whom nod in muted respect; and Viho, who brought me the pencil.

Alden wastes no time. "So, little child, you have seen it—the foul fortress of the evil one, standing here in the Kingdom of the Most High by your permission."

"Alden," Manuel interjects.

"No," he replies. "The youth must face the truth, Manuel. You have been kind until the present, but we must speak freely. The Beast knows our location. At any moment, he could strike; therefore, the time to be vague has passed.

"Now, little child—"

"I am not a child." I yell to the elder. "I am not ignorant. I know that this battle is the result of my choices. I know I let sin linger when I should have cast it away. And I know that matters are worse now due to all of my failures. Is that what you want acknowledged, elder? Is that what you want me to say? Then be satisfied."

I have the attention of them all, and I can see that Manuel is taken aback by this outburst.

"Forgive me, I—I just—I look to the enemy, and I cower to the center of my heart. Because I know—I know it took over a decade for that fortress to be built, with that monument to evil sitting at its roof, and I do not know how I shall stand against it, not tonight or any other. Fear drives me to rage, as it does many men. I am truly sorry for such disrespect. I ask your pardon, please."

Alden sits and stares. Agyei holds his hand at his mouth in thought. The others have similar responses, less Viho, who nods then turns to the other elders.

"He is ready," Viho says, before extending his arm to offer me Manuel's seat. I look to my guide who re-affirms the invitation, and I sit in his chair.

Viho takes my hand in his and looks deep into my eyes. "You have passion, which is good, and also meekness, which is better. If you can bind the two and keep them properly, you will be wise and a worker of fine deeds. Be mindful of this." He then squeezes my hand and nods before releasing it.

"Call the diakonae," Alden tells Manuel, who leaves the room to do so.

Given the brief respite, Viho leans over to me, "Oh, and also, 'little children' is what John called believers in his first epistle. It is not said with disrespect, and all of us use it. Consider its meaning before taking such injury."

I am reminded of my thoughts while following The Lamb—childlike thoughts of wonder. I feel even more embarrassed for my outburst, especially if The Lamb is watching. Perhaps the title of 'little child' is more fitting than I think.

Manuel returns with Makaio and Abdalla.

"Is this all that remains of your number?" asks Agyei.

"We are two of the three who survived," Makaio says. "Our brother Dashawn lies in wait, hopeful to speak at a later time. For now we shall tell all that we know in hopes that he can return and say more."

Cato turns to Gyan and asks, "All of the others? All four? Ravaged by The Beast so soon?"

"Yes." Abdalla interjects. "The Beast tore at them all and bested us. We had taken to the plains late in the eve, after meeting our charge in the room of waiting. Quick we were and vigilant, in hopes of spying the oncoming foe. We made our way through the mist into the eastern valley, and over marsh and swamp we trekked until we found our missing friends. Among them were two of the rahfaad as well as two of my own diakonae. Racked upon altars of stone they lay, but in the fog we saw no enemies.

"I approached and found them alive, waiting to be freed from the slab. I grabbed the rahfaad, yet by pulling him from the stone, I sprung the trap that wounded all. For on the top of the altar lay shards of rock, upon which all rested and tried to keep still. But each altar was hollow at its center, and through its core ran a vine of thorns, tied around the torso of each of our kin. A rope underground, beneath the traps, bound all of the vines together; and by lifting the rahfaad, I pulled down all the others, and pierced their flesh upon spikes of stone.

"Screams rang out and leapt on the wind, alerting The Beast that we had come. Sprang he did from the thickened mist upon Ivan, my largest aid. A moment flashed and he was gone, while Ivan lay dead at my feet. Laszlo was faster in thought than I, and he cut the thorns round the rahfaad. He did this as well for Toby, who was tied to the nearest altar.

"The Beast saw Laszlo's blade at work, and in his jaws he gripped the body bound on the altar furthest east. Four remained tied, and The Beast's maneuver pulled all their bodies against the altars, shooting shards into their backs.

"Laszlo cut them free as they screamed. I grabbed the first rahfaad with my right and took up Toby in my left. Laszlo cried for me to flee, and I obeyed him with the pair on my back. The mist was thick, but crimson eyes pierced it, for I saw The Beast reach the final altar as Laszlo also approached it. Seeing that the diakonae had bodies in wait, The Beast leaped upon Laszlo and cast him to the ground.

I could see little through the mist, but I heard a cry and a call to run.

"Makaio then sprang from the darkness, Laszlo in one arm and Dashawn in the other."

"I then screamed, 'All the others have been lost.'" Makaio interjects. "Let not Abdalla sound weak, for he moved with focus and the speed of the wind. Indeed, I followed in his steps though streams of blood poured from our wounds."

"How did you rescue Laszlo?" I ask.

"The Beast is cunning but arrogant. Near the last altar, he took one swipe to Laszlo's throat and assumed him dead. He then moved toward Abdalla for his next assault. This left Laszlo unattended, and I lifted him."

"How was it, Makaio, that you were not pierced to death on these altars?" Alden asks.

"The char'rashas make armor well, even if it is layers of hide. Mine had not been stripped by the crons. Fools they are—the lesser ones—and they paid little heed to disrobe Dashawn or me. This is why he survived as well."

"And yet seven still were lost," Cato states. He then looks to the others around the table. "Such has been the cost of *our* counsel."

All are silent.

After a moment, Alden asks, "Makaio, are you fit to speak further?"

"I come to serve."

"Tell us then of what you saw, before your capture and escape."

"My task was to scout the closest front—the village in ruin beyond the swamp. I moved through the mountains until making camp to the west of the villainous place. There I stayed, and much I saw.

"The village is filled with houses, schools, and other buildings of various kinds, but they are not ordered in a discernible pattern. An open marshland surrounds it, and a road runs north to south toward Mykmun. Each structure in the village is damaged, missing walls or bearing rooftops torn to kindling. Enemy minions moved unchallenged, both agras and crons were in the streets. The largest there are gehoonds of hell, who walk amid the ruined dwellings. Of their number I am uncertain, but I would testify to three-score, if not more."

"Crons and agras are of little concern," Alden begins. "Of course, a host of them could overwhelm our defenses."

"I do not believe that they will be of use to The Beast," Makaio replies. "They are far too foolish and short-of-skill to be anything but pawns to their cunning captain."

"Yet therein may lie their value—and in such numbers," says Si, the elder with a wispy Fu Manchu who had not spoken until now. "Tell me, Makaio, how did this legion spend its time?"

"In folly. Slinging excrement onto the walls and lighting fires where flame would catch. They also spent their hours in sport, mocking the heir through mimicry."

I look away from the others. I need not imagine what he saw, but I hazard a guess it was shameful.

"They acted as if unassigned to this war? That is good news to us," Gyan theorizes. "They may be ignorant of your presence." This he directs at me.

"Good," Alden says. "We can consider the village a haven for evil but not a front from which they will strike. At least we need not worry of that. Crons and agras are of no consequence when The Beast and armored patrols are abroad. As to the gehoonds, we shall ignore them as well; they are more of a nuisance than actual soldiers. Thank you, Makaio.

"Abdalla, what have you to share?"

"Excuse me," I say, raising my hand. "First, what's an 'ah-grah'? Second, what's a 'geh-hund'? Third, what's the significance of this village in ruin?"

"Both are demons of a lesser kind," Alden says, not wanting to waste a moment. "They are not of great importance in your present plight. As for the ruins, we were hoping that you could inform us of their meaning. I believe Makaio did renderings, did you not?"

Makaio lowers his head before answering, "Indeed. I drew for the better part of the day while the sun sat high before strolling west. The satchel that held them was lost to the crons, and I am sure the sketches have met the fire."

"Well then, little child, we can know nothing more of the structures other than what you saw above and what Makaio has spoken to us. Can this be sufficient for the present?"

"Of course. I am just glad that Makaio returned, drawings or not." This is true but much more gentle than the response I intended, for Alden is testing my patience once more.

"Good. Come then, Abdalla, tell what you can."

"I learned much from Toby's final words as I carried him to the ward.

"You should know, servant of Christ, he spent his last breaths passing his knowledge in hopes of aiding you in this fight.

"Toby's task was that of the Mykmun, but little did he learn of what lies within its walls. I assigned him to burrow in the southwestern swamp, across the road that leads to the stores. Under cover of shrub and dirt he sat, and there he saw the following: traffic enters the hall at the north and exits south toward the fortress itself, where the demon makes his bed. Of those who enter, two kinds are common. The first are clerks who neither deliver goods nor leave with them; he could not decipher their purpose. The second and worse are the ra'shrogs, of whom there were seven score at least—such is the number to which Toby attested. All serve as armored guards at the dwelling. The structure's length is ten times that of The Tabernacle, and two lone doors to it exist—one at the north and another at the south. He could say nothing of the nature of the Mykmun, but we can be assured of its security."

"I'm sorry," I say (half meaning it and feeling like I have done this far too much). "But what's 'mcmoon'?"

"'Meek-Moohn,'" Gyan says, "is your hidden treasure in Solsland. Not your ultimate treasure, perhaps not your conscious treasure, but it is something to which you hold fast. Something you will not release."

"And it must be altogether wicked," Alden claims, "for the enemy guards it in the shadow of your heart."

"Peace, Alden," Viho exhorts him.

"No. I shall speak—alone, if needed. Little child, you keep something we cannot know, and you enabled the enemy to secure it. Now they can use it against us all and bring you into further ruin. On this you must come to a realization in hopes of discovering what lies therein."

"Alden's point is well taken," Agyei tells the others.

Gyan, Si, and Manuel agree.

Viho also nods then looks to Alden, "Your thoughts are true, but bear in mind, truth can be brought in gentleness, especially to a willing ear."

"This is wisdom, Viho. I accept your aid." With this Alden stands and looks over the table. "I believe The Halls of Mykmun could confound us. Was there nothing more from Toby?"

"No," Abdalla confirms.

"Unfortunate. Then let us keep in mind, that whatever lurks in the halls may be our undoing. We shall approach them with caution. Abdalla, is there anything further?"

"As the zaquenan are aware, I assigned myself the first watch on the horrid citadel. Much I can say of that awful place, but I will begin with this: our fear is realized. A great creature, which we have all long hated, sits at the foundations of that fortress. He is not some inanimate thing as we had hoped—not some shrine or craft of stone. He is a ghoul of the pit, living and well, and he is not weak."

I am confused and consider the enemy lair in the east. From this distance I saw what appeared to be breath from an enormous, hideous, and wretched statue. Though I believed it to be stone, I thought I saw lungs of cinder heaving at its chest—as if it were sleeping, waiting to awake. But I fear Abdalla has now confirmed my suspicion.

"Wait," I tell Abdalla. "That is no statue where the citadel is built?"

"No," says Viho. "The creature is a demon, living and vile. Awthoomgaw is his name."

"Yes, and an abomination he is now," Agyei interjects, "though he was not always. He was beautiful in the Prehterra."

"Prehterra?"

"Yes," Agyei continues. "The time prior to the collision of the Heavens and the Earth—the ancient days, before we walked in your world. It was an era in which the entire host served and worshipped in the court of the Lord."

As has often been the case, my confused expression leads the speaker to continue.

"Is it not written in the Holy Scriptures, 'In the Beginning, God created the Heavens and the Earth. And the Earth was without form, and void'? Well, in the Heavens, this was not so. No, the realm of the angels was far from formless. There lived the Most High with his throne open to all, a place to worship at the foot of perfection. The Lord hovered over the waters, and in the Earth—that is, in your natural plain—he continued his creative work, and it was good. In the Heavens, however, the task was done, and we lived content in the kingdom Prehterra.

"Then our former brother, who you call 'Satan,' decided that he should be as God. Before Satan's treachery, the Most High alone dwelt within the Heavens as well as the Earth; but in his great defiance, the evil one did the same, usurping a right given to God in the first. He then became the adversary of the Lord and mankind, leading many of our brothers to their failure and deceiving the man and woman into sin. Curse the stone upon which he tread, serpent as he was in that day. He soiled creation, and ended the Prehterra—binding us all to an era of war.

"Now, we struggle with that wretched devil and one-third of our fallen brethren, and to them we have given new names—names they now know, for their former ones are lost to all but the Lord himself."

Agyei pauses. He has been calm and reserved to this point, but the flare in his spirit makes him larger and stronger. He rests his chin on his hand and stares while he muses. "I cannot recall Awthoomgaw's lost name. Long has it been since last it was said."

He shakes his head and collects himself, "I am sorry. I have digressed and spoken of things you cannot comprehend, for the Prehterra is hidden from you, and that which I have told is an echo of the real. Our world is kept from you for a purpose. All with which you need concern yourself regarding our kind is written in the Scriptures. Seek them for wisdom on this matter."

Agyei rises and walks to the windows overlooking the training and storerooms. He turns back to me and says, "One thing more shall I tell you: Awthoomgaw's good name is long lost, and his new one is both hideous and dreadful, for in the ancient tongue of Prehterra it is thus translated: 'The Full Craving of Lust.'"

My attentiveness turns to concern when Alden interjects, "The 'Full Craving.' Lust-everlasting, beyond satiation. This is a sinful hunger that does not rest. You know it—the craving with an inner abyss, and though you feed it day-by-day yet still it grows and demands more meals. Thus, he is Awthoomgaw. You would be well to remember his name, for it gives you constant warning."

We all sit in silence. This was a sore spot among the zaquenan, and I fear their opinion of me has been lowered. I do not believe I am possessed or that this demon has control; however, he is here. He is also set in his position with such fortitude that an entire structure can be built around him. I think of the torches moving at his torso and the fire burning in his lungs. I may have put him to sleep for now, but he lingers and desires to wake. My mind is set on a single thought: Awthoomgaw is a parasite, and I want to destroy him.

"Well, what say you?"

The question startles me. I have not been paying attention. Has Abdalla continued?

"I—I'm sorry. I was lost in thought. I didn't hear—"

"Well, a fine time you chose to daydream," Alden scoffs.

"I'm sorry. What was said?"

"A good deal," Manuel tells me. "Perhaps a few minutes of air will be useful before we decide what next steps to take."

The others nod, but Agyei has not returned to his seat. He has continued looking into the rooms at the east.

I apologize to Abdalla, who is gracious with me. Manuel then asks if I need anything, but I decline. I want some time alone (to recover from embarrassment).

I leave the war room and head through The Tabernacle to the low lookout. The exharts are gone, and the char-rashas watch.

"The prior guard are in the room of waiting," Cutler tells me. "They are considering how best to prepare you for the coming fight."

I nod to affirm I have heard him, then grab the ladder and hoist it over the wall.

"You should not leave; The Beast may lurk near us."

"I will not go far," I say, half-hoping I do.

As I walk over the side, I can see Agyei, who has moved into the high lookout, watching the east. Something about this revelation has struck him. I do not know why Abdalla withheld the information of Awthoomgaw's presence until now; perhaps he had no chance to tell them earlier. This does not matter. Such bitter news would have been as bad yesterday as it is today, and truth be told, I do not know how to deal with it.

7 : THE DESPAIR

Though our peak is not the highest of the mountains it provides an amazing view. I have passed from the sight of the char'rashas, having walked down a path on the descending western slope through a long line of evergreens. I figure that the west is safer than the east, and an area near The Tabernacle is not a place of danger.

In the valley through which I passed with The Lamb, leafless trees endure the cold in hope of coming warmth of spring. Beneath the endless sea of stars, the woodland testifies to peace, to serenity Solsland can possess when evil is not given ground.

When I recall the journey here, I reflect on the harsh terrain and my breakdown. Shame sits within me—over my cowardice, Awthoomgaw's presence, and a thousand nights before this one when I did not choose to fight.

But I also have the memories of The Lamb, and such recollections are a comfort.

After a moment of composing myself, I head back toward The Tabernacle. In the east I see flying creatures on the wind. I cannot discern if they wail or laugh, but they seem to be swooping at the peaks of the mountains. They are hunting for something. Or someone. Or me.

I then hear a voice.

"Wait," it says. "Please."

I see no one but sense … something. Eyes are on me.

"Do not yet return," the voice continues. "Please. Speak with me."

"Who are you?"

"I am Yaosh," it tells me, but no one appears. "I aid weary walkers on this path."

"Then show yourself, for I am weary."

"I cannot—not yet, but soon. For we must reason together."

"Reason together? About what?"

"This. This dilemma in which you find yourself."

"What dilemma? I am safe here."

"Exactly. You are safe." An aged white man appears, fighting his way through the dense foliage of the slope. He brushes needles from evergreens off his sleeves as he approaches me. "Safe because you are in your home, not in a strange land, and you are playing a mind game, not fighting a great war."

My look of curiosity turns to skepticism. "I know this. My quest here is an exercise, a means to an end."

"Right. And I am here to help you reach that end. The greatest end you can have to this battle."

"What is this? You are no angel."

"No. I am not. I am much more important. Come with me."

"I must stay near The Tabernacle."

This challenge to my journey seems out of place, and I return up the mountain when he follows and he calls to me again.

"Why do you want to leave? I am trying to help you."

"I doubt that."

"Wait." He grabs my arm and turns me toward him. This further raises my defenses despite his kind face and soft eyes. He appears unassuming and harmless, and once I face him, he continues with his plea. "I can guarantee you true victory—not on this evening alone but all thereafter. Please, if you will listen to reason, you will get everything you want."

"Which is?"

"Freedom. True freedom."

"I have freedom."

"Oh do you? Bound to fight a war you wish you did not? Forced to fight a desire ingrained into you? Longing but never having? This is freedom?"

He steps closer. "No. This is slavery."

"Why do you say these things?"

"Because they are true. You are a slave, not to lust but to something far more sinister."

He takes a step backward down the slope then nods for me to follow after him.

"What is this?" I ask him.

"This is your brain, rescuing you. Come. You have enemies here, and they are listening."

He is right. I sense something, and the hairs on the back of my neck stand on edge. I do not look back to The Tabernacle as I follow, unsure of what is coming but feeling I must face it. He is fast for an older man, and he leads me down the mountain to a clearing of tree stumps. We sit on two that are close to each other, and I begin to feel comfortable despite my prior misgivings. The forest surrounds us like the walls of a room, and the moonlight overhead creates a calm blue hue.

"Thank you," he begins, catching his breath. "Your willingness to lend your ear means much to me."

"You're welcome, but I'm unsure of your aim in this."

"My aim is simple," he says, taking my hand in his. "I want you to be done with this."

"This quest?"

"Well, yes—but not merely the present exercise. No, I want you to be done with all of this—this falsehood you embrace to cope with the truth."

"This is my imagination, but I would not call it falsehood. I do not accept this as an actual place; this is a symbolic exploration—for lack of better words."

"Yes, yes. Of course. I know; and as I have said, this is not the idea to which I am referring. I am talking to you about the grand idea, the great imaginative concept you embrace, not this little puppet show you are staging but the more explicit and dangerous web that entraps you."

He looks down then straight at me. "I am trying to get you to give up the idea of God."

"What?"

"God is the great imaginative concept. The master of enslaving falsehoods. The gravest of lies."

I chuckle. "Really? This is your gambit? That God does not exist."

"He doesn't. You know it, in the deepest recesses of who you are, you must know it."

"Do you think you would get me to accept this claim?"

"Yes, because it is true, and you are no fool, despite what that book tells."

"No. No, what *you've said* is the worst of lies."

"You are wrong. And you know you are wrong." He lets go of my hand before rising and turning his back to me. "Don't you know it, deep down inside? This is all a lie."

"Quite the contrary."

"Stop." He turns to me again. "You struggle day-by-day—some days worse than others, but it does not have to be so hard. If you would but listen to reason, you would be finished with this war because you would know the truth, that no war exists except the one you are creating in here." This last phrase he says while tapping his finger to his temple.

I rise before speaking. "Yes, I know that this present battle is all within my mind. The true fight is happening at my house, in front of a machine, where I am choosing not to sin."

"But that's it. That's what I am trying to tell you." He rushes to me and grabs my shoulders. "There is no need to vex yourself over so small a choice."

"I need to give up this addiction."

"Fine. But do it for the right reasons. Not because of some primitive, nonsensical belief but because you want it for yourself, because you have this one life and you want to make the most of it or because you fear the consequences, because of something real, not fantasy. If you are going to fight with yourself on this then by all means you have the right, but do so realizing you need not fight at all.

"You are not beholden to some creator watching you and awaiting your response. You are not bound to his expectations. You are free to fight, and you are free to fail, and if you do, you are free to love yourself despite it all. Embrace what you will, enjoy your life, and live it to the fullest without fear of judgment."

"That is not what you propose."

"No? I am the last bastion of sanity in your mind. I am the part of you that will not let go of that age-old, aching idea—the one that has truly given life to the masses and haunted your heart for years without end. The real chains around you are not your addiction to flesh but your addiction to spirit, to nonsense and foolishness of the most absurd kind."

"I will not accept that."

"Fine, then don't, but at least stop wasting your time tonight. It's getting late in the real world; get some sleep so that you can think with clarity in the morning. Maybe you won't step back into reality today, but if you would at least take one step closer to it, that would be a fine beginning. Perhaps tomorrow, you will entertain the truth, consider it, and maybe, just maybe, you can get your life back and do something with it."

"You speak much but say little."

"At least I am not wasting your time with obsolete rituals and the embellished history of some ancient tribe. At least I am not asking you to forego the pleasures and comforts of this world so that by self-denial you can be closer to an imaginary friend—a friend who you also believe will judge many you love and cast them into eternal punishment. At least I am not trying to break you of your inherent, undeniable human longings for sex, security and self-satisfaction."

He shakes his head at me. "My goal in this was to help you, but if you refuse to deny this ridiculous, childish nonsense, I—I can do nothing."

"This is not reason."

"It is reason. True reason. But you refuse to follow it because a lifetime of guilt and fear and shame have stripped you of your most important tool—your ability to think."

"I have thought on these things."

"Oh yes, you have, but then what? Fear brought you back to notions so foolish that you believe that they free you from death when, in reality, they lead you to it—death of your true self, your deepest desires, your human potential, and your worth to your species. Look at you, a fully developed male sitting in your house, making play-pretend with angels and devils that fight for your 'soul' that does not exist. How absurd. You could solve this whole I-don't-want-to-lust dilemma by going to bed, and yet you engage in this chicanery. Do you not see the self-refuting madness of this behavior?

"The only reason this fight is hard is because you won't surrender it. Think about it. Of course this whole world feels emotional; this battle feels mental, and this war feels real. You're telling your brain to run with this concept so that you can feel you've accomplished a victory, and it is obeying you because that is its job—to keep you alive, to inform your sense of self-worth and enable you to pursue the best version of yourself. And you've tainted it. Ruined it. You think that tonight's little game of play matters, and I am here to remind you that it does not, because all of this is a distraction from one habit to another. You are trading your addictions from the pleasure to the pain, and you have no idea how silly you will seem to any rational person who hears this tale outside of your circle of fellow lemmings.

"This is hard for you, I know, but since you persist in this delusion of grandeur, cold water in your face is my last option. Hear me right now. You are not an heir of a heavenly kingdom. You are not the result of some creator's hands. And you are not accountable to anyone for your life. The universe has shown us the truth of this. It answers all our questions and grants serenity that no archaic deity could. For to it we owe nothing and die into nothing; we are gone without regret, pain, punishment, or loss. This is reality, and you want to embrace it—to accept your longings and fulfill them with leisure. Your life is yours, and it's all you've got, so get your act together and live in the real world."

"Are you finished?"

He catches his breath and looks at me. "Are you?"

"I am finished listening."

Yaosh sighs. "Why are you so unreasonable?"

"I'm no genius," I say while approaching him, "but I know that you are no part of me, Yaosh, 'helper to the weary.' You have shown me your true face, and I am loathe to find it here."

As Yaosh spoke, his visage changed, and he has failed to realize it. With each passing word his vigor grew but his body shriveled to its bones. His face that first was clean and kind faded gaunt while his eyes went hollow. His voice that once was tender and clear turned coarse and full of bitter gall. He is now a shadow of his earlier form, and I can see there is no hope in him.

"Tell me, Yaosh," I command, "what is the meaning of your name?"

Out of breath, the creature stumbles toward me. "I am Yaosh, and I claim the truth to men, 'it is hopeless.'"

"Now *that* is true," I concede.

He smiles and stares in grotesque pleasure with tiny beads of white resting in deep black sockets. He thinks I accept him, but he is mistaken. All that is true of him is his name, and I explain to him why this is.

"Without a Creator's handiwork, without justice beyond the earth, and without a future to look toward in anticipation—all is hopeless. This planet is a speck of dust on cosmic carpet; and in the grand scheme of ultimate history, nothing we do matters, nothing we know is certain, and nothing we hold dear has value. All are atoms viewed in tandem, giving a false construct of meaning to an uncaring universe. If this is truth, you are right to be hopeless.

"But your grand design is self-defeating, for the finest thought that a being could have is nothing more than a synapse of a simple brain, handed down in a genetic code that indicts itself to inevitable demise. The entire world and all who inhabit it are less than a grain of sand on the endless beach of time. And even that revelation, within your construct, has no meaning whatsoever. You are despair, Yaosh, and I have no use for you. Leave this place. Now."

"See reason—the nature of reality."

"I see reality, and it is this: God exists, and God is good. I would much rather surrender my will to his than be left to my own unending self-worship. If I am the center of my world, it is a terribly small word, indeed. Therefore, go. Be gone from this place."

He continues to stumble down the slope, taunting me as he goes.

"God is a lie, and you'll know it before the end. Or you won't. Who knows with you. Like I said, you're unreasonable." He laughs to himself as he stumbles further into the dense forest on the mountainside. I give chase because I want to deliver him to the angels.

The angels.

Oh no.

He has led me down the western slope of the mountain. I know not how far.

What have I done? I am out in the open.

Then I hear it.

A rustling in the trees.

The growl of a lion.

A footstep that sends a tremble up my spine.

The Beast.

A plume of fire bursts to my left! A bush wreathed in flame sends a pillar of orange toward the sky. Behind it lie two crimson eyes and a gaping jaw full of rage and anger. The pillar burns, and The Beast swats at his eyes as they bleed from the potent, sweltering heat. He roars in frustration and flees to the east.

Yaosh returns and looks for his master. He hears the cries of the angels sprinting from the peak.

"Hold fast, heir of the kingdom," one cries.

I look for them, and Yaosh takes advantage. He stabs my gut with a rusted blade. I scream but hear only a humming in my ears; an unnerving din blocks all other sound. I grab my head and feel blood in my palms. I scream to no avail—no volume comes.

I look down at the dirk, and I must be hallucinating. The blade itself thrashes like a frenzied snake and whips the weak hand of Yaosh from the handle. The length of the weapon breaks from its hilt and burrows into my injured gut, like an eel driving through the sand at the sea floor. I grab at it with my fingers, but it festers inside me, and I realize I am grabbing at my own open flesh. I hold the wound and crumble to the ground.

Looking up, I see Yaosh reach to the ground for his bladeless hilt. Klahan appears from the darkness and collides into the gangling demon, sending them both against a tree.

Cutler and the char-rashas spring through the trees, followed by Jadon, Alexavier, and Tarak. Kneeling at my sides they speak to one another, but I can hear nothing but the same dim ring. Tarak takes my right hand in his and gestures for me to be quiet with his left. Deron stands over his shoulder and speaks, but I hear nothing but a constant hum.

Jadon puts the back of his hand to my cheeks and talks to the others, but their words are silent. The ring is closer. It stings my head. My face is clenched in searing pain. Jadon rips his sleeve and hands the cloth to Alexavier who wipes it beneath my weeping eyes. When he pulls it away, it drips with blood. My breathing is heavier, and all those before me are turning to silhouettes within a gray haze. Jadon motions to me to keep my eyes fixed on them. I try, but they are all shrouded in fog. The sound from the night is gone less the ringing, and I feel nothing but the gnashing of my own teeth.

8 : THE REVELATION

All I experience is the pain and darkness. I am being moved, but I know not where or how many angels are needed to do it. They are vague shapes dwelling in a thick, gray mist. Moment to moment I scream and cringe, but I cannot hear a sound of it—only the ringing. I know that acts of agony occur; I have felt a firm collision more than once, and I assume that the angels have dropped me due to my jolting.

The creature burrowing inside me is a monster. It expands and pushes my organs against one another. It tears through my tendons as my arteries snap. My limbs jerk in reflex each time I feel it. It is getting larger; and at this point, I would wager that it's the length of my torso.

An eternity seems to have passed when I see a glimmer of hope. A steady bulb appears in the distance through the haze. The beacon shines as a lighthouse in the morning fog. Brighter and brighter it becomes until I see The Lamb at its center. He neither speaks nor gestures; he watches.

All hope is shattered as I sense an expanse between us. The great chasm seems wider than the whole earth could hold. He is there but out of reach, visible but untouchable. I am yelling at the top of my lungs, but still I hear nothing. Why are we far apart? Why can't I be near him? What has happened to me?

The light is gone; hollow dark remains. I am freezing cold, but sweat runs from my pores. My tears are thick and sting as they stream. I cannot hear my own pleas for death. I exist in utter ruin—pain from my core to my skin. I am in torment. Alone. What have I done to myself? Why am I here? How did this happen?

A sullen voice I do not know whispers within the haze I inhabit. "Where is God now?" the voice asks. "Why doesn't he fix this? You don't deserve this. If God existed he would save you. If he were real you wouldn't be here. He would rescue you from this nothing. He is a lie; it's all a lie."

The words echo within the gray and seem to come at me from all sides. "You were right to doubt and embrace your own passions. They were all you had, and now they are gone. You are gone; lost without hope. All that remains are your thoughts of agony.

"You must hate whoever brought you to this place. If God exists, it must be he who condemned you. But if he doesn't, then who is to blame? Whose fault is this? You must hate him—the one who did it. Hate is all you have; there is nothing else here. You hate him, but who is he? Who is to blame?

"Why, it's you. It must be you. You deserve this, after all. Abandoning your faith. That's what this is. You get it now—this is your will, your doing. You have rejected God too often, and now he has given you all that you want. He is real, but you rejected him, and he has let you leave his world. He's given you all that you had hoped in your hours of sin and lust and depravity—a world without him, without his seeing. He has turned his face from you and granted all your deepest longings. Now you are alone. You have departed, and he has not pursued. You have fallen—torn yourself from his side."

The voice ceases, and the ringing returns. Wait. What is this new pain? Something gnaws at my skin. Something heavy and firm, a fist digging at knotted muscles. It is crushing and grinding.

Now, a numbing, but that is not all. The numbing takes shape. It cools and calms—a soothing balm upon my heart. And a sound. What is it? It whistles in contrast to the dim ringing; my ears cannot bear both. What is it?

"The Lord knows …" a different, softer voice says.

"What?" I scream, not hearing my own cries. "'The Lord knows' what?"

"The Lord knows …"

"'Knows' what? Tell me."

"The Lord knows … who are his."

Yes. It is true. I weep.

"God's solid foundation stands firm, sealed with the inscription, 'The Lord knows who are his.'" The voice is clear now.

Am I among—no, wait—I *am among* them. The Lord knows I am his.

"There is therefore now no condemnation for those who are in Christ Jesus."

I know not who speaks or how I can hear him, but his words are beautiful as they continue, "And we know that for those who love God all things work together for good, for those who are called according to his purpose. We are afflicted in every way, but not crushed; perplexed, but not driven to despair. May the God of hope fill you with all joy and peace in believing, so that by the power of the Holy Spirit you may abound in hope."

"Speak more to me please," I beseech the voice. My pain exists but not with acuity. I feel my body again, and I am kneeling on the floor.

Beginning anew, the calm voice says, "Beloved, do not be surprised at the fiery trial when it comes upon you to test you, as though something strange were happening to you. But rejoice insofar as you share Christ's sufferings, that you may also rejoice and be glad when his glory is revealed. And after you have suffered a little while, the God of all grace, who has called you to his eternal glory in Christ, will himself restore, confirm, strengthen, and establish you. For we did not follow cleverly devised myths when we made known to you the power and coming of our Lord Jesus Christ, but we were eyewitnesses of his majesty."

I am weeping, but the tears are not thick nor do they sting as they pass from my eyes. My head is bowed onto the cold, stone floor. The tugging inside me is present but less.

"More," I beg. "Please, tell me more."

"Blessed is the man who remains steadfast under trial, for when he has stood the test he will receive the crown of life, which God has promised to those who love him. Draw near to God, and he will draw near to you."

"Yes. Oh Lord, draw near. Forgive me, Father, for I am lost." I do not know if my prior words have been audible as they rushed from my heart through my lips, but with the next portion, I hear my own voice echo quietly in my ears. "Create in me a clean heart, O God, and renew a right spirit within me. Cast me not away from your presence, and take not your Holy Spirit from me. Restore to me the joy of your salvation; and uphold me with a willing spirit."

I feel sick—horribly sick. A new type of knot has formed at my belly. My throat contracts, and I cough at the floor. The dust blows from beneath me toward the sides of my face. I raise my head, and the gag reflex hits—strong at first, then stronger. I grab my stomach. A third heave chokes me, then the fourth hits. The gagging turns to vomit, and from my mouth flies a creature I have never before seen.

The villain writhes and wails upon the floor, and its violent hissing sears my eardrums. Its body is far smaller than I had assumed. In a single swift movement, Klahan arrives and cleaves the horrid creature in two. Hewn upon the floor, its face full of jagged teeth, the wormlike thing continues to screech into the night. With a firm foot, the angel crushes it into the floor.

Wait.

I can see.

The Tabernacle—I can see her walls, her tented ceiling, her blessed tenants: the forty-nine, or some of them, anyway. Klahan and Tarak, Jadon and Deron, Cutler and a handful of the char-rashas—all stand watching with looks of concern. Manuel and Viho watch as well, along with the few remaining rahfaad.

The dizziness of my trauma hits me, and I collapse back to the floor, dazed but conscious. I wish I had fainted; the fall would have hurt less. Jadon stands over me. Clement and Gakuto look over his shoulder. Manuel and the others stand behind them.

"What happened?" I ask.

"From what point?"

"I—I saw a knife. I was stabbed. My vision turned to haze—my tears were as blood."

"Calm yourself," Jadon assures me. "You wept nothing of the sort."

"I did. I saw it."

"You said that your vision went to haze. How then did you see your tears?"

"It did—I did, but before—but The Lamb. He was there, then—then gone, such a great space between us. I forsook him in my grief."

"No."

"I did." I am crying anew. "I did. I spoke not but hate and bitterest spite. Jadon, I blasphemed God."

"Not that we heard," Viho assures me. "And suppose in passing you felt such things; they were not your final thought."

"No. No they weren't," I answer.

"Of course, not. We heard your words, as did the one you serve; for indeed, he hears all who are his."

"But I—"

"Hush. You need to listen, now." Viho looks to the others and commands their testimony with a simple, "Tell him."

"You lack wisdom," Klahan begins. "You are blessed that the king has seen fit to call you, for of your own accord you are lacking in all things."

Viho glares at him to get on with it, and Klahan coughs before beginning the tale.

"The king alerted us to your trouble by means of the bursting fire. The char'rashas who stood on watch cried to us and fled downhill. I was speaking with Tarak, and we were quick to leave the hall. Jadon followed with Manuel, and all of us ran toward the geyser of flame.

"I arrived at the scene and struck Yaosh. He rose, but in his wounded form, he was no match and met his end. I sliced his head from his frail form and threw the skull at the vhulraks above."

"You were inconsolable, however," Jadon begins, "for though the demon was dispatched, his poisonous aid was in your chest. Yaosh impaled you with an exporex, a thing of dark design formed by the fallen for one purpose: to torment the hearts and minds of men. Yaosh is known to strike his prey and twist the dagger in his hand, gripping at the hilt to keep the blade from breaking free from his control. He prefers to unleash the poison slowly, but his demonic tool fled his hands the moment it had its venom in you.

"The exporex is a hideous foe, and it wrapped itself around your heart, blocking your eyes from all true sight. As it ate of your insides it gave you its waste, soiling your heart with visions and falsehoods."

Deron steps before Jadon and continues. "Four of us were needed to carry you, and you kicked us and ripped at our clothing in horror. Your voice erupted and begged for death, but we returned you to our haven. Here you laid in utter agony, calling to a specter we did not see. This was terror to us, and I speak for all when I say that our hearts broke at your pain."

"I was sure of your ending this affair," Jadon interrupts, "leaving this land and seeking respite. Much have I seen of men in despair, and many a time have they held to it—believing it freeing and becoming its slaves. But you—you had some zeal in you. In loathing torment and gall of pain, you begged and pleaded yet for mercy."

I cannot help but feel this praise undeserved. "I do not recall that," I tell them.

"Nor would you," Deron interjects again. "The exporex blocks you from such things while filling you with agony from itself. It grafts a thorn that perverts your thoughts, making them into realized terror. We tried to calm you, but you could not hear; thus, the rahfaad took drastic measures."

"This is how we combat the exporex." Jadon holds up a dagger weathered in appearance but shimmering beneath a layer of dirt. It connects at the handle in the strangest of ways. A thin three-inch blade extends from the mouth of a sculpted head of the body that makes the hilt. The molded grip is small, four inches in length, and the figure's outstretched arms serve as the hand guards. The human shape is wrapped in leather from the feet to the neck, and the overall appearance of the tool is strange.

"This is The Apostle's Edge," Jadon says, extending the hilt toward me. "Within it are held the words of those who walked with our Lord Jesus Christ, and when it strikes a person's flesh, the dirt dissolves, and the sharpened, double-edge pierces the heart. From the blade comes the doctrine, correction, and healing that combat the filth of the exporex. The joy of the truth burns at the worm, and the dark thing longs for fast escape."

"Hence your spill," says Klahan. "Once the edge had broken your skin, the exporex was sure to flee; and when it did, I was glad to greet it."

A moment passes as we turn to the aggressive angel, who smiles.

"Very well," Manuel says. "The tale has been told. The rahfaad will mend you for a moment, and we will double our defenses. The enemy will try again to subdue you.

"See to the upper and lower lookouts," he tells Cutler and the others. "We will call for you if needed."

Manuel remains with the rahfaad and me as the others exit the medical ward. They look over my wounds and check my throat.

I feel foolish and at a loss. How I wished I had fought the demon on the mountain. How I hate to be the victim once more. Too many times have I done nothing. Too often have I been unfit for battle. Too long have I failed to rise against my enemy. Jadon claimed to see zeal in me, but I do not know how he could. All I have done since arriving here is fall from one pit into another.

'Heir of the kingdom,' 'child of God,' 'servant of Jesus Christ,' they call me; but this is no way for God's child to live. We are not called to survive while the devil wages war on our hearts. Such is the life of a powerless victim, and that is not the life that Christ gives. The truth is clear to me now. As children of God and heirs of his Kingdom, we are called to do striking of our own.

And I shall.

From the moment I arrived, Satan has been on the attack. His minions have hunted, kidnapped, and pursued me—wounding me at every turn. I have been made the prey in this battle, ever on the defensive. Such has been the state of things tonight and on a thousand others like it.

I feel a confidence I have not yet known and look to Manuel, who stands beside me. "Call the legion, Manuel. Call them to the armory."

"And what should I tell them?"

"Tell them the truth. Tell them I'm ready."

"Ready for what?"

"For war."

9 : THE GATHERING

I am on the upper lookout when Manuel informs me they have assembled. The valley sits as a lake of gray mist, surrounded by the beauty of the snow-capped mountains. Despite the perfect night sky, the sight is soiled by that distant structure protruding from the fog. Awthoomgaw stands as a lighthouse to evil, and my desire to destroy him rises.

I run through The Tabernacle until I reach the armory, and I stand on the landing at the center of the room on which Manuel, Viho, Tarak and Jadon join me.

I look over the faces of the angelic host and with a deep breath call out, "I say to you, host of the Most High, all praise and glory to Him who is worthy."

"For to him is due honor from the first to the last." They respond in unison.

"Praise. Glory. Honor. These are due to our Holy King. These are his: praise and glory and honor.

"But I have not honored him. No. I have failed—failed him and failed you. For I have not fought for his honor. I have not striven for his glory. I have not praised him through deeds. On the contrary, I have lived in fear—of my old nature and the fight against it—terrified that I was going to stumble, horrified at the thought of a fall. I was desperate in my worry.

"But for this, I must repent.

"I must repent of mere defense against the evil one. I must repent of my fear of the evil one. I must repent of my focus on the evil one. I have come here expecting defeat. I have been anticipating the fall. I have hidden here hoping he will not come, but of all these things, I must repent.

"In the most clear sense of the word, I must repent—I must turn my attention from one thing to another and, therefore, act in an opposite way."

Alden nods, the first to see my point.

"I must shift my eyes from the evil one to the Holy One. I must change my mindset from being the prey to the pursuer. I must cease cowering and start striking back.

"Not I alone, but all of us. Do not focus on their attacks upon me; instead let us develop an assault against them. Yes, they have numbers. Yes, they have a fortress; and yes, at its center is a demon of lust, the likes of which I had never imagined. But we are warriors of The Lamb, and he alone is greater than all hell's minions.

"From the moment I arrived I have been made to fear, but that fear has been utter foolishness. The Lamb is king, and Solsland is his. Every inch of it. I have allowed the enemy to dictate terms and made this battle one of defense, but no more. Not one moment more. No.

"This war is against an invading force seeking to take land to which it has no right. Satan moves. Lust rests undisturbed. Demons strut across that plain as though they are its masters. I must repent of this state of things.

"So hear my words, noble warriors of heaven. Hear me now and hold me to it. I repent. I see the Truth; and through him, all things are made new. The dark of night will lift its curtain to day, and this stronghold will be dashed to pieces—by his might, for his honor, and to his glory."

More nods come from the others now.

"And in this we shall evade the devil's snare."

"Yes," says Viho.

"And in this you shall answer your charge."

"We shall," Klahan calls.

"And in this we shall see victory."

"Praise and honor," Deron cries.

Cheers rise from all corners of the room. They echo through The Tabernacle, and I am sure our enemies hear. I look to those with me on the landing, and the two zaquenan nod in firm support.

I look back to the remaining host and call to them, "Gather your armor. Take up your bows. Sharpen your blades. Before dawn, we march."

The angels disperse throughout the storeroom. Diakonae and char-rashas distribute weapons. Amunamai fit one another in armor. Arayil sling quivers of arrows to their backs.

Manuel steps toward me and clears his throat before he asks, "You mean for all of us to wage the offensive, then?"

"I called everyone here, didn't I?"

"Yes, and I must say, I am looking forward to it." With that, he walks off the landing and grabs Alden, who has been staring at me ever since the others dispersed. I let out a deep breath and turn toward Tarak.

"Well, I guess I need to find myself a sword."

"Wait," Cutler calls, running onto the landing. "Wait. Nothing here will suit you. Your blade still needs crafting—if you still wish to forge it, that is."

"I wish for nothing else."

"Good. Then follow me."

I take one final look at the angels at work. As one laces the straps of another's boots, a third fits armor to the first. A fourth stands near them placing helmets on each, and a fifth follows behind him handing them gloves. They work together like gears of a machine, each doing his part for the whole to function.

Fires blaze in the kilns of the forge, and an anvil rests at its center. A large basin of water rests near the wall, and raw metals sit awaiting their use. Cutler stands with an artisan at each side.

"This is Emmett of the hammer's swing and Ferris of the flame. They are workers of the forge." He then hands me a heavy metal mallet. "Listen to them and to me, and we shall make a mighty weapon."

I turn to Emmett, who directs me to the anvil.

"After I swing, you swing," he says. "On Cutler's orders, we cease."

Cutler then approaches us and looks me in the eyes. "You will labor, and you will tire, but this is now your task. Forge yourself as you forge this sword, and in time both shall be made stronger."

Cutler and Ferris work with the metals, while Emmett puts my hands in work gloves. He shows me the key striking technique. The hammer must glide in an even motion—forceful yet precise, firm but not blunt. No stroke should be wasted, and a wrong one can be ruinous. I must be willing to follow and obey.

The metals are heated. The room grows hot. Cutler places the first rods on the anvil. Emmett swings. I do the same. The process repeats. Over and over. The first several strikes resound through my arm, but fifty swings to the anvil, and my muscles adapt.

After a time, the blade is taken. It is heated, tempered, and hammered anew. New metals are added, and the flames are renewed. Cutler watches, inspects, and instructs.

Our methods change. Our swings adjust. One hammer is traded for another more fit, and the striking continues in rhythms and cadence. The heat grows. My arm fades into numbness and my hand locks in place.

I consider Cutler's urging to forge myself throughout this process. I recall a verse; I utter it once. I muse on its meaning. I whisper it again. One verse. Then another. Focus takes shape. My heart is renewed. Truth etches itself to the front of my mind.

> Whether therefore ye eat, or drink, or whatsoever ye do, do all to the glory of God.

> For God has not given us a spirit of timidity, but of power and love and discipline.

> Be strong and of good courage, do not fear nor be afraid of them; for the LORD your

> God, He is the One who goes with you. He will not leave you nor forsake you.

I do not know how long we have worked, but Ferris moves the sword to the basin once more. Steam erupts throughout the room, and we are further drenched in sweat. I am exhausted. My arms are sore. The moisture stings my eyes. Cutler takes my hands and covers them in a salve. Emmett needs nothing. He cracks his knuckles and sits on an unused anvil, waiting for the next phase of forging to begin.

Another of the char-rashas appears arrayed in armor. Gold chain mail covers his head to his knees. His pants are white and his boots, dark brown, which match the belt around his waist and the scabbard at his side. His pearl-colored breastplate and matching helmet have golden lettering I cannot read.

"You look good," Cutler tells him.

"We know our craft," he responds.

"Then put it to task once more."

The craftsman sits at a table at the southern wall, and Cutler brings him all his materials. Emmett comes to him, and the two speak, but as I move toward them, Cutler stops me.

"The rest you leave to us. We will finish."

"But—"

"You asked to forge your blade. I have granted you this, but other matters are pressing. Return to the others; they will want you."

I walk to the door but turn back; they cease their talking and look at me.

"Thank you," is all I say.

Cutler nods, and the others return to their tasks.

The storeroom is alive with the preparations of war, and a sea of gold and pearl armor moves beneath the torchlight. Islands of deep blue, forest green, and regal purple appear in the crowd. The various groups assigned by the zaquenan have all maintained their unity, and I identify each by its style as I walk to the landing at the center of the room.

Having seen one char-rasha in his armor, I recognize the remaining craftsmen, but their suits are complete. They too wear the golden mail, white trousers, and brown boots. Likewise, they boast the pearl plates at their chests and have similar helmets to the other I saw. In addition, they also have gauntlets of white with gold trim midway up their wrists, and each possesses a unique quiver of arrows slung at his back.

The next group I recognize is the exharts. Their outer robes of white are gone, revealing cream-colored inner linens. Over them is armor of gold—at the feet, the chest, the forearms and head. Each wears a deep green belt and scabbard, and dark green trim in the shape of leaves weaves its way around points of their armor and masked helmets.

The diakonae are the next I see, for their remaining three members are huddled at the landing. Their blue bodysuits have been replaced with white ones, accompanied by gloves and shoes of a pearl hue. The deep blue of their prior uniforms is now the color of their belts alone, and they do not wear a single plate of armor.

Each also has a memento to those fallen. Makaio has a single ripped piece of cloth wrapped around each of his legs and arms. Abdalla has four blue patches in the shape of wings sown into his right sleeve. Dashawn sits with bandages at his arms and left leg and a dressing around his head. Four blue chords tie around his left wrist.

Like the diakonae, the rahfaad are easy to find due to their lessened number. Also, they are dressed differently than the rest. Whereas the standard for the legion is white and gold, the rahfaad are adorned in deep, royal purple. Their robes from earlier have been removed, revealing linen suits of the same bold tone. They have shoes and gloves rather than boots and gauntlets, and the gold color of these contrasts the purple. They also have satchels slung at their shoulders and brown belts wrapped around their waists.

The arayil boast armor of pearl with golden trim that matches the mail worn under the plates. At their chests is an emblazoned gold cross, and on their backs are capes of the same color. They wear round helmets, the sides of which turn inward and curve, forming an opening in the shape of a cross that reveals their faces.

By contrast, the amunamai wear golden armor over fitted mail of pearl. Their breastplates are broader than any others I have seen, and their gauntlets are thicker as well. Their helmets are more pronounced and boast wings at the sides, flaring upward and back. The full ensemble creates a resolute appearance; each guardian looks like an immovable gold statue adorned with a cape of blue—except their leader, Alexavier, who wears a purple one.

The zaquenan bear their same white robes, over which they wear armor of similar color. They look like armored ghosts—light as a breeze but hard as a gale. At the front of their helmets is the crest of a cross that slopes to the back of their skulls. The same blessed shape extends from the openings of both their boots and gauntlets, wrapping around their calves and wrists. The single outstanding color in the ensemble comes from the thin golden tassel worn about each one's waist. The elders move in a specter-like manner, and they inspect and encourage each warrior in waiting.

"Quite a sight, are they not?" Manuel asks.

"Yes," I respond, somewhat entranced. I am reminded of when I first saw Jadon, Gavrill, and Adofo. I was taken with their regal appearance, yes, but this—this is wholly different, as if the angels withheld their true might and nobility until I was prepared to use it. I look to my left to find the counselor fully arrayed like the others in his unit. His bold, weathered face looks strong within his helmet, and a youthful zeal beams from his eyes.

He smiles and places his hand on my shoulder. "You, too, must be well-adorned if you are to lead them."

With this he nods to one of the char-rashas, who gestures in return and rises. The craftsman and two others behind him approach the landing, each of them carrying a covered object in his arms. The seven zaquenan make their way through the crowd and form a crescent that arches away from us.

"Raise your arms," Manuel tells me.

I comply, and Viho approaches after grabbing something from the char-rashas.

He wraps his arms and a plate of armor around me saying, "Protect yourself with the Breastplate of Righteousness, which is also called the Breastplate of Love. Let it be a sign to the enemy of your calling, a symbol of your seat in the court of the Lord. Bear it upon your chest and wear it as one purposed to rage against the enemy's evil."

He steps away, and Alden moves in front of me. "Fasten to yourself the Belt of Truth, for it will hold you firm in the face of enmity. Hold to it, lose it not, and it will be a source of rescue."

"And upon your head bear this mighty gift: the Helmet of Hope and of Salvation." Another elder says this as he and a fellow zaquenan hold the sides of said helmet and place it upon me. "Though at times it may appear to obscure and offer less vision than those who forsake it, be renewed. For it protects you from many a blow and keeps you secure from fierce attack."

I feel a tugging at my leg and look down to find Agyei at my feet. He has slipped a deep green covering over my foot and laces it as he speaks. "Upon your feet bear the Boots of the Gospel, to spring to the opportunity to praise and honor, to serve and to love, to share and to give. Yes, these are a wondrous boon to your footing, for they both quicken and assure your steps."

"And this hold in your weak arm," another says, handing to me a shield the length of my legs. "For in your weakness, it shall be made stronger. Yes, this is the Shield of Faith. Let many a strike be brought against it, for it will protect you if you hold it fast."

The shield is pearl in color, with a gold cross at its upper third, which extends in all four directions and wraps around the back. The angels all look at me with a strange expression. It is neither awe nor pride but a sense of calm and contentment, as if they are satisfied to see me this way.

"And to attack, you will require this."

Manuel steps before me, holding a sword. Its hilt is wood wrapped in leather straps, and words are etched into the hide. The blade itself is stranger. At its center, columns of metal extend but are scored and sculpted into words. From the base of the hilt to the tip of the metal, these strands of text extend like towers, but they form only the core of the blade. A clear, double-edged diamond prism surrounds the metal.

"This is the Sword of the Spirit, the Holy Word of God. As your Savior, Christ our Lord, used it to ruin the words of Satan, so too shall you wield it in defense and attack, to dash the enemy's schemes to rubble at his feet."

Manuel turns the weapon as he presents it, and the blade shows an altogether new beauty. The crystal casing serves as a lens that magnifies the tiny etched words. This makes them legible, and I realize that they are Scriptures writ in stone:

> For God has not destined us for wrath, but to obtain salvation through our Lord Jesus Christ, who died for us so that whether we are awake or asleep we might live with him.

Such is a single line of text, but each strand of the blade boasts another like it. Dozens of these long metal sinews stem from the hilt, bound together to create the core of the weapon, protected and enhanced by the clear encasing.

All eyes are fixed on me when Manuel returns to the line of elders. Cutler smiles toward me from the back of the assembly. He has put on his armor, as have Ferris and Emmett. I was the last, and now we are ready.

My armor is light, and every inch of it feels tailor-made to fit. The whole of the moment catches me, and I look down from the legion and shake my head.

"I am unworthy of this," I say aloud but to myself.

"You are correct," Viho says coming next to me, "but The Lamb is a good and noble king, and many undeserved blessings he loves to give. Be affirmed, little child, for the Lord knows who are his, and he does not leave them wanting."

"But this is much more than I –"

"Stop. All too often you children look at what you are given and claim your ill worth. Rather, accept these things from your Heavenly Father and live a life of thanks for them. Live as one who is worthy of them, for through Christ they are given. A focus on yourself and your shortcomings will lead to further failure, but a focus on the one who is right and pure will lead to a life well lived."

"Thank you."

"You do not need me to tell you these things. Look to the blade and the truth it bears, it will say the same."

The zaquenan stand at the head of the remaining forty fighters. All look to me, but I am out of speeches.

"We await your order," Manuel says.

"Then let us be off, to whatever end."

"No." Alden says, before coming toward me and looking me straight in the eyes. "Not whatever end. Tonight, we march to victory."

10 : THE MARCH

The night is still. The air is silent.

But the sound of fury stirs. A piercing, shrill horn fills the air, and the winged demons swoop from the dark clouds near the mountain. They are called 'stradains'—bat-like creatures the size of men that wear nothing but tattered loincloths at their waists and blank black masks that cover their foul faces.

In their talons each grasps a cron, and these hellish goblins stare at The Tabernacle with bulging, enlarged, looming eyes. Their pale green skin is covered in filthy rags, and their weapons are slipshod—shards of metal with cloths wrapped around one end as a makeshift hilt. The crons' gaping mouths bear uneven sharpened teeth, and a black tar drools from their chins onto their oversized shoes.

The attackers from the air are not alone. Up the western slope crons skulk toward the lair, and they drag torches along the ground to cause brushfires up the mountain. Whoever has led the charge is patient, and both groups descend on The Tabernacle in unison.

The stradains reach the camouflaged tarp, and they are quick to realize the deception. The dropped crons, however, are less savvy and stab at the canopy with their blades. Ignorant of their height, many fall to their doom. The attackers from the land hack at every inch of the lower lookout until they find the opening. Dozens stream through the forge into the other rooms.

What they do not know, however, is that the lair is empty—less gallons of torch oil brushed along the floors and ceilings. The angelic warriors and I have left The Tabernacle, and we stand in a grove down the eastern slope of the mountain. A shallow candlelight flickers in front of me, as I use my hand to protect it from the breeze. After dozens of enemies enter our lair, I lower the flame toward the forest floor. A dark path of oil carries the fire uphill to our camp, both onto its surface and into its rooms.

I imagine a hot wind stirs beneath the tarp, and the crons realize what has happened too late. Their torches must have been too far below the ceilings, and the demons themselves too roused to be cautious. As the flame arrives, not a single one flees. The Tabernacle erupts toward the sky as bursts of fire shoot into the air and hit several stradains who had not kept their distance. Small demons scream as they dive to the ground, their bodies wreathed in cloaks of fire. My hidden haven is now a ruin, crumbling atop the mountain.

"We must not linger," Manuel tells me. "More will come."

"Let them," I tell him, watching the scene.

"Boldness and arrogance are oft as twins, and few men can tell them apart at a glance. Be mindful, little child, we are here to counsel you."

"And you do, noble Manuel," I admit, having grasped his meaning.

"Good. Then let us continue."

The march down the eastern slope is hard, and the clanking of armor echoes in the night. The way in which The Lamb led me was not the easiest way up the mountain. This would have been much gentler. Abdalla and Makaio lead our forces through beautiful woods. The evergreens are thick and full, and they dwarf us with their towering height. At this elevation the mist is thin, and beams of moonlight gleam off our armor.

Behind the two diakonae are the pearl arayil and the char-rashas. Next in the caravan are the zaquenan. The rahfaad then follow, with the wounded Dashawn keeping a limp pace behind their step. The amunamai are second to last, and they form a ring of gold with me at the center. I feel more trapped than protected by them, and I cannot help but look for a hole to escape. Our multitude ends with the ever-patient exharts who were assigned to train me but were given no time. Nonetheless they do not complain and accept their new role as the guards at our backs.

Between the dense of the trees and the thickening mist, we must be unseen as we move further down the mountain. Though our course has been both long and loud, no further attack of the enemy comes. I would have guessed them to be on us by now, knowing that The Tabernacle lies in ashes.

The diakonae lead us to a plateau on the mountain, and the smoldering ruins can be seen high above us. Clement directs me to a pool, assuming that I thirst from our march. I bend down to drink the crystal clear water and notice that the fog has broken. The mist awaits us in the forest, but on this mesa it is gone. The enormous moon shines above us, and I see a most fascinating sight in the pool.

Me. Clad in armor. Before now I failed to consider that fact that I had neither the means nor time to see my reflection. I feel a great swell of dignity as I take in my form. I would have expected vanity or pride, but I feel neither. I feel "appropriate," as if this is how I should be—as if I am reflecting my actual status as an heir in the kingdom of The Lamb.

My helmet is bronze with three golden bands at my temple, and it reaches round my head and down to my chin. Its curved edges extend ahead of my cheeks and protect the sides of my face without encasing it. The breastplate covers the whole of my chest, extending from my shoulders down to my navel. This too is bronze and sculpted with musculature as well as an emblazoned gold cross at my heart. At my waist I wear a broad green belt that possesses a wide brown loop. This serves as the sheath for my sword, the tip of which extends to the top of my green boots.

I lean down to drink and set my shield beside me, but I keep my right hand near the hilt of my blade. I cup the mountain water with my left and bring it to my dried lips. The fluid glides through my parched mouth and renews me as it makes its way to my stomach. I take several more slow and careful sips, trying not to let a single drop escape my hand. I let the last drink sit in my mouth, not knowing when the next will come.

As the rings from my disturbance settle in the water, I see them—flying things, backlit by the moon. I thank the Lord for the lesser light and its unintentional warning to us. By the time I turn to tell the others, I realize how obtuse I have been. Several arayil and char-rashas have aimed their arrows at the enemy. The amunamai guardians form a crescent around me. The diakonae have sprinted further below the mesa, to ensure that the foes are not forcing us into an ambush. The remaining char-rashas have formed a line at the east, and the exharts have done the same at the west. The zaquenan also have bows at the ready in search of other foes above us.

A cry echoes from the devils.

Klahan of the arayil and one of the char-rashas release their arrows into the air. That of the former finds its mark through the wing of the closest creature.

"What are they?" I ask. "More stradains?"

"No. Vhulraks," Alexavier tells me, "weaker demons intended to watch, to spot us and call out the news to the others."

Two of the other arayil send another vhulrak tumbling into the treetops.

"Zaquenan, we should move." Alexavier cries.

"When the diakonae confirm the path is clear," Manuel claims as he watches above us.

As the vhulraks hover and our arrows fly, a shadow falls across the plateau. A gathering cloud of winged things approaches from the southeast, silhouetted by moonlight.

"More come," Alexavier whispers to himself.

"Amunamai," he declares. "Now is the hour to heed your task. Eyes alert. Arms at ready. Be savage toward wolves and watch over the sheep."

A bevy of arrows ascends toward the sky, and a number of flying demons fall.

"More vhulraks?" I ask.

"No, child of God," Alexavier says. "These are stradains, the fierce riders of the wind." He turns to me and closes, "These will be harsh toward us, and we to them."

The amunamai fire again. The elders and arayil do the same, alternating with the char-rashas who shoot as the others reload. The cloud of darkness gets larger, and the barrage of darts does not diminish it.

"Further down the slope we move," Abdalla calls as he exits the tree line.

"Clear of snares?" Manuel asks.

"As best we can see. The plain is covered in marsh and mist, their forces by land will not soon see us."

More arrows fly into the night.

"Then we move," Alden confirms. He barks orders, and the whole legion obeys, adhering to his every command. "Exharts. Char-rashas. Fire. Hold our foes to the sky above. Diakonae shall lead the way with arayil following at their heels. Zaquenan, stay near the heir and aid the amunamai as his shield. Go. Go now. Into the mist and wood."

As we run toward the trees more arrows pierce the air. Manuel grabs Jadon by the arm, "Rahfaad, stay close. Who knows what pain we shall endure."

The elders are before me, and the guards trail my back. We are near the trees when the enemy strikes. Swooping down, the remaining stradains hurl spiked orbs at us. I hear one of our members cry out in pain. I turn to look back, but Tarak seizes me without missing a beat as he strides to the tree line.

I try to struggle while I protest, "Tarak, let me go. We're not on the run."

I break from his grasp and turn toward the fray. The ring of guards grabs me and holds me down. I hear metal crash against their armor, and two of them cry aloud. The dome they have formed encases me, and their leader Alexavier also takes a blow.

"Please, child of God," Alexavier implores me, "we must run at present. Our prize is the stronghold, not this rabble."

The fear and confusion of the battle have taken me. I have lost all speech.

"Move," Alexavier commands his men.

Tarak pulls me up and holds my arm as we all enter the forest.

"I'm sorry. I'm so sorry." I tell them.

Tarak stays silent, but Alexavier speaks for all. "Keep your breath for the run."

I hear another series of cries echo from the clearing, and I hear footsteps at our backs.

"Are they following?" I ask.

"No, their wings are strong and made for travel, but their feet have long been scalded in flame. They may carry crons and weapons, but they do not step onto the land. I imagine those bold enough to dive were undone by our sword or bow."

"Then why did we run?"

"Because most do not dive. They glide high and throw their bombs from above, but they cannot follow us through the forest and mist. We are more secure now."

I hope he is right. In my periphery, Cutler and Deron make their way passed us to the front of the zaquenan. They give a status report as they run.

"Who is taken?" one amunamai asks.

"Only three—Arif by their spiking orbs and Saku by a talon's slash. Emmett, too, fell by their strike, but five of their kind it took to swarm him after a shot had slowed his step. Until the moment his presence left, he fought hard with his noble swing. Such shall be remembered in later days, when tales of valiant ends are told."

Emmett. Hours earlier, he was forging my blade; now he is gone from the land of my soul. His murderers stay and return to their fortress. Anger boils in my blood. I want to put my sword to use.

"Opportunity will come," Alexavier assures me. "I know the desire, child of God. Do not waste your tension yet. The time is near to expend it all."

We run in silence. I glance to my left. One of the hit amunamai has a dent in his armor where his neck and back meet. I cannot see the other that was struck. Alexavier has been hit as well, and I can see the wound at his side. My haste brought their hurt, but I do not know how much.

I feel as foolish as I ever have.

We have not left the forest, but the ground has leveled. The turf is softer. I assume we have reached the eastern valley, the dark sea of mist resting in a bowl of stone. The low laying clouds may protect us from the scouts, but they also blind us to incoming danger. When we emerge from the tree line onto the plain, the fog is at its thickest—ten feet in any direction is an opaque gray.

A few dozen yards further into the valley, the zaquenan suspect that we are not alone. Manuel calls our march to a halt, and using his spyglass, he looks in all directions.

"I can see nothing beyond us," he says.

One of the arayil is launched backward as I hear the burst of a cannon blast. This is a sound I know all too well.

An armored patrol has found us.

This time I have dropped to the ground, the soft turf cushioning the speed of my dive. The others have followed suit.

I look up to find vhulraks diving low. I can barely see them in the fog and assume that they can see us also. At least one does, and it caws to the patrols. Manuel looks in all directions to decipher from where the next attack will come, and the others look for the scouts above us. A youthful-looking amunamai named Edmund sees a vhulrak and nudges the guard next to him. One by one they warn their neighbors, set arrows in their bows and move into position. Each has shifted within reach of the others.

"On my signal roll away from my shot," Alexavier whispers to me.

I do not know what he means, but I follow his lead. He releases the arrow upward and away from our position. The moment the shot is loosed from his bow, he also taps his foot on Edmund, who fires. Alexavier rolls backward from the direction of his shot; after I move also, I notice the strategy. As each fires his arrow both upward and outward, he signals the next to shoot as well. The archer then moves inward, tightens our line, and resets the system. The other units do this as well. I am reminded of dominoes as the arrows fly, one after another after another.

Though the enemy is hidden within the clouds, many arrows hit their marks. Vhulrak bodies fall several yards outside our line, but they make no sound other than their thud on the turf. They are hideous demons up close. Enormous eyes bulge out of an oblong head that also bears tiny ears and a bump for a nose. Their beaklike mouths possess rows of small teeth, and their long, wide tongues hang between their gaping lips. The wings at their sides are large and feathered, giving them a greasy and ugly appearance. Despite their human shape, they are altogether beastlike.

Our caravan has gotten more compact as we lay in wait on the cold valley floor. Tarak is at my left, and Alexavier at my right. I am looking at the latter when he nods to those near me.

"What is it?" I ask Alexavier.

"They are coming—patrols, from the east and south, and they are upon us."

"What are we going to do?"

"My force and I will guard you when we strike."

"When will that be?"

"I assume right now."

As he finishes his sentence, I grasp his meaning. The walking sycoma eye and the marching cron appear within our pocket of mist. They had no idea what was to befall them. The whole of the legion, all thirty-six remaining, rise in a single wave of pearl and gold, crashing upon the devils while charging through the cloud. I hear neither gunfire nor the cry of death—only swords slashing wind and metal tumbling to the ground. Tarak has lifted me and pulled me into the fray, but I am too disoriented to be of any help. In a matter of moments we duck down once, lying close to one another as we await the next group. The minute that it appears, the legion rises and rushes it.

This process repeats itself as we cross the plain. Time gets lost between attacks, but the method remains effective. Though the marsh becomes deeper and the water is cold, we lose no more warriors to cannons or ambush. The crawl through the damp ground has been long and uncomfortable, but in time we come to hard soil in a grove of willow trees.

As we pause and await our next assault, the fog departs from the valley floor. The dark sky above houses brooding clouds that look ripe to release a downpour at any moment. The floor itself is clear and wide, and I realize something I did not expect. We are near the end of the valley's southern wall. Around the corner of this last slope, the south expands as wide as the east, and in that area sits the stronghold.

With the mist gone, I look back to the path by which we came. Mountains frame the valley on all sides but the east. A road of demonic corpses descends into the distance. Patrol after patrol lay destroyed along the ground, and I realize something I had long forgotten—my force is no rescue party of three. No, this is a battalion en route to war.

Jadon makes sure I get some fluids as Clement and Evan look to the injured amunamai. The diakonae scout our path, while the zaquenan and arayil take counsel together. The char-rashas and uninjured guards take time to rest and renew their strength. The exharts watch me but say nothing.

Our march has not been what I had expected. I had envisioned us walking across the valley unmet and unopposed until breaching their walls. I had thought we would move without wasting a moment, refusing delay as we trekked toward war. I had assumed I would lead with the others behind me, following my command. As I reflect on the battle we have waged, I realize I have not fought a single enemy.

Given this development, I make no predictions about the hours to come. My mission is clear, and my goal is firm. I should be secure in that. No matter what befalls us, I know what I must do: bring the stronghold to ruin however I can. These reflections renew my aim, and I am ready when the diakonae return.

Abdalla draws on the ground as he speaks. "If we come straight from our present course at the west, we should be able to seize the ruins at their sides, avoiding any forces watching on the road as well as catching them off guard."

"Hm," Viho says.

"What is it, zaquenan?" Klahan asks.

"An attack from the west would allow us to ambush, but I do not feel that is the young one's intent." He then looks to me. "Would you have us strike them where unguarded or attack them where their eyes keep watch?"

I am now supposed to voice my expectation, the one I had decided to drop. This is good, for it forces my gut reaction, and I am not surprised by it.

"I want us to attack them head-on," I say, looking over the legion for a reaction. "I recognize that such a move may not be wise, that in fact it may be reckless and brazen, but I cannot help thinking that it is honest—that it shows the enemy our courage. We no longer fear their number nor strength, and I feel the need to tell them this."

"I agree," Alden says.

"As do I," Manuel adds.

Viho stares straight at me and folds his arm while he lets out a long, deep breath. A smile cracks, "A noble desire—one I think we all had hoped you would have."

A few nods and affirmations arise from others.

Viho looks to Abdalla and Makaio. "Diakonae, your plan is shrewd, but this is a moment to be unabashed. We shall make known our coming. From here we move north before turning east to arrive at the road. We will then march in full force to the south at their front and make them tremble at our approach."

More nods and affirmations come, and Viho looks to me.

"I think it would show them your resolve, little child, if you stand at the front of our number. Let them see that your fears have passed. Let them know you intend to destroy them."

Indeed I do, and they will know.

11 : THE RUINS

Our approach begins by backtracking west to the site of the last patrol. I tell the angels to strip the cannons off of their bases until all that remains is a platform flanked with treads on either side. This provides us with a vehicle of sorts. I am rather proud of the plan, until I realize something disheartening.

"Wait," I tell them. "This isn't going to work."

"Why?" Alden asks.

"We have no idea how the cannon is driven or what propels it."

"Well," Viho begins, "you know that it has no driver, and its primary purpose was in seeking your capture, correct? Then it is possible that the mechanism is tied to some other agent or driven by remote."

At that moment, Klahan and another arayil drag a two-legged probing sycoma into a pile with the other dead;

and as they do this, the treads of the platform turn. All of us stop. Viho directs them to move the orb. As they carry the orb, the treads follow it.

"Ha." Manuel yells. "A fortuitous discovery. We could have spent hours looking for the remote."

"True," I interject. "Plus, we can manipulate this."

Using the spear of the nefqahan, I stab the head of the sycoma and jump onto the platform. The treads back up as I do this but stop when I land.

"This should work," I tell them, positioning myself near the front of the vehicle.

"The platform remains still, little child." Alden observes.

"Right," I tell him. "But—wait."

I hold the spear ahead of me, placing the sycoma orb in front of the platform.

The treads propel themselves forward which in turn propels the orb. The platform continues to move as long as the sycoma is ahead of it, but once I pull back the spear, the treads stop.

"Clever," Alden admits.

"No, it's not," I tell him. "I'm pretty sure farmers have been using a variation on this for thousands of years to get their mules to move. I'm just lucky it applies here."

We move to other patrols, and after stripping the cannons and prepping the treads, we pile the bodies and machines into heaps. Covered in oil from the mechanized suits, these bundles burn hot, and they send a column of black smoke into the night.

We arrange five platforms in the shape of a 'v', each one propelled by a spear stabbed into its front. Our legion moves northwest several hundred yards before circling back east and starting south. Four guardians and I ride the center vehicle, and two transports flank us on each side.

I overhear the angels engaged in conversation but glean no more than a phrase or two. They speak of other battles on countless other nights with other fervent saints who fought as I do. I wonder if on some other front, in some other battle ages from now, two will reunite and speak of me. I will be the one who asked to forge my own sword, who was later stabbed by the exporex, and who led them toward doom on chariots of the enemy's making. Or maybe I think too much of myself. This whole night may be long forgotten in the lengthy memories of their ancient minds. Regardless of their thoughts mine need to be focused, for we are close to the enemy.

The road looks south. The air is clear. The ruins are a ghost town on the horizon. Behind them the great storehouse awaits and after it lays the fortress of Awthoomgaw. From the road he appears as a statue of magma—distant but ominous, far yet too near. Closer and closer and closer we come. The larger he grows, the more perilous he appears.

However, the time to fear has passed. The time for excuses has run its course. Now is the hour of righteous anger. Now is the moment for fury to surge. All of the rage from the hours enslaved, all of the longings for purity lost, all the shame of abominable deeds—now they find a means to strike.

All else fades but war to The Lamb's glory.

I cannot wait another minute. The treads move but lack speed. I leap from the platform and sprint for the ruins; I assume the others follow. My armor, sword, and shield weigh nothing. My arms pump fast and propel my legs. My feet show swiftness I have not known. I look neither right, nor left, nor behind me. I stare forward at the site of our siege.

The sound of our transports is soon overtaken by the charge of three-dozen mighty angels. Metal boots stomp the soil and stone—booming drums of the coming assault. I cannot imagine what our enemies see other than a wall of pearl and gold.

Pale crons around a dying fire are the first to fall from our powerful strike. Arrows pierce them by the time they see us. I am the first to enter the ruins; the others trail a few steps behind me. Once our full force arrives, a tumult of violence befalls the tenants.

I see two crons run behind half a wall, and I pursue them with sword in hand. Coming around the brick and wood I find them hunting for weapons in the rubble. My first stroke shows my blade's sharp edge, for it removes the cron's arm from his body. A second swing detaches his skull from his neck. His partner turns and hisses at me, but he meets the same fate as the other.

I move from the building back to the street, and find the battle underway. Any surprise at our arrival has passed, and our enemies rush at us from all sides. I see what I believe to be the agras, the demons lower in rank than crons. They are little more than ravenous cretins, bearing no wings, weapons, or armor. They are wide-eyed, long-limbed, green-scaled upstarts, grabbing at arms to bite through armor or holding at legs to trip those in the fray.

I can see that the angels have no time for them. Klahan has one on each of his legs and another pair pounding their arms on his back. He ignores them and chases after crons and humanlike demons called "gehoonds." These latter villains have calloused burns covering every inch of their skin. They dress in tattered leather armor, and their weapons are daggers, maces, and chains. Most have sullen, sunken faces, but they are far more aggressive than the crons or the agras. Despite this level of increased hostility, they are not equipped for the force that has come.

The angels attack in efficient units. Two arayil rush into a building, and hiding crons pour from the exits. The demons are met by waiting char-rashas who slay them as the arayil move to the next structure. Zaquenan archers move back-to-back and make their way across the rooftops. The first one reloads as the second fires, and they cover those on the ground from oncoming attacks. The diakonae run to the fallen targets to reclaim the arrows that they can; if any ounce of life remains in the villain, the runners end him with a snap of his neck. The rahfaad search the field of battle for need, but at present our soldiers appear unscathed.

The amunamai and exharts have become a single force and hold a line around me while I attack wherever I choose. Given my impetuous charging, they rescue me from constant ambush. While many of them keep a distance, Alexavier, Tarak, and Alden stay close.

A crash echoes from the northern end of the ruins as our abandoned chariots arrive. Until its sycoma eye is stopped, each vehicle charges on our behalf. I doubt they damage any structures, but I am sure they run down a few crons and agras.

The light from the lanterns, torches, and fires has created endless shadows within the ruins. A pair of gehoonds spring from a corner before me. My guards charge one while I engage the other. Our eyes meet as he grabs my right arm and keeps my sword from finding its mark.

"You are not as strong as you think, believer."

Deron comes upon us and crushes the demon under the weight of his mighty blow.

I nod in thanks but concede, "I think he had a point."

"No," The exhart says. "He was a liar, and you would have ended him within a few moments. Remember, son of the Most High, you are far stronger than they will ever say."

I accept the lesson but make no response.

"Therefore," he continues with a smile, "do not let them speak. Do not hesitate; strike hard. In time, they will know your strength."

From the corner of my eye, I see a few demons moving toward the outskirts to escape.

"There," I yell to the others before I charge the rogues. The defenders follow at my back, and I come upon the villains—four crons and a gehoond. Remembering Deron's exhortation, I drive into them swinging and kicking. The first cron is booted into a wall as a second is cast aside with my shield. My right arm makes a swift arch out, and the back of my hand strikes the larger foe. The momentum of my swing shifts my left side forward, and the counterstrike from the gehoond rebounds on my shield. I pivot and thrust my sword into his gut and turn the blade as I pull it back. I thrust aside right and stab a third cron as it tries to return to hiding in the ruins. As the fourth takes its second step into a run, I throw my sword at its pale back. The blade fails to stab him but cracks his head, knocking him to the rocky ground. I pick up the sword and flip it blade-downward, then stab it into the cron at his neck. I rise to find several angels behind me, watching this conflict with silent approval.

Alden tilts his head to the left to usher us back to the heart of the ruins. On the way, we charge into houses, slay villains, and exit onto new streets. The pattern is confusing, and I lose my bearings. By the third house we attack, I cannot tell east from west. With me at all times are Alexavier and Tarak as well as Deron who has stayed at our rear. I assume the other defenders are close, keeping unseen villains at bay.

Minutes pass before we arrive at the village square where our offensive forces stand in a sea of corpses. Agras, crons, and gehoonds by the dozens were driven here and hewn to pieces.

I pause to reflect on the victory and look at the many buildings that surround us. In a frightening way, I know them all, but I cannot place the reason why. With each that we entered, I had moved on instinct. I knew the layouts, hallways, and doors. Since arriving I have been led by others, but here I seemed to lead by default.

I realize something both strange and horrifying. The house at the south of the square is familiar—in fact it is the house in which I was raised. I do not know what the others are doing, and frankly I do not care. I sheathe my sword and run toward the dilapidated structure.

Upon entering, I find the hallways in shambles, the kitchen neglected, and the den destroyed. I move upstairs and look to the end of the hall at the room that was mine until I left home. The other rooms I pass are battered and disheveled in the same manner as the main room downstairs. My parents' room is ignored, same as the kitchen. My room however is drenched in filth—blood and dirt are on the walls (or rather, what is left of them). The room smells of foulness and melted plastic. It may be the worst place I have encountered in Solsland.

Then I see something worse.

Manuel lies against the wall, suffering the death of a thousand wounds. I rush to him, grab his right hand, and look in his eyes. They are fading gold amidst a tortured face.

"Manuel. Manuel, please. Hold on. I will get the rahfaad."

"We cannot help him," I hear from behind me. I turn to see Jadon in the doorway but return my focus to the dying zaquenan.

"How did this happen to you?" I ask.

He shakes his head "no," but I dismiss this and press him.

"Tell me. How many? Where are they?"

He coughs blood and closes his eyes as he pushes his arm toward me. This presses my own hand over the cross at my heart, and he nods as his grip goes limp.

"Manuel?" I ask. "Manuel, please. Not this soon. Not you. Not—" Tears well in my eyes. I look away from him and set his hand upon his lap. I rise and turn to Jadon, who is now joined by Alden.

"Did we kill all of them?" I ask.

"Those who did this? Yes," Alden responds. "Klahan confirmed it. He told us that Manuel grabbed two arayil to pursue many crons that had run into this house. The demons led them up the stairs to this final room where the ambush waited. The zaquenan foresaw the scheme and blocked the arayil from entering herein. He locked himself inside the room before any of the demons could swarm at the others. The crons broke loose, but all were destroyed once they reached those in the hall."

"I need to look at the other houses," I tell them.

"If we are to assail the fortress, I advise we do not linger here."

"Alden, please. I need to see the other houses. I just—I need to know something before I go further."

"Do as you must, but be aware, with each minute our foes regroup, and the next front will be more defended than this."

"I know." I head down the stairs and leave the house through a back door.

The next building I find is another I know—a neighbor's house. I run into it to find a similar scenario. Certain rooms are ash and ruin; others are unkempt and neglected. I go to the third home, that of a childhood friend, and the scene repeats itself. The fourth house is a relative's house, and the fifth, another friend's. The next building I come to is a dilapidated storefront and after that another local shop. All are echoes of how I remember them. In the western corner lies the largest building, and it too is a location I recognize—a school.

The sun has begun its rise, but the cloud cover permits not but a foreboding gray sky. I turn around and look back over the streets full of dilapidated homes and buildings. I know them all, and I know why they are here.

I return to the square to find the others waiting. The rahfaad tend to minor wounds, and the char-rashas hammer dents out of armor.

"We are fortunate," Agyei says walking toward me. "They have sent no second force; perhaps they think we will end our march here."

"No," I tell him. "They know as well as I do that this is just the beginning."

"What do you mean?" Jadon asks.

I look to Alden, "Should I tell them?"

"You are our charge. No new knowledge changes this. The Lord saw fit to assign us to you, and we shall remain until he takes us home."

"Tell us," Klahan barks.

"This village is made of many houses. These were good homes and places full of memories, but they are also seasoned with poison. These places should never have been connected with lust, and yet they were in thought or action. These are the ruins of what was innocent, of what was good at an early time before I perverted it on the road to addiction." I sigh and remove my helmet. I turn from the others and look down the streets, reflecting on the sheer number of structures, considering how far my carnality spread, remembering how it knew no bounds. This village is made of many houses. Far too many. I feel the angels stare, but I do not face them.

A hand is on my shoulder. I turn around to find Deron, whose strong but kind face smiles at me. "We await your next order, son of the Most High."

I look beyond him to the rest of the legion. Their gaze has not turned to condemnation. Their eyes show no sign of contempt. Either they have seen worse, or they do not let this affect them. Regardless, I stand and keep my eyes on theirs. A bright beacon in the distance stands against the gray sky behind them. They are not the only ones who have seen this battle. I replace my helmet and turn from the square, looking to the road that leads south toward the warehouse.

"And now?" Alden asks.

"Burn it."

12 : THE ARCHIVES

The ruins go up like kindling in a fireplace. From the top of the citadel, I am sure it looks awful—a sea of ashes coughing smoke into the air. A playground where the demons roamed is now their graveyard burnt to dust. From the southern end of this lost terrain the demons see a wretched thing—a worm of pearl with a head of gold, with a copper nose and eyes of purple. This shining devourer of the horde moves with speed toward Mykmun.

We approach as our foes would—fearless and bold, ready to destroy any enemy that crosses us. None emerge. The path we take to the warehouse is clear, but the air upon it is heavy and damp. Stagnant pools of sludge and mud lie in the fields at each side of the trail. We stay upon the trodden road and march to a destination that appears deserted.

"The diakonae said this place was well defended," I tell Alexavier.

"Then perhaps we are being lured into a trap."

"True."

"What will we do, child of God, if the threshold to Mykmun is open?"

"Proceed but with caution and expect a trap."

"Do you think that is wise?"

"Well, no but—maybe. I don't know. What else can we do? We came here to destroy this place, regardless of their forces here. If they give us entry, we might as well take it, maybe we can exploit it somehow."

I hear a strange noise—a *poonk* or something similar. An angel behind us falls to the ground, and the march of the remaining soldiers stops. I turn around to see what has happened and find the rahfaad standing over the fallen.

"What is it?" I ask.

"He has been shot," Clement tells me.

"From what direction?"

"It came from the south. Passed right through his mask and stopped within his helmet. There is no exit wound."

They have a sniper, and he has a powerful rifle.

"We must get to cover," Clement tells us. "Now."

Another *poonk* and Zaquenan Cato falls to the road. I waste no more time.

"Into the warehouse," I call.

We run south toward the building and find the door open.

"You are right," I concede to Alexavier. "This is a trap. We have no cover but here. The sniper wants us to flee toward this place for a reason."

"Then we shall spring the trap before breaking through it."

"Amen to that."

The road widens into a gravel lot, and the building on it is a large rectangle. The color of the structure is rust over orange, the shade one may see on a long-abandoned tractor left to decay in some farm's backfield. The depot shows only one portal to the outdoors—a single large door that has been raised.

We maintain vigilance as we move inside the warehouse. Two were slain to drive us here, and the unseen enemy awaits our entrance. All the char-rashas arm their bows, while everyone else draws his sword and shield. We are ready for an ambush to come from anywhere (or everywhere).

But it does not. All we see are pallets, boxes, and shelves. Lights hang from the ceiling thirty feet overhead, and they illuminate the space with a synthetic glow. Catwalks and ladders rest high above us over the towers of amassed objects. The stacks show no order and create a labyrinth impossible to navigate. Nowhere can I see a door or the building's outer walls; the contents are too tall and dense. If I did not know better, I would think this place is just a huge distribution center. Though its size is disconcerting, nothing in it feels evil.

"Of course," I whisper aloud.

"What?" Alden asks.

"The catwalks, the ladders, the disorganization from the floor. We are in the wrong place. From where we stand it is a maze, but from the walkways above us, I'll bet all is obvious. I'm guessing everything is labeled looking down from above, yet on the floor one will be lost. They'll be surrounding us from the higher ground. If we flee we will run without direction, and they will follow our every move."

"How do you know this?"

"They seem to be good at guessing my dread, and the idea of such a trap terrifies me."

"Why?"

"Because I have no idea how I … would … escape." I see something. Something wrong. I change my mind; great evil *is* here.

Alden can sense it, and he shakes my shoulder.

"Wait," I tell him as I walk toward an open box tipped on its side with contents spilled. I stop as soon as I surmise what they are. I look back at Alden.

"We were right to fear this place," I tell him. "We need to get out. Now."

We have made our way too far inside the hall. I do not know how to get back to the open door.

Alden looks beyond me to the box.

"Yes," I tell him. "It's what you think."

"All of it?"

"Yeah."

"Surely not all of it."

"Check any box. Check every box. Every last one will be filled to the brim."

The diakonae scouts, Makaio and Abdalla, walk past me to shelves of content on either side of the two makeshift walls. Each opens a box and looks within it.

"What did you call this place?" I ask Alden.

"The 'Halls of Mykmun,' the last word being Prehterran for 'hidden treasure.'"

"And so it is," I reply as my eyes meet Abdalla's. He shakes his head in disbelief then looks down the corridor of shelves in shock. Makaio keeps his head low, staring at the contents.

"Well tell us what they contain," demands Klahan.

"It—" Abdalla stutters, "they are the—but they cannot all be full?"

"They are," I answer. "All of them. Full of pictures—actual pictures or mental pictures—copies of images or echoes of imaginings, my mind's long memory of a lifetime's addiction."

I rise and face the men as I speak. "These are my stores, Klahan. This is my Mykmun. A man can go for some time without seeing new filth, but much of the old remains burned in his mind, captured and stored right here in his heart. We can change our behavior but that does not erase its scars. No. Our sinful nature keeps a catalog.

"And that, my friends, is our challenge now; I could get lost in here forever. If I look in any direction, a single image could catch my eye; and if it does, I could run us in circles in hopes of a second sinful glimpse. Or I could just let go of pretense, surrender, and run to see what else I can find. Within a moment my entire endeavor could shift from being free to enjoying the snare.

"I cannot lead us through this place."

"Nor will you have to," a voice assures me.

All the angels and I look up. The trap is sprung. Along the catwalks stand demonic foot soldiers clad in crimson—more ra'shrogs. From knee to neck they stand in scarlet, slacks at the legs and vests at their chests, with black armor beneath and crimson gloves at their hands. Their boots are black and covered in spikes. They have the same filthy, unpolished chrome faces of those who stood in the cellar of Mokmah. Each of them bears a large, imposing rifle, and they are at least a hundred in number.

Their leader's basic uniform is the same, but he boasts a gray cape and a red officer's hat. His head is like a skull sculpted from obsidian stone, and his taut, thin skin is stretched around it. His eyes are bright red and his mouth full of teeth, straight but black as thick crude oil.

He makes a foul grin as he speaks, "You took back the ruins, we will grant you that."

"But that has not satiated our thirst for your destruction," Alden responds.

"Our destruction? Here? In this land? You are as foolish as you were the day The Lamb formed you. Do you think that we will be driven from here? Do you believe you will gain any more ground? You have lost, angel. You lost the moment you arrived."

Agyei then comes to Alden's side and calls to the speaker. "You are not as invincible as you feel. As you said, we assailed your first post. Now this and many more await our wrath."

He waves his hand to dismiss Agyei's claims. "You defeated a rabble of mindless fools, a horde of useless fodder and bait. Do you not see that we gave it to you? Why else would we not defend our claim if not to draw you into our web? You think you defeated the patrols in the valley? Ha. Sacrificed pawns to align you in our sights. All of your victories, we permitted. But no more."

I want to cry out, but shame forces my silence. The battle has ended, and we have lost. I might fall into sin after the fact since I am in a headspace to rekindle temptation. I need only a moment to start the process.

I look over my force that stands ready for combat. The loaded bows of the char'rashas are aimed toward the overwhelming force. The arayil have done the same. The others wait with swords in-hand, prepared and determined to fight to the last. The angels have not surrendered like I have.

I notice that Viho's eyes search for mine, but I glance away to avoid a connection. I can feel his stare, and it draws me back to him. The moment our eyes meet, he winks and screams a battle cry in a language I do not understand. A barrage of arrows launches from the floor toward the ra'shrogs, their leader, and the lights.

The brightness of the hall near us goes dim, and I see my legion about their work. Taking flares from the rahfaad, the remaining zaquenan set fires to the stores. They stab the flame into the stacks and knock shelves and boxes onto the floor. The archers continue their assault on the lights overhead and the demonic soldiers. By the time the enemy fires on us, the amunamai form a circle around me while our remaining force scatter throughout the warehouse.

"Thane, your aid." Alexavier calls. With that the exhart with the red beard takes to the shelves, hacking and smashing and breaking and slicing. The other exharts follow his lead. With fervor and speed they cut a hole through the pallets, tumbling boxes here and there. We move from one makeshift corridor to another.

I assume we are lost and trapped anew, but the arayil surprise me. While some use their bows to attack from the ground, others climb the stacks to the catwalks above us. As the exharts cut our path through the maze, the arayil tell them the direction to go. My guards and I follow the demolition crew and slay clerks who pass by us en route to save records.

These clerks are some of the most hated of the demonic legions. Alexavier refers to them as "a cowardly lot." They make no direct efforts of their own against men, but through their knowledge they aid in evil. They keep records of wrong, search men for weaknesses, and provide information to the warrior hordes. Believing themselves innocent of actual wrongdoing, the faceless figures dress in white, topping off their ensemble with pristine gloves. This specific use of color is a perversion to the angels, and the amunamai revel in destroying these vermin.

Overcast daylight hangs in the air a few dozen yards away from us, and I realize that the southern door is open, having been used by the frantic clerks. The wearied exharts are renewed by this and break through the corridor barriers with vigor. They break shelves to planks and shred boxes to splinters—a path of destruction rests behind them. The arayil have continued to battle overhead, rescuing us from unseen enemies. Through the coordinated efforts of the legion, we have almost escaped the trap.

But I am not ready to exit this place. I want to stay here and destroy this Mykmun, to burn every image and forget every memory, but I have no control of my path. The amunamai around me force my direction, for their goal is set on ensuring my survival. Though I have enough space to move and attack, I cannot halt us or change our course.

The pale light that shines through the door is brighter than the glow of the overheads. Freedom waits beyond two walls. If I plan to stop us, I must do it soon. A group of clerks sees us, and they turn for the exit, but the exharts and amunamai pursue. Once the clerks are slain, we move, but I stop in sight of Deron and Tarak. The others break through the wall, but without a word I slide outside the protective ring.

Deron grabs my arm. "We must keep moving, son of the Most High, lest we find ourselves trapped again."

"No," I say, before assaulting the records. "I cannot let these stay here, Deron. They must be destroyed. All of them."

"And they will in the end," the exhart assures me, "but at present such cannot be done."

"It must," I cry. "I don't want them here. I can't have them here."

I unleash my frustration on other cartons, kicking and grabbing and throwing and smashing. A flurry of paper and splinters flies into the air. I use my elbows and the point of my shield to crush through wood and knock down the stacks. I battle the contents until exhaustion takes hold. I fight it, but soon I am a mess on the floor surrounded by piles of rubble I have created.

I look up to find the exhart and guardian who have watched my complete and total breakdown. They are not alone. Realizing we were absent, the others returned, having made a path from here to the door. The zaquenan have arrived by a route through the maze. The char-rashas are trickling toward us, and the arayil stand overhead on the catwalks. A few members are missing from our ranks, though I know not who. The survivors watch and await my next move.

I kneel in the sea of my ruined Mykmun, but I do not look down to savor it. I have no desire to see the remnants. Shame and pride contend within me. I feel glad to have fewer images than I had minutes ago, but I am embarrassed at their being here at all. I stand and look at the legion without word, and I target the next stack at the wall.

"Wait." Alden cries. "We have earned an escape but not total freedom. If we stay here, they will renew their numbers, and there will be neither parlay nor posturing. They will destroy us. We must gain the upper hand by continuing our siege."

"I can't, good counselor. I am sorry. I want to be rid of all of this."

"You will be," Viho begins, "but that is a longstanding work; one the king oversees alone. This is not your task in the present battle."

"But how can I go on, knowing this is here, available to me at any time?"

"You *have known* that it is here, yet you have not used it," Viho replies. "At least now you know that you have held it secure, and you can open yourself to further cleansing."

"I want to be free of it now," I protest.

"So do all men who fight as you do, but that is a portion of their just desserts—you cannot undo a decade of wrongs in one night, no matter how fervent your longing to do so. Only the king does such a work, and he does so in his right and good timing."

"We have our exit to an open plain and the next obstacle on our course," Alden states. "The time for discussion has ended; the time for action is at hand."

I glance at the small pile of refuse at my feet, then toward the rest of the warehouse. Fires have caught throughout the space, and our path of destruction has caused great loss. The building holds more content than I can bear to keep, and I want to stay and make our stand here. Perhaps we could burn it as we did the ruins.

A banging strikes the western wall.

"Too long have we lingered," Alden whispers.

A second banging occurs and the brick begins to crack. This strike is followed by a third, and with this final sound, an enormous tentacle breaks into the warehouse, making a hole in the wall.

The hideous, red appendage bears a diameter of several feet. Extending several yards into the stores, it wraps around undamaged boxes. With pores in its skin, it clasps the items and holds them in place with spikes on its surface. The rescued contents are pulled back through the hole, but a few random images remain and float to the floor like dead leaves stirred by wind. We do nothing but stare in stunned confusion.

From the eastern wall another tentacle enters the room. It completes the same task as the first, grabbing a pallet's worth of boxes and pulling them outside the warehouse.

"Nofayn. The eye awaits." Agyei cries.

"What?" I ask (since I saw a tentacle, not an eye).

Alden ignores my question and addresses Agyei. "If he is here and this is his doing, then we must find and destroy him as well." Alden wastes no time and heads for the door; the others follow with their weapons ready. Alexavier and the other amunamai wait for me.

"Who is No-fah-een?" I ask.

"Continue your siege, child of God, and you shall see." This answer gives me no comfort, but Alexavier continues. "Be strong and of courage now, for in this hour you shall need it."

That does not comfort me either.

13 : THE EYE

We charge through the path created by my allies and exit the wretched Halls of Mykmun. The cloud cover looms in the sky overhead, and a sullen gray daylight shines on the plain. From here the road continues south leading to the moat that surrounds the fortress. The distance is no more than a hundred yards.

From here Awthoomgaw waits like a statue carved from active volcanic rock. He is at least one hundred feet in height and his skin appears as fading charcoal. His massive wings rest at his back, but his arms are extended—left forward, right upward. Each holds a watchtower in its hand, and similar ramparts reside on his shoulders. A crown-like tower rounds his horned head. I would fear my contest versus him if I were not focused on the next structure in our path.

Taller than the warehouse but a fraction of its width is a new breed of evil. While one might surmise it to be a tower, it in fact is something much more hideous—a creature upon a podium of sculpted black stone. The bottom of its base is round and wide, surrounded by a wall of tall obsidian shards. Inside the wall, a pedestal slopes inward, and the entire post is covered in spikes that crawl across its rising, slender surface. This base alone extends the height of the storehouse, and at its peak sits a basin surrounded by upturned black horns. Some sort of green fluid spills over the dish and rains onto the walled-in base below it. The structure itself is an enormous chalice.

Of course, the horror comes not from it, but from the demon, Nofayn, who sits in the basin. His form is that of a bloodshot eye with a dozen tentacles extending from its back—as though he were ripped from a human face with the nerve endings and blood vessels intact. The demon's face is an immense central pupil surrounded by a crimson iris. The horrible eye pulses with life upon its seat—watching and waiting and seeking.

Its tentacles are those we saw in Mykmun. The two active ones we encountered are longer than half the distance of the plain, for they pull archives from the storehouse and move them across the moat to the citadel. Another half-dozen of these appendages are wrapped at rest around the base. They appear short and stocky, but they show endless folds that imply they can reach as far as those at work. The structure in its entirety is half the size of Awthoomgaw, but it pulls my attention and captures my focus.

Nofayn's pupil connects with my own, and it dilates in hatred. The remaining tentacles flare from the base, and all of them extend in preparation to attack. The eye itself is pulsing faster as the pupil darts right and left at its targets. The first assault comes when the tentacles lash at the ground like enormous whips of a giant. The wicked thing strikes one of the char-rashas, and a tremor growls through the plain. The pores of the tentacles breathe and expand as the limbs are pulled back for a second offensive. This one comes with as much gall as the first.

Nofayn, however, is not our only concern. The spikes on the pedestal have ceased their shifting. They are demons in black armor that jump from the stem. These warriors are ra'shrogs by their size and build, but their black armor covers any traces of skin. Tusks from their helmets drip the green fluid, and they appear as beetles on their hind legs (missing a pair of limbs, of course). With crooked swords and pikes pointed forward, this next batch begins to charge toward us.

"The eye is yours, little child," Alden declares. "We shall clear the path ahead while you and your guardians dispatch the enemy."

The armored ra'shrogs and bold arayil collide and engage in their violent conflict. The char-rashas try to take shots at the eye, but the tentacles block them and retaliate. The remaining zaquenan rush to strike the limbs, and the diakonae and rahfaad aid wounded members of ranks. I then hear that same *poonk* as I did earlier, and the rahfaad Gakuto goes limp and falls. The sharpshooter hides, but his attacks continue. All manner of evil is upon us.

My guardians and I are six in number, having lost one member to the sniper's fire and another to the blitzing limbs of Nofayn. We break through the battle and race to the pedestal. At our rear is Viho, who has decided to join us in bringing down the one called "The Adulterous Eye."

Two of the amunamai create footholds with their arms and hoist Alexavier, Edmund, and Tarak onto the jagged wall around the chalice. The three then lift Viho and me, and the five of us lift the remaining two. We all then jump from atop the barricade into the area in which the pedestal stands. The slope up the tower is now smooth and much thinner given that the hidden guards are gone. Few places to grip are available to us as we try to make our way to the underside of the basin.

Things get worse when the tentacles thrash at us, knocking Tarak and Edmund from their climb. I look down to see the ground shift beneath them, and a creature in hiding emerges from the earth. The gangling demon is sinew and muscle, with a long gaunt face and pitch black eyes. He stands twice the height of the dazed angels and lashes at them with a whip in each hand.

As I turn from the sight, a new dilemma presents itself: there is no way to climb the underside of the basin. Its smooth and hard stone will provide no grip, and I look to Viho and Alexavier who are realizing the same. A tentacle whips at me, but Viho parries it with his sword.

"Child of God," Alexavier yells, "we shall keep the arms at bay. Climb to the enemy alone."

"I don't know how." I tell him, as my foot slides down the pedestal.

"Take a moment—a short moment—and think," Viho commands.

"Think" he tells me. *Think*.

The first idea that comes to mind may be the worst, but time is short. I hold to the tower with my left arm, and draw my blade with my right. I hack at the basin with the sword, but it does not leave a dent. With a sigh in order to regroup my efforts, I slice at the chalice again. A hunk of black rock falls beneath me. Blade in hand I extend further, and swing at the bottom of the basin once more. Another chunk plunges to the fray beneath us.

I return my sword into the scabbard. Despite my substantial fear at this height I reach to the first nook that I cut into the chalice. Finding a grip, I swing to the second. Here, I hold with my left hand alone, and take my sword again in my right. Swinging it with all my strength, I hack another hold. After returning my sword to my side I reach out to the grip and hold it with my right hand in order to give my left a breather. I switch hands and grab my sword with my right and stab not one but three holes in the basin, cutting enough to find a hold but not to the extent that it leaks the fluid.

I rest my sword into its sleeve and move to the first of the three new grips. I hold with both hands and also look down, which is a mistake. Trying to shake off the terror at this height, I swing my right hand to the next wedge. I release my left hand and swing again, finding the next hold at the third dent. I feel the sweat pour down my forehead, and it begins to burn my eyes. I close them and breathe, but to little avail. I know I am going to lose my grasp.

In desperation, I reach toward my sword. I swing the blade both forward and up, jabbing two cuts into the basin's curve. I relieve my left arm; and though the stronger right is holding, I can feel my fingers loosen their grip.

The world now seems to slow to stillness, and I see a bright beacon on the nearest hill. The Lamb stands and watches at this desperate moment—calm and assured I will complete the deed.

Of course he is certain I will succeed.

He has prepared me to do so. Upon the mountain under the rain amidst the dark with both hands bleeding, I climbed a path not unlike this one, and yet my strength withstood the test. Blessed be The Lamb for tribulations, for they train his servants to survive new tasks.

Certain that he sees, I nod in his direction then reach upward to grab the next two holds. Hanging at the curve of the side of the basin, I swing myself toward a horn that extends from the bowl. I kick, but my legs cannot reach. My fingers tighten at this failed gambit, and I look to find The Lamb. He does not falter. He watches, and he waits.

I swing back and forth to build my momentum, and with the third swing I kick again. The moment I feel my knees round the horn, I release my hands and my momentum shifts forward. My legs lock around it, and I dangle upside-down staring several stories above the plain. With my arms depleted from their hardship, I allow myself a moment to rest.

The battle on the ground is chaos from this angle. The sky expands as a wide gray carpet, and the hard, brown soil is a vast rock ceiling. On it two armored forces clash. One appears as a swarm of angry beetles and the other as toy soldiers of pearls and gold. From this perspective they fight without gravity, walking and leaping and sticking to the ceiling over a widespread sea of clouds. It is disorienting and hypnotic (though that could just be the blood rushing to my brain).

I shake my head and hoist my body upward, gripping the sides of the horn with four limbs. I pull myself round it so that I hang no longer, thankful my helmet has been strapped in place and my shield and sword have survived the acrobatics. I lift my head and face Nofayn. His massive pupil stares at me. The arteries and veins pump through his round body, and he pulses with a rekindled rage. I stare straight back at him as I climb from the horn and step onto the basin's rim.

The perimeter of the bowl is about a yard wide and will provide me some running space should I need it. The basin itself is a few feet deep, and it is full to the brim with the green broth. Nofayn fills it less a foot-wide moat that runs between the rim and his body. I have about four feet of working room. Things could be better, but they could also be worse.

While I have been working these dimensions in my head, several of his tentacles have risen near me. I sense one at my back and see four behind Nofayn; the others must be contending on the battlefield. The limbs I see are retracted and thick, with folds hiding the pores and compressing the spikes. A single strike from any could destroy me.

This close to the demon I can smell him. The odor of skin after a bandage is removed hangs in the air and fills my nose.

The lidless pupil contracts as Nofayn focuses on his target. The tentacles mimic cobras waiting to strike. I focus and take my sword in both hands, leaving my shield slung at my back.

The overpowering stench makes my eyes water.

With a deep breath I circle around the demon. The eye follows as I speak.

"I doubt you can hear me, but I assume you read lips."

No reaction, but the eye stares.

"You have pulled my attention far too often and forced my focus where it ought not go. You are the conductor of my heart's deepest shame," with this I stop walking and close with a promise, "and this day, I will slay you."

The first whip-like crack of a tentacle comes, but I dodge it. A dent lay in the chalice where the limb struck, and green stew splashes upon me. The liquid does not burn—not acid. I am lucky. Also, I am assured the moat can be used to my advantage. A second appendage comes toward my back and extends with a vicious thrust, but I duck. Rising, I face Nofayn with caution, and I notice three more massive tentacles in wait—one at the left, another at the right, and the third inching behind the despicable orb. They creep toward me with calculating menace.

I move on instinct and adrenaline, stabbing my sword into the edge of the pupil and breaking through its surface but not embedding into tissue. In shock the tentacles pause, and I sprint to my right, dragging my blade at the cornea of the eye. I scrape it and keep the cut shallow. The limbs are overactive; they whip and flail. They slap the side of the basin and strike the eye itself.

I duck low into the green liquid, and it has a horrid, filthy quality. The iris glides along Nofayn's surface; and when it spots me, I jab at its pupil. My sword breaks the surface, but does little damage. I retract my blade and hold it ready. The frantic tentacles try to strike. I run round the rim of the basin to the point where the limbs meet the orb. They block the perimeter. I have nowhere to run, so I do the next best thing.

With my teeth clenched I slash at the tentacle then hack at it until it is hewn. Dark green blood bursts from the gash, but I maintain my assault at the oversized limbs. My sword is strong, and its edge cuts through another.

I feel a presence behind me, and I turn but not with the needed speed. A tentacle grazes me into Nofayn's body. The wind leaves my lungs as I collide into him and collapse into the chalice's stew.

I lurch as my stomach tightens in pain. My heart beats in panic. The pulsing of the eye carries through the fluid, and the tremors make me fear the coming blow. Rather than wince and brace for impact, I react with another desperate offensive.

I emerge from the liquid and thrust my sword deep into the demon's pupil. I give my blade a firm twist upward as I let go of the hilt and collapse back into the basin.

All the tentacles whip downward at the chalice, and I pull my shield to my chest. The great limbs strike, but the impact reverberates off the shield and through the fluid. I am neither broken nor smashed further down, but I am stuck within the soup.

Then the shield gives me an idea.

Staying low in the muck, I position myself. Nofayn neither attacks nor takes notice. He is preoccupied with the sword impaled into his horrid face. I seize this opportunity and jab the shield's pointed end between Nofayn and the bottom of the basin. My feet planted at the rim of the chalice, I push with all my upper body, but the demon remains unmoved—until my legs assist in the thrust. With their backing, I feel movement of the demon from the basin's floor.

As his tentacles thrash at my embedded blade, I reposition for another push. My legs extend, and I give the scream of a man using the last of his strength. The demon shifts up the curve of the bowl, exposing a drain his body had covered. The green fluid pours through the opening, and the assistance provided by the liquid is lost. The full weight of Nofayn begins teetering toward me. I give my shield another push, forcing it forward until I stumble.

As Nofayn rolls upon the edge of the rim his weight snaps the horns, and he falls from the pedestal. The tentacles flail and reach for the bowl, but they move without focus and find no grip. When the demon strikes the ground a shock ascends through the tower.

I lay upon the pedestal alone.

The odor hangs in the air, and I am covered in muck, staring upward into an overcast sky. I then remember that such a respite cannot last, for the demon Awthoomgaw awaits in his fortress a few dozen yards from the place where I rest. I wonder if he saw the destruction unfold. I wonder if he is angry at my assault. I wonder if I will survive this battle and meet him face to face in the end. How will I fight him if I do?

A knock alerts me from beneath the basin, and I knock in return. A moment later, a blade stabs through the bowl several feet from where I lay. It slices up and down, cutting a hole, and in minutes a portion of the black rock falls. Viho pops his head through the opening.

"Well done," he says.

"Thank you," I reply, rising and slinging my shield on my back.

"You smell awful."

I just give him a hug, and he laughs.

We descend the tower, and when we reach the ground, Tarak hands me my sword. I regret letting it go and gladly accept it back. The minions of the eye lay slaughtered like exterminated insects. Huddled at the pedestal, behind Nofayn's broken body, our ranks can recover for a moment.

The pause is sobering.

Fourteen have fallen since the ruin, including several of our healers—Gakuto, Clement and Evan the Compassionate. Taking these deaths into account, I realize we have but one healer remaining, and he is injured.

Several of the survivors get behind Nofayn, who heaves as if he were clinging to breath. They roll his oozing body toward the ravine surrounding the citadel, and his limp tentacles flare from time to time—a reflex or last attempt at defense.

Though the moat is our next obstacle, it will serve first as a grave for this demon. Despite enemy fire from the fortress walls, we send the wandering eye over the precipice.

This is when Nofayn takes his revenge.

14 : THE PIT

I am pulled straight downward to the barren soil, and the world goes black when I strike the ground. I am dazed but can feel my body being dragged. Nofayn's tentacle is wrapped round my legs.

I grab at air with half my faculties, and the limb jerks me over the ledge of the moat. My hand finds a lucky grip, but I will be unable to maintain it. If the tentacle continues to fall, it will yank my body from this hold.

Once Nofayn hits the floor, the appendage goes lifeless and releases its grasp. Given my own exhaustion, however, holding myself is too much strain. After a moment, I lose my grip.

I fall a few inches, but Tarak grabs my wrist. I dangle suspended over the pit.

The floor of the ravine is dank, dark, and foul. The walls are not as jagged but rather similar to those of a tunnel burrowed by a worm. The bottom of it rests a few dozen feet below me and is filled with dark brown fluid. Judging from the way Nofayn's body sits, the sewage fills about a yard at the moat's floor. This fluid moves, but I cannot be sure if it is due to Nofayn's floating tentacles or some other evil.

Of one thing, however, I am certain. On the citadel side of the ravine, a few feet above the surface of the fluid, a storm drain trickles water into the moat. From here it is hard to gauge its size, but next to the hideous form of Nofayn, it appears wide enough that a man could pass through it. We could use that entry instead of storming the walls.

As soon as I have been returned to firm ground, Tarak takes my arm and leads me toward the west side of the citadel. I see no other angels near us and ask the guardian where the others have gone. He says nothing but continues to run. Gunfire from the fortress walls impacts the ground and ricochets off his armor. Their rifles must not be as powerful as the sniper's.

After several seconds of sprinting across the plain, we round the northwestern end of the fortress. I find a small force surviving the fray, but their circumstances are as dire as mine were. Having shot their arrows at guards on the walls, the angels stay alive by shielding themselves behind the dead. From the jagged ramparts of the fortress the enemy fires bombs, bullets, and boulders. I see dozens of ra'shrogs coming across the moats on zip-lines, their arms brandishing axes with crooked, rusted heads.

Unlike the crimson soldiers of Mykmun or Mokmah, these ra'shrogs are clad in armor. Their plating is rusted and worn, with replacement pieces affixed onto marred originals that appear to have been long abused and neglected. Their appearance is similar to an amunamai, if he had been buried at the ocean floor and battered by hidden things in the deep for a century. The moment the ra'shrogs get their footing on our side, those at the castle cut their lines. Despite their numbers, these latest foot soldiers continue to be ill matched against the angels. They attack, get slain, and are used as shields.

Alden is the first to meet us when we arrive, and we are all forced to fight off ra'shrogs while conversing.

"Is this all that remains?" I ask the elder.

"No. Another force of our same size is making way to the south to attack at the enemy's rear, if they can reach it."

"And what are your men doing?"

"Waiting for you, and we cannot do so for long."

"I know this, zaquenan. What is our plan?"

"The pit."

"What? We cannot dive into the moat."

"Dive, no. Climb, yes. We cannot remain here any longer, little child; the fire from the enemy will overtake us in time. Of that we can be assured."

"But how will we do such a thing? The walls of the moat offer few places to grip; climbing down free-handed will not be possible."

"No, it will not."

"Then what?"

"We lower ourselves down with the remaining arrows."

"With arrows? That's insane."

"No more absurd than staying on this front, getting destroyed one-by-one. We have lost one noble amunamai, and others will fall if we do not flee. Once we reach the moat's floor, the sewage tunnels will offer entry. Our forces await my signal."

"What signal?"

"This," he says, dashing away from us. Despite his age and armor, Alden escapes the fray and outpaces any foe that chases him.

"To the task, all you angels," he yells. "To the task."

As the other warriors hear his call, they make their way to the moat. The fight has developed into madness. Our enemies fire upon many of their own comrades on approach. Meanwhile, more boulders and arrows rain toward us, and as the angels move near the edge of the ravine, the fighting becomes more condensed and compact. Every launched projectile now hits more combatants, but fortunately for us, they are of the enemy's ranks. Alden is right; we cannot do this much longer.

The zaquenan commands the others as Tarak and I reach the edge of the ravine. Here we find Zaquenan Si, who gives us each a pair of arrows.

"I thought you guys were out of these?"

"Alden held a quiver full for this very moment. Put them to good use, little child."

The arrows are sturdy with heads that bear hooks, and he assures us they will hold our weight on the climb.

"Are you coming?" I call to Si.

"Alas, little child, I cannot obey," he says as he throws a ra'shrog to his death.

"Why not?"

"Because none but Tarak is to follow until we are assured that you are safe on the floor."

"No. There's no time."

"Less if you argue. Heed counsel. Go."

Tarak nods to me and throws his legs over the edge while stabbing the arrowheads into the ground. I follow his lead, and within moments we have begun our descent into the ravine. My guard remains several steps ahead, and I follow as quickly as I can. The sound of the battle echoes off the walls, though we can see no more of the conflict.

After a few brutal minutes of descending, Tarak drops from the side and into the sewage. The second his feet break the surface of the water, strange and horrid creatures emerge to attack. The guardian finds himself thigh-deep in filth, assaulted by this breed of demons I have not seen until now. I leap from my present position ten feet above them and land on two of the pit-dwelling rogues. We all fall beneath the surface of the muck, and the stench of it almost leads me to vomit. When we return to the air, the creatures assail me.

Two more golden figures whip their legs over the ledge. They belong to Alexavier, whose dreadlocks stick out from his helmet, and another amunamai who I cannot name. They descend the wall much faster than we did.

The villains of the moat are tall but not gangling and strong without heft—“svelte” may be the best term for them. Their pale, green skin of upturned scales is visible beneath the sewage covering their bodies. Striking with their elongated arms and biting with gaping mouths full of fangs, these demons scream through wide, drooling lips, and with long forked tongues they lash at our faces.

I slash and kick, but they are much more adept at fighting through the muck than I. While one pulls me under the surface, another stomps at my legs, and a third punches my breastplate. In desperation I stab the last and break the stranglehold of the first. Rising from the sewage, I decapitate the second and find myself besieged by a fourth. By this point, the other amunamai have arrived, and they now rush to aid Tarak and me.

They are stopped, however, by a horrible new foe.

A great worm rises from the sewage between us, and it wraps itself around the second guardian. This worm bears the same pale color as the other demons we are fighting in the trench. The creature appears at least six feet in length and wider than the torso of a fully-grown man. The end of its body, which I assume is its head, now takes aim at the arm of the angel in its grasp. The face of the creature splits in two, and it engulfs the guardian's arm from the hand to the shoulder. Once the arm is in the open snare, huge teeth emerge from the perimeter of the mouth. With a firm snap the demon clamps through the armor, ingesting the appendage to the bicep. The amunamai stabs at it with his other arm, but the demon worm continues to have his feast. By the time Alexavier has fought off his own attackers, the creature has eaten the full arm of the angel, an amunamai called Alastair.

Alexavier chops the worm in half, and bright green blood sprays in all directions. Before he and the injured guard take another step, more of the demons leap on their backs. Tarak and I have no chance to reach them, and I feel this plan may be our undoing. Our foes here overpower us; this is their lair, and they have every advantage.

Beneath the sewage, a worm wraps my legs and pulls me under the surface of the muck. I cannot kick in hopes of escape. I feel the arms of numerous attackers slam into my chest and helmet. The dark sludge creeps into my nostrils and sneaks into the corner of my mouth. All my wrestling and struggling is futile; these pit dwellers have me at their mercy.

With no explanation, the hitting ceases, and an arm grabs my breastplate and pulls me back to the surface.

"You are not dead yet," Exhart Deron tells me before turning and striking one of the demons in the skull. "And we must move."

More of our allies have reached the moat floor, and they have clustered in order to defend themselves. Along with Deron came the Exhart Thane, plus Viho and Alden, the two zaquenan. Edmund of the amunamai is here as well, and Rahfaad Jadon has also joined us. Zaquenan Si, I do not see.

"Where is Si?" I ask Deron.

"He has stayed to guard the ledge, to ensure that no ra'shrogs could follow."

"If he is alone, then how will he join us?"

"He will not, son of the Most High."

I have no time to lament his loss, for the attacks continue without pause. As they did upon the mountain, the angels form a circle around me. The guards on the walls rain down rocks and gunfire, and the demons of the pit assail us. As if the enemies were not enough trouble, the putrid stench of the pit makes me nauseous.

We reach the sewage drain near Nofayn's carcass. It sits ten feet above us. The mouth of the pipe spans about five feet, a size in which each of us can fit. From it streams a dirty fluid, and I do not want to know what it is.

The angels form a crescent in front of me, its curve facing away from the drain. Despite the loss of his entire arm, Alastair has continued to fight, and he now volunteers to be the stepping stool and squats against the wall. Tarak climbs on his shoulders and leaps at the opening; once he pulls himself into it, he disappears.

After a few moments, the guardian returns and affirms that the path is safe. Alden motions for Viho to follow. When the zaquenan leaves, the line of angels step backward to close the gap and hold their defenses. A worm breaks past Thane, but I smite the villain before he can cause any ill to our party. I hear Viho's call from the pipe; my time has come.

I look into Alastair's eyes before climbing. "Thank you for this sacrifice, guardian of the kingdom."

"I do it in joy, son of the Most High. May the Lord bless your efforts beyond today's battle."

With such kind words he tilts his head upward, and Viho awaits me with an outstretched hand. I leap to reach it, and when he grabs me, I look back to find the others maintaining the line. All seem immovable despite the constant assault.

I climb into the drain, and yell, "I'm in."

I then hear the voice of Alden cry to Jadon, telling the wounded rahfaad to join us.

"Reach down your hand to lift him," Viho commands me.

I turn around and pull the healer into the pipe. He gets his bearings and does as I did to aid the next ally. We shift further into the pipe as more come, Alexavier follows Jadon, and Deron enters thereafter. Alden and Edmund are next to join us, and Exhart Thane is the last to arrive.

"Jump now and reach," he yells to the guardian below us. A scream rings in the distance, and Thane calls forward, "They have taken Alastair; we must flee. They are using their dead to build a mound toward the entry."

I can picture it now: the ravenous demons drag the hewn corpses beneath the pipe, and with Alastair's body at the center, they heap the dead upon each other and create a means to give chase in the tunnel.

We move faster through the pipe as Thane gives another call. "They are lifting the worms into the drain."

"We have faced enough of their wicked number." Viho replies. "We must hurry."

The further we get into the drain, the more pungent the odor becomes. I can almost taste the garbage, but it is accompanied by a sweet scent—like a single stalk of incense trying to mask the stench of a landfill. Because the lesser fragrance has no power over the greater, everything smells worse and more unnatural. I gag and pause.

"Keep moving, young one," Deron calls. "Enemies pursue, and we are near the end."

"Push forth," calls Thane. "They are coming."

"I can't make it; I'm going to puke. I have to stop." I admit this even as I crawl as fast as I can.

"You will make it," Deron tells me. "Speak to me further. Have you any injuries?

"None of which I am aware."

"And your helmet and shield and armor? Are any lost or destroyed?"

"No. I have them."

"And your sword, have you kept your sword?"

"Yes. Yes, of course." I tell him.

"Good. All is well?"

"No, I'm going to be sick."

"Beyond that however?"

"I suppose all is well; I am not hurt."

"Excellent. Have you any questions for me?"

I did not think I did, but one strikes me. "Yes. How and when did you all coordinate the escape from Mykmun? I heard no plan before we entered."

"What do you think we discussed on the road from the ruins toward the hall? As soon as we burned the city to a cinder, the elders knew we were walking toward doom. They were certain we could escape as long as we held until the right moment."

"And how did you know when that was?"

"I looked into your eyes, little child," Viho interjects, "and I saw that hope had fled them. Your doubt might have led to a hasty surrender as well as your seeking a release thereafter. Such a fate could not come to pass; hence, the time to act was at hand."

"Does that answer suffice?" Deron asks.

"Yes, it does." And I am thankful for the angels once more.

They ask about my battle against Nofayn. I inquire about their conflict with his minions. Much is told of acts of valor and angels who died so others would live. Praise is given to The Lamb for the victories. The desire to complete our siege is rekindled.

In time, Tarak kicks a drain at the top of the pipe that opens into a small room. We have entered the lower dungeons of the citadel. The air is stale and old and dank, but at least it is better than that of the tunnel.

The tunnel.

I have passed through it without being ill. A shrewd move from Deron has allowed me to endure, and I realize a most intriguing thing: the exharts may have been unable to train me, but they are a key component of my force. I suspect they may prove more important than I thought.

This is confirmed when Thane emerges, covered in bits and blood of the pit worms.

"They were bottle-necked and forced to cannibalize their own," he tells us. "But these demons are as repugnant to each other as they are to any of us, for they turned round once the task called for their feasting."

His smile from the first time we met returns, and I greet him with one of my own. The gesture fades, however, when I am struck with a harsh reality. We are standing inside the stronghold, within the hidden depths of my soul. I shudder to think what we will find, particularly in the stack of old, damp boxes in the corner.

15 : THE CORRIDORS

We stand together in a dank, neglected room. A single dim torch sits beside the door. A faint glow spreads through half the space, and the other half is masked in darkness. Stacked boxes like those from Mykmun rest in the shadows, a hint of them visible by the light. The smell of wet cardboard and mold fill the air, and the clamoring sounds above us echo off the walls.

Viho moves toward one of the boxes and looks to me for permission to investigate. I nod in return, not knowing what he will find.

"These are not pictures, little child," Viho says in surprise.

"What?"

"This is something else."

"Should I look?"

"Well, I do not think it will cause you to stumble if that is what worries you."

I look inside a waterlogged, cardboard box to find notebooks—stacks of notebooks. I open one to the middle, and I find the page full of my handwriting. I scan the next few sheets, but I see neither dates nor times. I read to myself.

> Attended sleepover but did not want to. Would have much rather stayed home, but they had access to cable and go to sleep faster than I. Waited until they were in bed then crept downstairs. Surfed the guide and premium channels. Stopped at …

I close the book and then my eyes.

"Stories?" Deron asks.

"Memories. A fair amount of them from the look of things," I admit. "Instances I want to forget."

"Hm," the exhart says, taking the book from me and scanning its contents. "You have many, but all are forgiven."

"I know."

"Perhaps you need not be ashamed, then. Regret them, yes; lament them, of course, but you should not keep them hidden—for in darkness they are useless." He closes the notebook and returns it to its box.

"Come," he says, "we have greater needs to address."

We exit into a wide hallway, different than I would have expected. Chandeliers line the ceiling in both directions, but they are missing many limbs and bulbs. The tilting fixtures provide a dim light but also create an imbalanced look. The walls are covered in floral carpet, and black pillars a few yards apart extend from the floor to the ceiling. Between them hang damaged paintings with torn canvases set in broken frames. A lavish crimson carpet lines the ground, but it is waterlogged and stained. From where we stand, we are in the middle of the hallway. Looking left, we see that the corridor begins to curve left; looking right, it bends to the right.

It appears this lower level was once important to me, but it has since fallen into decay. As we make our way left I glance at the paintings. My quick looks are enough to get an idea of their contents; however, any anxiety over them is misplaced. The paintings convey the landscapes of rooms—rooms I recognize but have no obvious spiritual meaning to me at the moment. One is a dorm room, another a bedroom; one is a home office and the next, a bathroom. This cue seems redundant from the village, but I dread that it has some other painful significance.

I look to the walls for a door but find none, and my confusion grows as we walk. I have no idea what all these rooms have in common or why they were once esteemed but now go ignored. These and similar thoughts fly through my mind when we reach a door I am hesitant to open but feel the need to investigate.

The door swings ajar the moment I touch it and leads into a large round room. The floor is a pit of sand less a brick walkway that lines the perimeter of the wall. Without stepping into the room, I close the door and continue moving as though I had left it ignored. Viho peers inside the door then asks me if I grasp its meaning.

I don't (and tell him as much).

We walk through the corridor and follow a curve through an identical extension of the hall. When we arrive at another door, it too opens into a room of sand, similar in every aspect to the first.

"That is a strange thing," Viho says. "Is it the same room, little child?"

I look over it once more, take a moment, and nod. "I believe it is, but let's test it. What is something we can afford to lose? Do we have any extra arrows?"

"No. I am sorry."

"Well, let's take one of the paintings from the hall and toss it in here. Then we'll round the next bend and see if we come to another door. If we open it and see the same painting, we'll know."

Thane and Edmund pull a landscape that shows my bedroom as arranged throughout my teens. The canvas is torn, and the frame is rotting. We place it to the right of the door inside the room upon the rock path that lines the perimeter. I close the door and run round the hall. As before, it bends left, and we come to the next door. I kick it open and almost tear it from the hinges. Once more I see a pit of sand with a stone path along the wall. The painting sits to the right of me.

"Huh," I say.

"Same room?" Viho asks.

"Same room. And I think it is the only one we'll find."

"If we cannot proceed, we could go back to the first from whence we came," Edmund suggests.

"No, I don't believe we could," I tell him. "I have an aching suspicion the way from the closet is gone, and this room is our sole exit from these halls."

That being said, I enter the room and hug the wall as I move along the pathway. The others follow me in the same manner, and in moments all nine of us are lined at the wall, looking at the large round pool of sand. Once the last angel enters the room, I ask him to close the door.

The moment he complies, a wall of brick matching the rest of the room blocks the threshold. The sand then gives a dull luminescent glow, and we can see one another though all is dark above our heads.

"Yeah," I say with a sigh, "that figures. Well, now we need a way out of here."

Alexavier grabs the painting and throws it into the sand. It begins to sink.

"Of course," I say. "You know, it's moments like this I wish I were normal."

"Are you not?" Deron asks.

"No. It takes a certain strangeness to imagine this type of place. So, who wants to take the plunge? Should I?"

"Tarak will venture first, as he did into the drain."

"That will not be necessary," Alden interjects. "I will go." He removes his helmet and takes a handful of sand in his palm. "You think, little child, that our portal lies through this sand?"

"I am certain of it. Quicksand terrifies me, and the idea of passing through it is a challenge I would invent."

"That is not reassuring," Alden replies.

"No. But it looks like you all have to trust me," I tell him. "The pit will be deep, but I believe that the sand will carry you through it, as long as you do not fight back."

"But we cannot be sure of this?" Alden asks.

"I'm sure enough," I say, launching myself from the path into the pit, much to their surprise.

The journey through the sand is odd. I assume I should be suffocated by it, but instead I feel that a thousand tiny hands push me downward from all sides. In moments I feel my feet break through the sand. Thereafter my legs are also dangling in the air, and soon my entire body is loosed from the pebbles. I fall about ten feet, but not a single grain follows me.

I land upon a large pile of sand and look up to find a portal in the ceiling. From it the room bends downward into a dome, and it is illuminated as the prior chamber was. I roll several yards down on one side in time to avoid Tarak's fall through the opening. The other guardians, Jadon, and the exharts follow. The two zaquenan fall through the opening last. No sand has come through the portal with them, but a large mound of it covers the room from edge to edge.

"Hourglass," I say aloud but to myself.

"What?" Alden asks me with a chuckle.

"It's an hourglass," I tell him.

"Is that significant?"

"Yes."

"How so?"

"Not sure."

"Well then I think we must ask the next pressing question. How do we get out of it?"

A strange idea enters my mind, but I tell myself it is not possible. Nonetheless I test it, and I kick the wall. The stones explode away from my leg with a sound of shattering glass. The noise echoes through this chamber as well as that outside of it—an immense open space with high vaulted ceilings and walls of enormous stones.

I look through the opening and realize we are twenty feet above the surface of a lake that extends to the edge of the room. I see no landing, less one, a small isolated deck of old wood across the water. At the point where it connects to the wall, a faint bit of light shines above a tall mirror.

Casting aside the fact that the water could be shallower than it appears, I leap from the opening created in the hourglass. I crash through the surface and sink, for the water is thick and heavy, with the pressure of a wave when its crest breaks. The weight of it forces me under the surface, but I strain upward and find air. I hear Deron's voice.

"Child of God," he calls, "You must not— "

I am sucked beneath the surface again, and the crushing weight of the water pushes me downward. I move as well as I can, fighting a powerful undertow and current that should not exist in still waters. Once I reach air I take a deep breath and swim toward the dock. Before being sucked under the water, I hear several splashes behind me. The others must have leaped as well.

The battle through the heavy water taxes my body. My legs seem leaden and my arms sapped of strength. The wounds of prior struggles and the exhaustion of the present combine to drain me of any momentum. Stroke upon stroke I fight the pool that drags me toward its pressing depths. While the actual distance could not have exceeded fifty yards, the swim from the hourglass has felt as long as a mile. I am famished when I reach the wet wooden planks, and I kneel on them while coughing for breath.

Moments pass before my eyes look toward the mirror and find a sight that is not welcome. I am looking at a reflection that looks right past me. It sees something beyond my shoulder, but its eyes are wide and full of anticipation. I wave, but the reflection's arm does not mimic my movement. Rather it lifts a remote to some device and clicks buttons to affect the screen it sees.

The pupils of the reflection dilate, and its face becomes vacant, as though entranced by what it sees. I step closer to the mirror, and the reflection moves toward me. Its breathing quickens. As I turn to check if the others are seeing this, my counterpart in the mirror looks off to the side as well.

I am getting anxious. I do not know what is happening, but I am sure this is not my reflection, not my present one anyway. I look at the doppelganger once more and find that it is spellbound. I feel as though it has lost itself, and whatever is coming I fear to watch. Though my hands have stayed at my sides, those of the reflection move. Its breathing has begun to hasten more, and its hands have now found their way toward its waistline.

I cannot bear a moment more. I am not certain what will follow, but my assumption warrants action.

"No," I say to myself in a whisper, before punching straight at the face of my reflection. The mirror cracks and splinters, but the outcome is not at all what I had hoped. Rather than break the scene I have compounded it, and each fragment of the mirror shows a different reflection. One of these is seated at a computer; another holds some magazine out of view; a third lies upon its stomach watching something on a screen. Other doppelgangers are similar, but each vision is unique. All of them look out toward me, though it is clear they are seeing something else.

I do not want to watch any more and slam my elbow into the mirror. Once more, the reflections splinter, forming smaller images of my sin. Again I strike, and I do not stop. I thrust with my knee and follow it with my elbow. I break into a full assault on this mirror, and with every ounce of strength I try to shatter it. Exhausted, I let my head fall forward, and when my helmet hits the reflective surface, the entire mirror falls to pieces, creating a new doorway.

Short of breath, I close my eyes and feel a hand upon my shoulder.

"What did you see?" I ask.

"I saw a man defiling himself," Deron says, "enjoying his sin though knowing it was evil."

Tears form inside my eyes. The shame I bear does not have words. The mirror showed nothing more than myself, who I was for a very long time—who I could be again, on any future day.

"But then I saw another man," the angel continues, "and he would not tolerate the other's sin, and he struck at it with everything he had until his strength was finished." I wipe the tears from my cheeks and refuse to face him as he continues, "I saw a man forced to confront his own sin, and he was loathe to bear the sight of it—a development that I think is most encouraging."

At this point I turn to him with an expression filled with despair. Beyond Deron's strong countenance I see the view of the entire room. Seated in the wide subterranean lake is the shape that I knew it held—an enormous hourglass of stone with a hole in its lower chamber. The odd structure sits at the center of the circular room, the floor of which is water, less the landing on which I stand. The lower chamber of the hourglass sits in the lake while the upper chamber extends to the height of the ceiling. I assume that the higher chamber is the one into which we dove; and if that is indeed the case, we are a level below the halls and have descended further beneath lust's stronghold.

We pass through the opening created by the mirror into pitch-black darkness. Each of the warriors puts his hand upon the shoulder of the one who walks in front of him, and our caravan moves with me at its point and Jadon at its rear. I find a wall and move along it with caution, hoping not to walk us all over a ledge. The journey feels long, and the thin air gives the impression that this tunnel might extend forever. After the rough, intrusive sand and the heavy, invasive water, I would think that such air would be a respite, but the chilling void of life in it makes me feel as if we were walking through a vacuum in space. I hear nothing but the steps of our company.

For one who takes his sight for granted, traveling in blindness is terrifying. I feel as though each step could be our last, and I have no hint of where to venture. I walk along the wall, hoping for a doorway to present itself, but all I feel is the cold face of stone.

"I believe I have found a stairway upward," Alden calls to us all.

But I do not heed him.

"Halt, peacemaker," Jadon cries. "I believe we have a way out of this darkness."

I hear them but ignore their words as I skulk forward, feeling near to a necessary destination. My hand reaches a different material, not stone but wood.

"Peacemaker, please. The stairs," Jadon pleads.

"No," I tell them. "This is the room we must enter next."

I push the door open, and a harsh red light spills into the corridor. I lead us into the room, but I feel something horrible is about to happen.

Torches of red flame line the wall in between mounted chains and shackles. I see stocks and a chair with holding straps. Poles with restraints stand in each corner, and a table with fetters rests at the room's center. This type of environment has always terrified me—even in my sin I avoided visuals like this.

"What hideous chamber have we entered now?" Alden asks.

The answer comes with such haunting clarity that I fear to speak it aloud. "This—this is my reward. This is my final destination in my sin." My hand runs across the implements on the wall. I think I am going to be sick. I see flashes in my mind of beatings and whippings, of my body laid bear before the hands of the ra'shrogs. I see myself entering, weeping and sweaty, binding myself to the post at the wall. I see myself handing the demons a whip, while I place my head inside the stocks. I see a thousand memories of events that never happened, but I know all too well the significance of this place, and I know why I have come here now. After the mirror, how could I not?

"Tell us, peacemaker," Jadon begins, "why you have led us here?"

I continue my tour without a response.

"Little child, answer the rahfaad," Alden cries. The elders voice has a fear I have not heard until now. "Why have you brought us to this wretched room?"

I stop and turn to look at them all. All eight of them have stayed with me, and they are owed an explanation.

"You have all been gracious in coming this far. You truly are servants if you are willing to bear such a struggle on my account. But I have led you here because this is where I belong. I cannot fight a war that I do not deserve to win.

"You have traversed with me through a valley of sin—through the places I embraced it, the images which enabled it, the wandering eye that fed it, and the pits full of its refuse. You saw the heaps of lost time and experienced a drowning guilt that leads to a momentary fleeting pleasure and results in this aftermath—a blinding, vacuous darkness and hollowness in the human soul. Where else could I come but here, to have my guilt assuaged by pain, to sit in my anguish and be tormented for the wickedness that I embraced? We are here, good angels, because I need to be punished for all the sins of every night before this one."

With these words I bind my wrist in a fetter and stand bound to the table at the center of the room. I look to them, and they look back in horror.

Deron rushes to my side, "Son of the Most High, what are you doing? This is madness."

"Getting my reward, good angel." I look past him and speak to the others, "Flee. Flee now. Abandon me."

Alexavier and Edmund stand at the door, and I hear a banging on the other side. My tormentors have arrived.

"Let them come." I whisper, with fresh tears in my eyes. "Let them do what they will."

"No." Deron says. "Look at me, son of the Most High—hear your title, now. You are no longer bound to your guilt nor a slave to sin and its just desserts. You are redeemed and ever renewed. This torturous place is not your fate. This is a lie, a grievous deceit."

"No, Deron. This must be done."

Thane rushes to us, "Please, son of the Most High, listen to him. You need not do this. You are redeemed."

"I am sorry, good Thane." I shackle my other arm to the table. "I am sorry, but I am neither worthy of the title you speak nor of the mercy to which I bear claim."

"You are deceived," Deron cries.

I lay upon the table, and in the back of my mind I hear banging on the door. Jadon and Alden argue nearby, but I cannot discern what either is saying. Ever calm and collected, Viho walks toward me. His somber face gives no hint of his feelings, but I assume he understands my actions. I nod to him in solidarity, but without a word he lifts his sword and swings the back of his hand at my skull.

INTERLUDE

And I open my eyes.

My computer is a foot in front of my face.

I take a moment to accept that my journey is over, and I have returned from Solsland to my room. I could not complete the task at hand. I could not take the offensive and tear down the stronghold. All I could do was surrender to guilt and admit that I feel an endless shame—a self-imposed sentence for my perversion. I have failed to do right all over again.

And now my thoughts drift to old desires. I am reminded of the temptation that I tried to remove. I think back on the events and all that I considered, the great battle in my soul and my ultimate surrender. Here I am, defeated.

Why not at least get some pleasure for my trouble?

I know it will mean more sand passing through the hourglass. I know it will create another reflection in the mirror. This choice will lead me into darkness and guilt, and I will sit and wallow in my own self-loathing, letting all manner of humiliation run rampant through my soul. I will let the devil's minions wreak havoc on me, and I will wake up tomorrow, broken anew.

No.

"No."

"Lord God, no, Please. Don't let me fail you now. Not now. Help me. Bear me forward unto victory. Forgive me for refusing the peace of your redemption. Forgive me for holding to a need for self-punishment. Forgive me for carrying such deep-rooted anger and hatred for one who you have redeemed.

"The enemy knew how to wound my spirit. The enemy sought to destroy my will by bringing me low and feeding me lies. But he has not yet led me into sin. Let me, in this moment—if never again, at least in this moment—let me overcome, please. Give me the strength to complete this task, to the praise and glory of your Holy Name.

"My eyes have not sinned; I have not fallen. Help me to stand. By your might and power, renew my mind, that I may worship you. Grant me victory that I may speak of your deliverance. Hear your child's call, Lord God, that these hours of struggle would not be in vain."

With such prayers and passion, I close my eyes …

16 : THE RETURN

And I awaken in Solsland to the sound of destruction. Steel strikes iron and cuts through wood and leather.

I rise but am whipped backward, and my head slams onto the table.

"Forget something?" Jadon says while working at my chains.

"Use my sword," I tell him.

He slashes the cuffs at my wrists, and in moments I am free. The fetters have no strength against the words of the Lord.

I look about the room to find the other angels at work. They have chopped the stocks to a pile of timber and broken many of the furnishings in the room. The chains have been ripped from their walls, and the whips have been sliced to pieces. The banging at the door continues.

"We saved the table's end for you, young one." Viho says, placing his hand upon my shoulder. I turn and look at his aged, kind face. He has the hint of a smile, and I hug him.

"Thank you," I tell him before stepping backward to get some distance from my target.

"Your sword gave you release from your chains," he tells me. "Now let it destroy them also."

With a swing, my blade cuts through the table and continues downward all the way through to the floor.

"You came back," Alden says with a smile.

"Yes."

"What brought you?" Thane asks.

"A need to finish this thing—to complete the good work The Lamb began."

"Then let us see to it."

Alexavier and Edmund have continued to hold the door, and I nod to them to release it. The moment they step away from the threshold the large wooden slab swings toward us. From the darkness leaps the first ra'shrog and many more follow after him. Their charge is fueled by desperation and fury. Picking up pieces of chain or wood or anything they believe they can use as a weapon, the ra'shrogs swarm the room and assail us from all sides.

These are a strange and horrid lot, new in some respects yet similar in others. Like those from Mykmun they wear the crimson uniforms over body armor of black. This new breed, however, has neither gloves nor boots, and the talons of their fingers and toes are exposed. Their uniforms are torn to tatters, and their featureless faces are dented and cracked—revealing that the unpolished silver appearance has been no more than a mask. Some of these faceplates are missing chunks, and the gaps expose charred patches of flesh.

Though the demons attack with far greater numbers, the angels are quick to ensure I am safe. They circle around me, as per usual, but I do not accept their protection this time. I break into the line, stand beside them, and face the door to engage the horde.

Slamming my shield into the first villain, I daze him and cast him from my path. I kick the one who enters after him and then slash forward with my sword. As this second enemy falls, I backhand the third and kick him with my opposite leg, stepping further toward the threshold. This third falls into another who enters, and I bring my shield to my front in preparation. As these two regain their footing I thrust my sword into one of them; then as if my arm is a gear in a machine, I pull it back into position and drive into the other.

I step over the fallen demons toward the door anticipating the next attack, and in the moment before it arrives, my allies have taken action. Having dispatched the first wave of the horde, the angels have prepared for the darkness we will encounter. Each of them holds a red torch in his hand.

"We are ready to surge at your order," Alden says, handing me a torch of my own. I sling my shield onto my back and take the torch in my left hand. My sword remains in my right.

"Consider it given."

I lean the flame forward until its red hue crosses the doorposts and illuminates the hall. The floor is formed of cobblestones, and the ceiling is arched and low. As I charge through the threshold, I swing my torch left and right. An army of the ra'shrogs waits at all sides. With their claw-like hands they cling to the walls and ceiling and floor upon all fours, as if they were lizard-like rather than human. They watch and stir, poised for attack.

Why the demons wait I do not know, until I realize that the others have followed me. They too stand with their torches extended, and we form a wall across the hallway.

"They abhor the flame," Alden says. "We must press this advantage."

Back-to-back with our torches outward, the angels and I keep the ra'shrogs at bay. As a single unit we move down the hall toward the stairwell Alden found. The demons follow and surround us. Their faces are visible where the chrome masks are shattered, and hateful eyes framed by scar tissue follow us. I feel oppressed by their fuming gaze.

"What are they?" I ask Alden as we march.

"They are the demonic horde without deceitful dress. You now see them as they are, neither refined nor powerful nor bold nor impressive—no, not them. They are terrified of the fire, knowing the eternal flames will come."

"I would think this fire would have no effect, considering that this dungeon is theirs."

"Yes, but you forget, little child, that in our hands the flame is redeemed and transformed into a tool for good."

Too focused on the malcontents, I had not noticed the shifting hue of the fire. A more intense heat now radiates from the torch, but it carries a different tone. What once glowed red and grim and threatening, now bears a flame with a soft blue glow. The demons do not fear me in the least, but this new blaze scares them to the core.

I then realize it may not be the torchlight itself but the way in which it shines through my blade. I see the words projected onto their faces. The Scripture reads:

> Behold, I have given you the power to tread on serpents and scorpions, and over the power of the enemy, and nothing shall hurt you.

I can imagine what the demons see—words of Scripture pouring through the prism, surrounding us and bouncing off our armor and the walls. They are right to fear.

We come to the stairwell to find it has an entrance at least fifteen feet in width. I glance toward the steps, which are tall and steep, and like the floor, they are laid unevenly. Being sure-footed on them will prove difficult.

Deron's back is against mine, and he must sense my caution. "Purpose in your heart to complete the climb," he tells me, "and lead us all to do the same. We will follow you."

I close my eyes, take a breath, and commit myself to the task. No matter the height or number of steps, no matter if I trip forward or stumble back, I will charge up them until I reach the top; I will neither turn left nor right nor back.

My eyes open and adjust to the soft blue light as I turn and sprint toward the rising passage. With my left arm outstretched I extend the blue flame at the faces of the demons that watch and wait. The quickness of the light both blinds and disorients them. I am on the first step, then the second, then the third; and adrenaline propels me at a speed I did not expect. I do not look behind me, but I hear footsteps at my rear.

Alden arrives beside me and keeps pace as I run. "Alexavier and Deron are behind us," he reports, "but the injured Jadon has slowed Viho and Thane. They remain in cadence with him several steps after us to ensure he does not stumble backward. Tarak and Edmund are at our rear, each with two torches to keep our enemies at bay. A dozen steps lie between you and them."

I know not how many stairs we have run, but the fatigue begins to settle in my legs. They become heavy with each lift of my foot, and I doubt I can sustain this pace for the ascent. My torch of blue shines ahead of us, but it does not show any signs of an end.

The stairs climb and curve. The hall is wrapped around something circular, something huge, and my guess is that it is the open space that holds the hourglass. Given the height of that horrible place, I assume the steps soon will come to a landing. Exhaustion is at the forefront of my mind, but I renew my purpose to finish the climb.

My hypothesis of the stairwell's end proves correct, but not without consequence I had failed to foresee. A disorienting spotlight shines on our faces.

I stop, and Alexavier runs into my back. The shift in light blinds us for a moment, and before I can get my bearings, a demon pulls me downward. We collide off each stair as we descend down the passage, and I punch and kick until we roll into a wall.

My torch lost in the fray, I am in the darkness. The lone light is a reflection off the demon's chrome mask. He hisses with a mouth that I cannot see, and I return his greeting with a kick to his chest. The demon topples backward down several more stairs, but his success is clear to me when I turn to look up the hallway. He has brought me away from the circle of fire and through the line of demons that have followed our ascent. They are all now turned toward me with their backs to the angels. The light is all behind this wall of countless silhouettes.

I hold my sword in both of my hands. The dim light from behind the legion catches my blade, and a bright light with shadowed text echoes off the walls.

> He gives power to the faint, and to him who has no might he increases strength.

The ra'shrogs are stunned, and I charge. I cleave heads from necks and arms from bodies, and they shriek and hiss and scratch and bite. Holding a low and centered stance, I move up the stairs while I slash at their ranks. I feel their claws slice me, and in time I am surrounded. All is darkness, but I am not swayed. I ascend one stair at a time despite the assaults, and the dim blue hue of the torches reappears.

The demons before me are cast aside, and Alexavier pulls me from the horde. He leads me upward into similar peril, for the light does not subdue the demons at the plateau. They are waging a campaign versus the other angels, and they are gaining the upper hand. Two of the ra'shrogs stand over Jadon, and I decapitate one before crushing another between the shield at my back and the nearby wall. I then kick the brute down the stairs into others.

Their lieutenant watches from upon the landing. I can see him in glimpses. His lipless grin of perfect teeth sits beneath slim and upright nostrils; squinted eyes with crimson pupils stare at the violence with satisfaction. I recognize him. He survived Mykmun, the leader of the party sent there to destroy us. The light echoes off his black translucent skin and reveals the sinews of his face. His cape is now tattered; his hat is gone, and his head is covered in a thousand scars. He looks less regal but far more sinister.

Making him my next target, I take my shield from my back and charge up the steps. At the sight of my attack he exaggerates an expression of fear that I know I do not instill. I take my blade to his chest, but he dodges it and stabs me in the back with some type of weapon. I turn to discover that he is wearing gloves that feature jagged knives for fingers. We face each other on the plateau, our two forces waging war on the stairwell. His grin stretches ear-to-ear when he sees me wince in pain.

He renews his attack and is faster than I. His slashing dents my chest plate and helmet, and he exploits the lack of armor at my arms and legs. He never goes for a fatal wound but a thousand stinging, shallow cuts. All the while he laughs and taunts, and I cannot connect my blade in defense. I feel the blood pulsing through my veins and past my skin as the wounds drench my clothes.

I stumble, and the villain leaps backward twice in succession, building momentum as he lunges off the wall. He is now a human spear, his body a plank with his arms extended. I get my shield to my chest, but the claws stab through it and send me to the floor. The demon stands over me and continues jabbing downward; his assaults pierce my shield and scrape my armor as he scoffs

"We have ruined more men than you've known in your lifetime, and we will ruin you."

I kick him in his back, and he flips over top of me. This gives me enough time to rise and turn before he begins his next offensive. But I do not get to finish the fight, for the sword of Tarak swings into the demon's chest. The ra'shrog lieutenant's movement carries him through the blade and slices him in two, showering the angel and me with his blood.

I pay no heed to my fallen adversary but glance back to the stairwell before leaving it. A sea of dead villains remains on the steps, but all of my company has survived.

We run on the next level of the citadel and find two staircases at the far side of the room. One flight sits in each corner, both leading toward a centered balcony. On each side of elevated deck sits an oblong pillar formed of orange light overlaid with dark stones. These two structures fill the room with a dull glow. Wrapped around each support is a staircase of stone, not built against the structure but erected around it.

We race up the stairs on the left side of the room, and upon reaching the balcony I examine the pillars. The orange light they give flares and dims, and something about them looks familiar. They smell of ash and firewood, but there is neither flame nor sign of smoke. I have little time to muse on this, for a shriek resounds throughout the room.

"More ra'shrogs," Alden observes. "And their numbers will be great. Come. Up the stairs."

Once we ascend around the pillars, a strange idea enters my mind. I tell myself it cannot be, but nonetheless I must disprove it. Without breaking stride I swing my sword against the pillar at my right. The orange light flares, and an increased heat emanates from cracks between the stones. These pillars are alive (or belong to something living).

At the top of the stairs we are funneled into a hallway, and on either side, the pillars continue. They are wider than those on the lower level and built into the corners of the room—in fact, they cover much of the back of it. I describe this as the "back" of the room because on the opposite side stands an enormous door, held closed by planks that form a lock.

We run toward it as shrieks echo from the stairwells. The amunamai and exharts make fast work of the boards, and the cries of the horde get louder and closer. I wrap my hands around the two large rings that serve as handles for the tall, wide doors. Deron places his hand on mine.

"Before you open this door, purpose to be undaunted no matter what enemy on the other side awaits us. We have fought hard, but the battle is not won. You will need a renewed mind for this next stage in your journey."

I nod, and he does the same.

I grip each ring and pull them toward me, straining hard as the door begins to budge. My arms go limp, and my lungs search for air.

Deron speaks next to me. "Remember your commitment, son of the Most High. We do not rest until they are destroyed or we are slain in our attempt to defeat them."

I take the rings in my hand again. A tumult rumbles in the back of the room.

"Release us from this evil fortress," Deron yells beside my face. "Do all that you said you would do and more. Now is the time of strength and valor. Now is the hour of courage and might. Pull now. Pull. Pull. Pull."

I obey, and the doors move further. The momentum of the swing opens them fully, and cold light hits me as my arms extend. A harsh wind gusts through the great gates. As the ra'shrogs attack at our backs, I see another force awaiting us in the courtyard.

17 : THE COURTYARD

"Ha ha," someone calls from the outdoors. "I knew you would return."

That voice is familiar. I blink; my eyes adjust to the light, and the speaker comes into view. He stands with dented armor, a broken shield, and a broadsword that drips with blood.

"Cutler." I call to him.

"Yes, I have survived; though I was beginning to think you did not."

"You were almost right."

"I am glad to be wrong. Half our number were lost in the siege; but as you can see, our rivals suffered also."

He is not exaggerating. The door from which I exited faces toward the northern wall of the citadel, and Awthoomgaw towers behind us at the south. The interior of the courtyard is an obsidian prison, with jutting stones at every wall. To the southeast where the other angels attacked, a great section of the fortress is dashed to rubble, and the body of a dead giant lies hewn in the gap. Throughout the courtyard lie many ra'shrogs, hideous and malformed like those in the dungeons. I also see two of our number among them.

"What does the new creation request now?" Cutler asks me.

I point my sword at Awthoomgaw and respond, "That we send *him* back to the abyss."

"So we shall."

Considering we are about to charge anew, I look about the courtyard for Jadon to bandage me. He was the last surviving rahfaad, but he is gone—as are Alden and Viho. The remaining amunamai surround Cutler and me, holding a line to protect us as we speak.

Meanwhile the exharts Deron and Thane run throughout the courtyard to distract our enemies; they pull bows and quivers from the dead and battle ra'shrogs with efficient blows. Seeing them at work jolts me back into the fray despite my concern for the unseen angels.

I run to Alexavier's side and stab a demon approaching him.

"Where are the zaquenan and Jadon?"

"They have passed from this realm, child of God."

"What? Where are they?"

"Locked within the citadel."

I then look to the threshold from which we exited and find the great doors closed. A banging comes at uneven intervals, as though something is trying to break through them.

"They locked themselves in?" I ask the guardian.

"Alden said it was your time to lead. Viho agreed and stayed with him. And Jadon, being almost to the point of death, believed he could aid them in their purpose."

"What purpose?"

"They have barred many foes from reaching us, and we must honor their sacrifice and march toward victory."

"Yes, child of God, heed their wisdom," Edmund adds. "They have fallen that we should not, and now you are left in command."

Time slows as this responsibility strikes me, and I glance around the courtyard to assess our plight. Ra'shrogs pour from the east and west walls while stradains and vhulraks swoop overhead.

But these familiar enemies are not who I fear.

A new villain skulks throughout the court, a giant similar to the dead one at the east. Nearly twenty feet tall, the creature is clad in discolored armor that is bent around him and bound together with long, thick nails. A forged helmet bearing a large, up-turned horn sits upon his foul head. Were he on all fours he would appear as a rhinoceros sculpted of scraps from a junkyard, but walking on two legs with a large club in hand, he is a monstrous ogre with a sole purpose—the destruction of the angels and me.

From the scaffolding around Awthoomgaw, I see another brood of evil. One of them catches my attention and hisses at me with a gaping mouth. His head is an eel's with catlike eyes that flank each side of his narrow face. Gnarled, rotten, jagged fangs protrude from lips that drool deep crimson. Beneath his layered cloaks of black extend long arms with talons for hands. A tail lengthens from behind his waist, and his large, scaled feet show at the bottom of his robe. The color of his skin is sallow green, and he wields a javelin, pointed at each end. He is but one of a force of several dozen.

The surviving angels have drawn back to me, and we are now eleven in total. Each of us is soiled from the ongoing battle but ready to contend with this latest evil horde.

The robed demons waste no time once they see us. They leap, crawl, and sprint from Awthoomgaw's towers, speeding toward us with rage and malice. As I watch this new wave of foes approach, a still, calm voice echoes in my mind.

Have faith in God.

They are coming, but I feel frozen in fear.

For the Lord will be your confidence and keep your foot from being caught.

I can feel the ground tremble at the nearness of their charge.

And behold, I am with you always, to the end of the age.

The first eel-headed demon reaches me, and I lunge forward with my shield, striking the villain in its chest. He falls backward to the ground, and I sever his head from his lengthened neck. A dozen serpents bleed from his cloak. They slither around me and snap their jaws, but I pay them no mind as the fighting continues. I have a demon of lust to defeat, and I am tired of his endless minions.

I press forward without hesitation and move with the courage of my steadfast conviction—Awthoomgaw will fall as soon as I reach him. Of this I do not have any doubt. The fray is thick, and our foes are many, but I feel a prodding at my back that pushes me through the congested battle. Every swing is a killing blow as I maintain my focus on clearing my path. My momentum peaked and my confidence high, I charge toward the enemy I fear the most in the yard.

The giant greets me with the swings of his club, first over my head, then downward at my side. The world seems to shake when the blow strikes the ground, and I stutter-step while I dodge a swift kick from his leg. With a keen eye that I have never possessed before now, I see an opening in the demon's armor. Between two plates beneath his left arm, his sagging skin is exposed. As he lifts his club for another swing, an arrow finds its mark there.

I glance to my left to find Cutler behind me, his bow doubling as a staff as he battles the horde. The demon giant drops his club and reaches to extract the barb. This reaction reveals a gap at his neck, and another arrow flies into it.

Cutler rushes past me, calling backward, "When he falls, put your blade through his skull." The char-rasha thrusts his shoulders into the giant's knee, and the demon stumbles backward over the soldiers behind him.

The battlefield shakes when the giant strikes the ground.

I jump upon him and run toward his head. From the side, a cloaked demon leaps toward me, but I slide beneath his attack and rise, finding myself at the neck of the giant. His malevolent face is visible within the mask. The giant's scarred visage is warped and weathered, missing an eye and his nose.

I raise my sword to end this monster when an idea forms in my mind. The harsh walls of the citadel will be difficult to scale, but we need to move upon them if we want to reach Awthoomgaw. I second-guess whether my ruse will work even as I commit to it.

I jump from the demon and sprint toward the wall. Eel-heads and ra'shrogs step into my path, but I charge past them without breaking stride.

A furious roar comes at my back. The giant follows.

I run to the courtyard's edge and stop; his legs pass over me. The demon halts, and I flip my sword and stab behind his knee. He turns toward me with his back to the citadel, and I strike the joint with my shield. He stumbles backward against the wall, and I roll beneath him and retrieve my blade.

Like Adofo at the riverbed, I climb the armor of the villain. When I reach the demon's shoulders, he screams at me, but his talk is met with action. I pierce his wicked skull with my blade then return the sword to my side. Taking his helmet with both my arms, I smash it against the wall. Its sharpened horn embeds itself into the obsidian stone.

Thus, his body becomes our means to climb atop the wall.

I step from the giant's shoulders onto his head and leap to the citadel. Removing my sword from my belt, I cry, "Servants of The Lamb, rally to me."

But I have forgotten myself—or, at least, forgotten my shield. I must have dropped it when I climbed the monster. The first javelin pierces my right shoulder, and the second embeds itself into my leg. A third strikes my head but is deflected off my helmet. I crumble upon the wall with two spears piercing me (and no healers to come to my aid).

Deron is the first to rush to my side, and Tarak and Alexavier follow. I am stunned and do not move. I lay. Deron tries to focus my attention, but my eyes turn toward the courtyard. Dead bodies and a sea of dark blood coat the ground, and the ra'shrogs break through the gates blocked by the elders. Thane alone remains in the square, and as he climbs the giant I hear the *poonk* from earlier.

The exhart stops and reaches for his head. In shock, he blinks. While still comprehending the fatal wound, a javelin plunges through his chest. He loses his grip and falls back toward the horde. They swarm upon him, and I turn away.

Deron grips my hand as he pleads, "We must not stay here, son of the Most High. The shooter's aim was poor in the fray, but once we pause he will find his mark, just as he did on noble Thane."

"I can't."

"Cannot what?"

"Go on. Not up there." I reach for breath, but the air is heavy. "I'm done, Deron. It's over. I got—I got nothing left."

"That is a lie."

"No, Deron."

"It is a lie."

"No. I'm spent, and it's too high."

"Look at me," he says grabbing my shoulders. "Look. At. Me. Nothing is too high for your king to climb. Nothing is too large for him to conquer. Nothing is greater than his power to—"

"But I'm not him." I cry, gasping for breath.

"No. But you have claimed his Spirit. You are his adopted son, and you are marked with his Noble Seal. Let him do with you as he pleases, and be the vessel for his good work."

I look down and shake my head in defeat as the others defend us and the exhart continues.

"Are you weakened, son of the Most High?" he asks in a calm and genuine tone. "Are you weak, right now, in this moment?"

"Yes," I tell him.

"Good," he says. "Then that is how he will show you his power. Your weakness, his strength. Your frailty, his might. His honor. His victory. Is that not your aim? Then come now and rise. Stand and trust him, fight to a triumph for his wondrous glory."

"I am going to bleed to death, Deron."

"That is fine. Raising the dead is no problem for him."

I smirk and chuckle. He does the same.

"Forget about the body you have in this place," he tells me, "and remember the real battle that is at hand. Renew your mind. Retake your sword. Your king will see you to the end."

Over his shoulder a distant light shines, and I am reminded of who watches over me. Deron is right. From the wounds I incurred while climbing the mountain to these injuries sustained in the siege, my pain here is only as powerful as the attention I give to it. This is not my real body; I am not bound to its wounds. If the spirit is willing, this flesh is afterthought.

I rise and crouch behind the amunamai. The imprints of bullets dot the backs of their shields. The sniper has continued, but they have stood firm.

We must move now if we are to survive, for the onslaught of the enemy grows, and the dark clouds above us unleash their rain.

18 : THE DEMON

Across the top of the wall we march, beset on all sides by the demonic horde. Enemies from the courtyard climb toward us, and eel-heads charge from the scaffolding. Stradains and vhulraks fly overhead, and the great villain Awthoomgaw glows brighter. The rain turns to steam as it strikes his skin and envelopes the demon in a sweltering mist.

We match their hostility with fervor of our own. By my order, Klahan is at our point and slays the attackers, followed by Makaio, Abdalla, and Cutler. At our sides are Agyei and the three remaining guards while Deron and I propel the unit at its back. The fight surrounding our group is fierce, but at least the walls of the fortress are stable. Once we reach the body of the demon, the path running up him will be less sturdy.

"More gebelayals are in the towers ahead," Agyei calls over the clamor of the battle. "Little child, they will be reckless. Do not fight them; run toward your goal."

"Who are these 'geh-buh-lie-ulls'?" I ask.

"The devils who struck you with their spears. If you pause, they will end your charge by any means—destroying the construction to crush you if they must. Do not heed them, not for a moment."

"And do not heed us, son of the Most High," Deron says, placing his hand on my shoulder. "A moment's respite could cost us all; thus, mind not the fray surrounding you. Run until you reach the heart of your enemy."

"And then what?" I ask, as I step onto the scaffolding.

"Bring his body to ruin with the strength of your blade."

Such is my goal as I head up the ramp that is strange and uneven and flimsy and dangerous. The damp planks are not as wide as the wall of the citadel, and we can no longer maintain our defense. The remaining angels and I spread over the construction, each of us finding our own path upward. The demons have built several ramparts on Awthoomgaw—at his back, shoulders, arms, and head. Parapets and balconies and watchtowers await us, but only a weak assembly of boards and rods surrounds his torso.

I climb several levels and hurl myself onto a landing. The raindrops tap on the boards above me, and I am accosted within moments. Five of the gebelayals have been coordinating an attack, and my pause has given them a means to ensnare me. Two scamper on the construction, and they block my path at both sides. Two land on the boards above me, and the final one climbs from below. Trapped, I lash at them.

I hear a great thud from the ceiling, and I see one gebelayal fall. The next one drops dead above me, and his blood drips through the boards. The others glance at the ceiling for a glimpse of the attacker.

"Go, Child of God. Go now," a voice cries.

I run to the edge of this platform and leap, grabbing a nearby beam. I swing to a landing below me free of the hunters. I look back and find Alexavier restraining the demons, but a stradain swoops behind him and grabs his shoulders. The demon glides away from the assembly and drops the leader of the guardians to his death. I watch with horror as Alexavier plummets. He crosses his arms at his chest as rain pelts him, and he falls many stories to the ground.

The same stradain turns and flies toward me. An arrow pierces its head, and its wings go limp. I look to the direction from whence the arrow came, and I see Tarak load for another shot.

I climb around the side of Awthoomgaw's torso and find a deck that extends the full length of his back. Before I reach it I hear a great crash, and a horrific event occurs at the demon's other side. Several pieces of wood and metal fall through the scaffolding, accompanied by gebelayals and Diakonae Makaio, who screams in joyous victory as his mission in Solsland ends.

The rest of the structure begins to shake, and the orange hue beneath Awthoomgaw's hide burns brighter. The heat from the demon sends sweat down my face, stinging my eyes before I can close them. Rain falls in sheets as I cross the boards, and I keep my shield at my side to protect myself from bursts of flame that exit the crevices in his skin. A gebelayal before me catches fire and screams. A sudden gust pushes me against the deck's railing, and I hear the dreaded *poonk* that meant the death of many others.

In the structure resting on Awthoomgaw's right shoulder, I see a sharpshooter in a gray hooded cloak. The sniper camouflages against the steam, but a single, crimson eye glows beneath his dark shroud. His shots come courtesy of a long-barreled rifle enhanced by a silencer and complex scope; a belt of large bullets extends from the stock. He aims the gun at me once more, and I realize I have provided a perfect target—the unguarded front of my face. A bull's-eye. Our eyes meet as he settles into his shot, which will hit me before I hear it.

From the steam Cutler appears at the sniper's side and hacks through the gunman's arms and the rifle. In shock, the villain turns toward his attacker, whose blade then disconnects the demon's head from his body.

Cutler gestures for me to come join him. I mount the scaffolding toward the rampart when a flock of stradains lands on it. Cutler engages them, and they are not alone. A pack of gebelayals and ra'shrogs have reached me and begun attacking my back as I climb. I kick one from the framework and grapple with another. Every foot I gain is earned through a clash. I am able to reach Cutler, unsheathe my sword and join him in fighting the flying rogues.

"Our time is short," he says. "Strike at the demon now while you can."

"Where are the others?"

"Keeping you alive, unseen and at a distance."

"Why have none gone after Awthoomgaw?"

"Your blade alone has been forged for that task. Its core and its cover are built for the deed. We are here to assist you, but he is yours to wound. Go now. Cut him down."

The rain creates an oppressive steam, but I spring from the parapet and move along Awthoomgaw. My boots protect my feet from his surface.

I should have known it would come to this. The angels were here to aid me, not do my job. By the strength of the Lord and for the glory of The Lamb, I am the one who must slay this great evil.

With my sword withdrawn and my shield at my back, I reach Awthoomgaw's steaming neck. Before I can consider where to strike, a gebelayal trips me onto the hide. My blade leaves my hands and falls from my sight. Lunging upon me and thrusting his neck, the demon snaps his grinning jaws. I remove my helmet, club him with it, and roll onto a deck at Awthoomgaw's chest.

The damp wood provides a moment's relief when an arrow passes the side of my head. An archer is positioned in the tower of stone held in the palm of Awthoomgaw's left hand. Masked and clad in a tattered cloak of black, the bowman reloads and takes aim anew.

Awthoomgaw's left arm extends forward, and the archer is too far for me to engage. The lone way to reach him is the uneven path of metal nailed to the demon's arm. Thinking about this has left me vulnerable, and the bowman fires but misses by an inch. I return my helmet to my head and grab my sword from the platform. A third arrow comes, but I deflect it.

Another will follow, but my attention turns to the demon of lust I have come to destroy. I position my blade to stab the base of his neck. As I thrust my sword forward a black spear strikes it down, and I turn to find a demon similar to the archer.

I take a stance to face this new challenger, but a sharp pain stings at my back. I glance over my shoulder to find an arrow embedded through my shield and into my skin. The spear-wielding demon seizes this opening and thrusts the edge of his weapon toward me. I parry left and right, but another sting erupts—this one behind my leg. Wounded, I stay low and lunge closer to the spearman. With no space to build momentum behind his strikes, the confused soldier ceases his attack. I spin around him as the next arrow reaches us. The head of the barb sticks out of the demon's back, having entered through his gut and sliced his innards. He stands stunned for a moment before crumpling off the landing, and I look for the archer's next shot.

Instead, I find Agyei waiting with a bow, and the dead demon's body slung over the wall. The angel then fires above me at a gebelayal climbing up the right arm of Awthoomgaw. The great limb extends upward into the sky, ending with a tower held in its hand. In the structure stands Klahan, surrounded by decimated corpses.

"Now is the time," the arayil calls.

I flip my blade downward and place my hand on the demon. The heat scalds my palm, but I endure it. In a wide, swooping arc I swing the sword and thrust it into his chest. I know neither how my edge can pierce him nor why it wounds him so, but it passes through him without resistance and settles in his flesh. I pull the weapon lower to deepen the incision, turn the hilt, and rip it from my foe.

A hissing scream echoes on the air as a spray of blood exits from his hide. With a single snap, Awthoomgaw clenches his fists, crushing the towers he holds in his hands. I find Klahan holding the demon's right arm. At the left wrist, Agyei grips the metal. I look to the rampart on the opposite side, hoping to see that Cutler has survived. He fights gebelayals without regard for the shifting frame beneath where he stands. I run from the landing at Awthoomgaw's chest as his wrath sends a tremor throughout the platform. Stabbing my sword near his shoulder, I hold to it then climb.

Awthoomgaw lowers his left arm; the nailed sheets of metal fall. The parapet at this shoulder drops, and I watch debris rain onto the courtyard. The demon steps from his foundations settled deep within the earth. His legs break through the walls built around them, and the evil fortress implodes at his feet. Once he extends his legs their full length, I am another fifty feet above the ground.

Jerking his neck to the left, the demon breaks the rampart at his head. His white eyes open but contain no pupils, and his gaping mouth cracks as he stretches it. The horrifying demon tilts his head and dislodges the remaining battlements.

As the tower at my enemy's shoulder snaps, I see the last of the char-rashas. With one gebelayal's throat in his hand and another demon trapped by his legs, Cutler plummets toward the courtyard. To the bitter end, he fights. The ruins from Awthoomgaw's rampart follow him, and I cannot bear to watch them fall.

In a single terrifying breath, Awthoomgaw flares his wings and roars.

I close my eyes at the horrible sound, and a sudden grip on my shoulder startles me. I turn to find Agyei, who is wounded.

"We have no more time, little child. Slow him. Weaken him. Cut at him further. Do all you can to—Look out."

A burst of flame ignites beside me as I am pushed from Awthoomgaw. I land where the wing joins his body; my sword remains gripped in my hand. I look up to find the elder on the demon's shoulder. His body is scorched along one side, but he rises eye-to-eye with his enemy.

Agyei stares as he proclaims, "I will not slay you but another shall, and you will burn in the abyss once more."

I hear a growl rumble through Awthoomgaw's torso. With a quick snort of his nostrils, he shoots fire at the elder. Agyei is blown backward off the demon, and his charred body disintegrates as it falls. Smoke rises from the wicked villain's nose, and in anger I stab him in his back.

But Awthoomgaw ignores me.

Looking upward to the clouds, the demon of lust raises his wings. He roars at the world; I stiffen in fear. As he crouches low, I brace for shock, and Awthoomgaw launches to the sky.

19 : THE FLIGHT

The citadel shrinks beneath us, and we enter the billowing gray. Bolts of lightning flash at all sides, and the raindrops sting like slivers of glass. Awthoomgaw rises through the storm and into the open sky. The day is bright; the air is cool.

Above the tempest, the demon flies, and we pass over the sea of clouds. The sun at his back and the blue expanse before him, he soars above the ashes of The Tabernacle and the trees of the wintered valley, taking us toward a region of Solsland I have not seen.

Five remaining angels hold to the villain: Tarak and Edmund of the amunamai; Klahan, the last of the arayil; the injured diakonae, Abdalla; and Deron, the head of the exharts. They maintain their grasp to the body of the demon, their gauntlets protecting their hands from his heat.

Awthoomgaw's wings beat the wind with hatred, and he throws his hands at his back in a rage. He roars in frustration and tries to swat us from his form. Edmund is the next of his victims, struck from the joint where the right wing meets the shoulder. The amunamai does not fall but flies backward as the enemy soars. This sight makes me close my eyes and cling to my sword, still impaled into the demon's back.

Wind cuts my face as the flight continues, and I hear Deron's voice in the air.

"Son of the Most High," I hear him call. "Son of the Most High."

I open my eyes to find him hidden at Awthoomgaw's right side. His sword has been broken, but he has wedged the hilt into the demon's skin.

"Hew the wing." The exhart yells. "Hew the wing."

I shake my head in utter terror as Awthoomgaw's right hand swings near me.

"All will be lost if you cower now. Finish the course." Deron cries. "Keep your faith. Do this to the glory of the kingdom. For the praise of him who is worthy. For the honor due him from first to the la—"

Awthoomgaw grips and crushes the stowaway, and the exhart's eyes widen in disbelief. The demon casts the broken corpse over his shoulder, and Deron descends behind us.

Two of our six have fallen, and to my dismay I know what I must do. However, I do not know how to do it. I am at a loss for any plan, and if I fail to obey Deron's order, we will be destroyed one-by-one.

With determined eyes, Tarak appears from Awthoomgaw's side and climbs toward me.

"I shall hold you in safety, child of God, but you must not hesitate or falter. Take your sword in both your hands, and hack at the wing until it is loosed. I will not let you fall."

"How can you promise that, good Tarak?"

"As we trusted you, trust The Lamb."

He takes my sword and stabs it through the wing tissue near the bone. Awthoomgaw screams and swipes at us, but we evade his grasp. To aid us, the others draw his attention to their position at his waist. Tarak returns my weapon, and I pierce the villain again. The amunamai ties the remains of cape through the hole in the enemy. He lies on his back, faces upward, and digs his heels into the demon's skin.

"I am strapped to him," he says, wrapping his arms around my ankles and holding to his own wrists. "I will not let you go. Rise now and strike."

"I can't."

"Rise and strike."

"No."

"I am not asking you to trust *me*; I am telling you to trust *him* who is worthy. Fear not. Be bold and courageous."

I nod, stand, and remove my sword from Awthoomgaw. Tarak maintains his grip round my legs. At the demon's waist, I see the others; they call to me to attack.

Far below us, beneath passing clouds, I glimpse other realms of Solsland. Calm lakes are settled within walls of stone; gentle flowers abide in lush fields. Rolling waves drift to a shoreline, and forests stand upon rising hills. But I also see pits and dried riverbeds, groves of dead trees and large heaps of chaff. Fires burn in a meadow and smoke plumes into the air. Other enemies exist in my soul.

Thoughts of elsewhere must be forgotten, for the demon of lust must fall first. Awthoomgaw has increased his speed; beating wings hit me with gusts of wind. I breathe while raising my sword above my head. My eyes fixed on his wing, I align my stroke.

"Show me your glory," I whisper.

I swing downward with conviction at the joint, and the shockwave reverberates through my arms. My blade did not pierce the skin.

"Show me your power," I say much louder as I land a second slice on the target.

"Shower me with your grace," I scream with a third stroke. "For am I undone—lost to a foe I cannot defeat." With this proclamation, a fourth desperate slash falls, and the demon's blood sprays into the air.

Awthoomgaw's wing stumbles, and he careens through the clouds. My body slams against his skin, but my legs remain secure. The demon hisses, grabs over his shoulder, yet I am out of reach. He spins in order to loose us, but we find our grip and stay. As he descends, he grazes a cliff, but his efforts are in vain.

Awthoomgaw levels on the air, giving his injury a respite. His flight now slowed, I see an opening, a final strike to end him. I am sure this gambit will fail, but I can think of nothing else. I recall the voice that calmed me as the demons charged the courtyard. 'Have faith in God,' it said.

With that in mind, I call to the guardian, "Tarak, Let me go."

"What? Why?"

"I'll show you."

Tarak releases me, and I rise and run against the wind. Dashing the length of the demon's back, I dig my sword into his wing. I run with the blade embedded, lacerating the appendage. At the end of the connection, I stab his back and halt. The sliced wing now attaches only at the joint I wounded earlier.

The strategy takes a moment to work, but the wind tears at the slash. As the tissue flails, the air rips the entire wing from Awthoomgaw's frame. The dismembered demon tumbles; the jolt loosens my sword from his skin. Blade in hand, I fly backward through the air.

A second jolt stops me in mid-flight, and I see a hand grabbing my belt—Klahan's hand. With one arm held to Awthoomgaw's hide and the other holding me, he grimaces before his finger loose their grip of the demon, and we find ourselves in flight once more.

I pierce the back of our enemy's leg, and my blade runs along his uneven skin until it anchors us at his calf. As the villain descends, we stay with him. I clutch my sword; Klahan holds my belt.

The ground gets closer. The demon hisses in fear. The wind tugs at my grasp and pulls at us. The plain is dark, gray, and barren. Awthoomgaw roars as he crashes into it.

The impact throws me forward and rips my blade from the enemy. I am tossed through the air, and pain erupts as I ricochet off his hide. The collision sends a cry from my throat when the last air leaves my lungs. Something snaps at my arm and my back, and I tumble onto the ground.

I do not know what has befallen the others, nor do I know if Awthoomgaw lives. My eyes open, and I find myself on the desolate plain. I chuckle in relief at my survival but realize something is wrong. I can move neither my arms nor legs nor anything below my neck.

A heavy tremor rumbles beneath me; a powerful presence shakes the ground. A demon whose wing was stolen from him rises several yards away. He looks to his left and his right for the escaped assailant. In frustration, he shakes his head. His back faces me and bears a great wound the full length of its left side. A river of unnatural green and orange flows from it and drips to the soil.

Awthoomgaw stops and sniffs at the air then grumbles as he looks over his shoulder. His white eye focuses on me as my own eyes widen in horror. The moment is brief but feels eternal. My journey has come to its end. I have made direct and irreversible contact with the enemy, and he is very angry.

20 : THE WASTELAND

Awthoomgaw turns toward me. Having his single eye find me was terrifying, but having both focused on me is worse. He can end this now if he chooses.

"Hey. Look here," a nearby voice yells.

I see Abdalla run toward the enemy. How the injured scout survived the crash I cannot guess. How he has the strength to run bewilders me more. But the most compelling aspect of his present state is how he charges toward his end with such abandon. He does not flinch as he speeds toward death. With a snarl, Awthoomgaw lifts his leg and stomps at the tiny challenger. Abdalla leaps out of the way then runs across the demon's path.

As the diakonae draws the enemy's attention, I am pulled backward along the ground. Klahan has grabbed my left arm, and Tarak has grabbed my right. They lift my limp frame from the barren surface, and the arayil cries in pain (also injured in the crash, I assume).

"Come now, heir of the kingdom," he barks. "You can aid us a little."

"I'm sorry, Klahan, but I can't. I have no feeling in my legs."

"Ridiculous. The sole reason you do not move is that you think yourself injured. If this realm is not bound by natural laws, then why force your body to be broken?"

He has a point. I do not need to experience injuries here the way that I would expect in the normal world. I know this, but he does not give me more time to process.

"Hurry, we must move."

I struggle to walk as the others lead. My armor is dented; my shield is damaged. I drag my sword behind me (it feels heavier now).

"Good. You are doing well," Tarak says.

"So, what made you decide to start talking?"

"I could always speak, child of God, but I had no need while the others lived. Once my voice became necessary, I used it."

I look back to Abdalla's contest with Awthoomgaw and see the villain raise his foot to strike. The diakonae lies twitching on the ground, and the demon watches him struggle for a moment. Our enemy then lands his killing stroke.

"Turn and watch where you are going," Klahan calls to me. "Seeing Abdalla's end will only wound your spirit."

I comply and face forward. Now we are three. Without sanctuary or any real chance of escape, we move across the deserted flatland. I do not know why we bother.

Some leader I have shown myself to be. All but three of us are gone, and we are in no condition to fight.

"His eyes are upon us," Tarak states. "Klahan, the task falls to you."

"I know it."

"No, Klahan," I plead. "We stay together."

"Alas, we cannot. I must draw his attention, for this is my final task: to buy you time."

"Time for what?"

He smiles and places his hand on my shoulder. "Time in order to finish your course and give praise and glory to him who is worthy."

"For to him is due honor from the first to the last."

"Funny thing," Klahan says as he heads toward the demon, "just when I start to like you, we are forced to part ways."

He smirks and runs toward the demon with Tarak's broken sword in hand. I now see that the armor at his back is crushed inward, stabbing him with each move of his upper body. Ignoring these injuries, he charges into battle, the last of the arayil.

"That blade cannot pierce Awthoomgaw," I tell the guardian.

"No, not his skin, but Klahan is skilled and shrewd in attack. He may yet find a way to strike. But we shall not see it; we must flee."

We turn our backs on the noble warrior, and I hear his war cry echo behind us. Despite my mental block demanding my legs remain injured, Tarak and I get some distance from the fray. The voice of the arayil carries over the plain as he condemns the "vile one" and "wicked servant." Within moments, his yelling ceases, and we know Klahan has passed from Solsland.

Tarak and I are the last to remain. All other servants of the kingdom are gone. The final angel lets out a sigh as we run.

"And now I must leave you, son of the Most High."

"And then what?" I ask.

"You do what you must. We were charged to aid you in this battle. Thus, we have."

"But my battle is not over."

"Our part in it is."

"I do not understand. Why has it come to this?"

"Because this is the way by which the king gets the most glory."

"But once you are gone, I will be alone, and I am too weak to defeat this great evil."

"I know."

"Then how can you leave?"

"Because I also know something you have forgotten."

"What?"

"That you never could defeat Awthoomgaw—not with forty-nine thousand and twice their number in reserve. He is too great for you or any one man."

I stop at this and catch my breath. "Then this was all for nothing?"

"No, it was for good."

"How?"

"I cannot tell you; my time is at hand. But you will know when you need to know." With that he looks to Awthoomgaw and then back at me to give his final command, "Look neither right nor left, but run. Run east toward the sun with all your strength."

"And what do I do when he reaches me?"

"Run."

I fail to obey; I watch. The final member of the forty-nine charges an enemy twenty times his size. The angel has no weapon, and his armor is in shambles. His cape is tattered; his helmet is lost, and he does all he can to catch Awthoomgaw's eye.

I turn to the east to follow his command, and the roar of the demon jolts my body to action. I sheath my sword and dash as quickly as my mind will allow, but in truth I feel as weak as I ever have (and more alone than I expected). My adrenaline wanes. Pain hits me. I should have known I could not win this battle. I cannot overcome this addiction. Tonight has delayed an inevitable fall, but it changes nothing.

A tremor runs through the ground and travels to my core. Awthoomgaw has come.

He steps over me and blocks my path. I stop and stare upward at him. Everything about the demon is overwhelming and awful—his size and appearance, his strength despite injury, his hatred for me and his longing for my fall. Of course I could never have defeated this villain. This exercise was a sojourn and a dream. I was beaten before I began; at least I tried, I suppose.

The demon leans toward me with a sinister grin. Inside his mouth lay countless, searing fangs with which he will tear me to pieces. His eyes meet mine, and he snarls with malice. I shed a tear at my defeat.

"I hate you," I tell him. "I hate you so much."

Awthoomgaw snarls, returning the sentiment.

"I know," I reply.

He grumbles, stamping his fist into the ground.

"You are angry at me?" I ask in retort, looking straight into his eyes with indignation. "*You* are angry at *me*? Why? Because I tore down your lair? Because I stabbed your heartless chest? Because I hacked off your wing, is that why? Huh? Is that why? Because that's nothing. Nothing.

"You—you," I am too enraged to think, but my words pour through my lips like raging water through a broken dam. "You took years of my life from me. You stole them. You drew me away from my Lord and pulled me into despair. You seduced and coerced and cajoled and harassed me. Night after night and day after day, you demanded my attention. You crushed me under your constant demands and bullied me until my will shattered.

"Angry at me—you are angry at me? No. I gave you passage. I let you linger. I let you take root here. This soul was bought and paid for with blood, but I kept letting you roam. I let you stay, but you were never satisfied—never content in the shadows. Never. You showed me no mercy and kept taking more—more time, more thought, more confidence, more joy. You begged and were fed, and you took, and you grew.

"Oh but you gave, too. Yes, you gave. You gave me self-hatred, self-loathing, and shame. You gave me anguish and all manner of guilt—badgering me for an inch then taking a mile while I would brood in self-contempt. You made me hate myself, and you loved every minute. You got everything you wanted, and you are angry at me?

"You are as spoiled and awful as I am. Maybe that is why I indulged you so long. But take note, Awthoomgaw: your rest here has ended. Do you understand me? You might crush me beneath your fist or swallow me whole in your hellish throat, but you will never again get passage here. I will not indulge you. Every day from this night until judgment, I will rage against you with all the hatred I can bear. I will hunt the pockets of lust in my soul, and I will strike with zealous fury. I know you now, and I fear you no more. You are a cancer upon my soul, no longer a tyrant that will sit unchallenged. Do you hear me, villain? Your time has passed. Send me away that I may show you my resolve."

Awthoomgaw's hue has shifted to red. Hatred burns in his eyes. He moves to kill me when his whole body stops, and his eyes shift to something behind where I stand. His face contorts. Focusing downward, he rises to his full height.

He roars into the air and swoops his arm to the ground. I close my eyes; my body tenses, and I brace for his crushing grip. I feel the heat from his hand emanate behind me, but in moments it is gone.

When I open my eyes, I see bright rays of light escape from a source in the demon's hand. Awthoomgaw lifts his claw to his face and opens it, releasing a great radiance into the air. The demon roars at the captive but turns his head from the blinding light.

I hear a cracking and glance down to find Awthoomgaw's legs have changed. The bold red heat beneath his stone skin has solidified to gray. The transformation continues up his torso, and I see that it has occurred at his arms. Awthoomgaw roars as his legs crumble under him, and his remaining wing snaps from his back. The shift in equilibrium sends his torso forward, and in moments, the huge demon implodes to rubble.

The hand holding the bright light stays intact as it falls several stories to the ground. In it stands The Lamb, white and unblemished, victorious and unharmed. I smile to him as he looks at me. He walks from the palm, and it shatters. The Lamb never lets my eyes leave his; he holds my gaze until he stands before me.

I fall to my knees and wrap my arms around him. I bow my head as I speak through my tears, "Thank you. Thank you. Oh, Lord Jesus, thank you. Praise your precious, holy name, for it is deliverance to those who believe. Ever do you rescue your servants from their despair."

"Despair?" A sinister voice asks.

I look up to find that The Lamb and I are not alone, for upon the remains of Awthoomgaw stands The Beast, charcoal-toned with crimson eyes and gritted teeth.

"You have not yet known despair," he tells me (and to be honest, I believe him). "Lust's power may be tempered in your soul for the moment, but you must bear the legacy of his presence. You must answer for the building of the citadel. You must answer for the breadth of this wasteland. You must answer for the sins of your youth. And once you do, you will know despair."

21 : THE BEAST

The Beast fixes his eyes on us as he moves down the broken form of Awthoomgaw. He walks with confidence and an air of superiority despite his disheveled and maimed appearance. Smaller stones burst into clouds of dust beneath his heavy steps, and his contempt for us is palpable as he reaches the bottom of the rubble.

The Lamb remains steadfast and unmoved, and I sense no fear in him. The emotion I gather is anger, a fierce wrath toward The Beast for his presence here. I cannot explain how I perceive this sensation, but the tension between these two forces is kinetic, as though their very coexistence breeds turmoil throughout this world.

“This one is mine,” The Beast says with a growl. “He may speak of you and your kingdom, but his heart belongs to me.”

These words do not come from his lips. He bears his teeth and snarls as he asserts his claims, but the sound seems to dart from his crimson eyes, which smolder as they stare at us. Smoke from his nostrils accompanies his words, and the smells of fire and burning flesh surround him.

The Lamb says nothing but places himself between the accuser and me.

"He is no fruit-bearer nor a sower of seeds," The Beast continues. "He is a selfish malcontent and a coward who shows no mark of your servants. He is, at best, an adequate actor but he only plays the role of the saint. As such he is a hypocrite and also a fool—not one of your dedicated would-be martyrs."

He begins to circle us as he continues, but The Lamb keeps in step and remains at a distance.

"Three falsehoods underlie condemnation," The Beast claims like a lawyer at trial. "Three desires lead your creation to reject you. Lust of the Flesh. Lust of the Eyes. The Pride of Life. This last was mine, and I live condemned. Not I alone, but those who followed me. For one of the three we are exiled from you.

"This one, however, has committed them all. Not in succession, not one-then-another. No. He is guilty of all at once. You know of what I speak, pure one. His actions and deeds may appear as one of yours but the heart of this man has revealed he is mine.

"Lust of the Flesh. Need I give you examples? You know well of his longing throughout his life. Since his childhood he has hoped for adulterous encounters."

I lower my head, and The Beast scoffs, "I see you know your depraved mind well." He pounces at us and snaps his jaws, but The Lamb stands unmoved. I step backward.

His physical attack thwarted, The Beast renews his verbal siege. "Consider his many past desires for the women around him—friends, friends' sisters, sisters' friends, friends' mothers—the wives of others—and teachers, bosses, classmates, and acquaintances. He wanted to use them, wanted to seduce them, wanted them for his own sinful ends. He longed to know them beyond what was righteous—he longed for their touch, their embrace, and more. You know this to be true of him. His mind and heart were carnal theatres. Day and night, he lusted, longed, and wronged with illicit, secret thoughts. He was a villain despite his deeds, for his fantasies alone were a den of debauchery."

I am feeling the shame of this trial. Knowing one's sins is difficult; hearing others reveal them aloud is devastating. Within the construct of another's description, an entertained thought has all the stain of an act. They say fantasy hurts no one but that cannot be the case, for something so ugly and foul must injure—if not the other person about whom it is crafted, at least the soul of one who thinks it (and the Creator, above all else). I hope this first diatribe was his strongest, but I know at my core that it is not. His next two will be more damning.

"Lust of the Eyes," The Beast continues. "Oh, how his eyes burned with sin. Observe the power the demon had; see how large this one's longing became. Awthoomgaw grew twenty times the strength that he might possess in the average man.

"Let us begin with the most obvious failing, that of letting his lust drive his sight. Nofayn had a long reach into his mind, and this one's eyes wandered, seeking opportunity and hoping for a glimpse of some sexual thing. He was not on watch for others in need, to help the lonely or aid the broken. His sight was zealous for the low-cut blouse or the slightest hint of indecent dress.

"And that is in public—need I remind you of the dark? His habit in seeking both pictures and more that the culture itself deems immoral and vulgar? His hall of Mykmun was tall and wide, and the archive within it was full. Remember the contents that he would sneak, the files he would hide in secret. Recall all of the sites that he would visit and the scenes that would be depicted therein.

"Think of the time he wasted in want. The hourglass was full. You gave him life, and he used it to sin, to spit in your face and disparage your cross.

"And this is only the lust toward sex. We ought not forget his covetous eyes toward endless goods for his own gratification—entertainments, games, garments, and gadgets. Time after time he looked and longed. He lusted for greater wealth than he needed. You blessed him with money, and he craved more treasures. Week after week your creation suffered, and he went about his way enriching himself, harvesting more material idols he knew to be empty but dulled his shame. He did not long for righteousness; he did not want your glory. His lust was for goods and for tangible prizes that he could buy, place into a box, and forget."

The Beast is not showing a hint of mercy. He is shaming me with all that he can. I am sweating more now than during any other contest, and I feel more broken than at any prior encounter.

"And, of course—of course—the Pride of Life. Is he not guiltier than I? Listen if you will to his list of accolades. First, his narcissistic delusion of thinking that he is above your other servants, as though you have a special design for him and that you orchestrate events for his good. He believes himself a great asset to your kingdom, one who will do great and wondrous things—not by your power but by his own."

"No," I cry, "I have not thought such things—"

"You cannot lie to us, boy," he growls, baring his teeth with contempt. "We see your heart. But if you decry this initial claim, then I will bring another. This coward who says he is your servant, who acts as though he loves you—his heart brims full of hate towards men, for he believes himself better than most. He fails to maintain your simplest decrees, yet he holds himself up as 'virtuous.' He claims to pray for the salvation of others while also longing to defeat them in dialogue. He thinks himself more handsome than some and hates those he feels more handsome than he. He covets his neighbors' homes and possessions, believing himself more worthy of their keep. He looks upon those with whom he disagrees as foolish, selfish, and arrogant. He derides the indulgent spending of others but creates systems of merit to allow it for himself. He feels he is owed blessing and praise from all as encourager, counselor, and aid—holding his false generosity as a badge of self-exaltation. He demands worship far more than I and looks for ways to gain it by ill, if needed."

The Beast snaps at us, but The Lamb does not grant him contact.

"You think this one is your servant, pure one? You think this one is not one of mine? Have you not heard all that I have said? Have you not considered the case against him? He is not a holy creature. He is not a noble man. He is a villainous, foul brigand, not unlike the Sadducees of old. Cast him from your presence now, for he belongs to the pit and to me. This is justice: that he should burn."

With this final burst The Beast lunges and is not rebuffed by the stance of The Lamb. He continues his assault, and my protector allows it, walking me backward and keeping the attacker at a distance. The Beast is too slow and thoughtless in his charge. The Lamb stares straight at him in constant resolve.

"The Lord knows who are his," The Lamb says. Like the accuser's, my savior's words come not from his mouth but from his piercing eyes.

The Beast roars and lunges, but The Lamb stomps his foot, and the ground trembles beneath it. The wool of the pure one begins to glow. My foe bats at his eyes and turns his head. He roars as he swats his front paw at my savior.

"All that the Father gives me will come to me," my protector claims, "and whoever comes to me I will never cast out."

The Lamb stomps his foot again and glows brighter. The Beast stumbles sideways. The Lamb stomps a third time and becomes more radiant than I have ever seen him before now. My enemy roars and tries to step toward us, but he cannot. The Lamb's light halts the devil's advance.

"I am the good shepherd," The Lamb says with his eyes fixed upon The Beast. "I know my own, and my own know me."

The Beast roars with such hatred that I step backward but do not fall. The Lamb responds by becoming so bright that I too must shield my eyes from him.

I then hear The Lamb yell, "Be gone, Satan."

My eyes closed, I hear a final snarl followed by fleeing steps. Realizing that the battle is lost, The Beast retreats from Solsland.

I open my eyes, and The Lamb turns to me.
"Resist the devil, and he will flee from you."

22 : THE SAVIOR

I fall to my knees and collapse toward the ground when The Lamb catches me upon his back. The exhaustion and pain from the quest have returned to the forefront of my mind. I know not how I stood versus The Beast and his assaults, given the beating I have taken. I should not have been able to stand at all. My body is shattered, and I rest on The Lamb. I weep.

"Thank you," I tell him. "Oh, Lord and Savior, thank you. Praise your holy name." His recent words ring in my ears—that I am 'his,' that he knows me, that I know him. "Thank you, Jesus, Holy Savior. Thank you for not casting me from your presence. Thank you for keeping and holding me. Thank you for loving me. Thank you for your grace, your kindness, and your compassion. Truly you are mighty. Truly you are pure. Truly you are worthy of all of my praise.

"Holy. Holy. Holy are you—a blessing to all who hear your voice, a boon to all who call your name. Blessed are you, my Lord and my God, my rock and my salvation. I love you."

My body may feel broken, but my shame has subsided. My fear is gone. Abiding in this place with The Lamb, I feel a deep swell of satisfaction, as though I was made for this. My spirit is now refreshed and renewed, and I have not but solace and joy in my heart.

Rays of sunlight strike fallow ground as the overcast sky begins to open. The sheet of gray breaks to soft tufts of white, and a bright blue expanse reveals itself behind them. The sun sits high in the east, and its warmth touches my tired face. The landscape of a serene and new morning takes shape.

Within the rubble of Awthoomgaw's form, a single flower blooms. A few other shoots crawl from the barren ground throughout the plain. Their healthy stems are green and bright, and they sprout small branches at their sides. All the vegetation seems to bend toward The Lamb as if paying homage to his majesty. He seems to nourish them more than the sun, for as they lean, they grow.

I pull away to make eye contact with The Lamb. I need to do more than thank him. I must apologize.

"Lord, you have delivered me despite my lack of virtue. I beg you for your forgiveness now, for I have allowed evil to endure in my soul when I should have purged it in pursuit of righteousness. Forgive me please for my great insult of being a man of contradictions, who praises you with his words but disobeys you with his eyes, who learns your commandments only to undermine them. You deserve a better servant, and in my own strength I am nothing.

"I am sorry for my addiction. I am sorry for the stronghold it formed. I am sorry for wasting the time you granted me, for using it to sin against you. I am sorry for treating your image-bearers as objects and failing to value others as your precious creations.

"I repent of allowing this evil to endure. I repent of pursuing sin instead of your glory. I repent of placing your creation ahead of you. Lord, please, forgive me now. Create in me a clean heart, O God, and renew a steadfast spirit within me, for I love you and long to know you more."

The Lamb looks into my eyes. "Be at peace; your sins are forgiven you."

I hug him once more and feel a breeze at my back. Behind him I see the wind move with purpose, for it carries the ash from this wasteland and clears the rocks from the plain. What began as soft and cooling air now becomes harsh and beats upon me, but once I see the effect it has, I do not mind the discomfort.

The rocks and depleted soil are expelled like dust is blown from a neglected shelf. Once the fallow layer is gone, the entire land has a new appearance. Lost is its gray and ashen face; instead an inviting surface spreads as far as my eyes can see. Deep brown topsoil covers the ground, and flowers of varied kinds grow on Awthoomgaw's grave. The shattered demon's form is now a tribute to this night, a picture of the beauty that follows evil's end.

I kneel to the ground and scoop a handful of the dirt. I sift it in my hands and rise. The soil bears a dark and healthy tone; its minerals will nurture and strengthen life. This is the earth one hopes to have, the kind that yields a bountiful harvest.

Before bounty, however, much work must be done. More seeds must be planted; the ground must be tilled. I look forward to all that will come—the trees, the plants, and the ongoing life. This part of my soul is no longer wasted, and I look over the plain with great anticipation. The land once dead has been redeemed, not by me but by the one who makes all things new. The Lamb has awoken and healed this land, and the ground is ready to be used.

The last grains of earth leave my hand, and I look down toward The Lamb once more. But he is moving elsewhere through his kingdom, and I am alone on this hopeful plain. He knows other strongholds require his attention. Perhaps they will not be as brazen as lust, but many more sins wait unchecked in the shadows. The Lamb moves against them in his time for his glory, and I realize tonight's quest in Solsland is complete.

I close my eyes.

EPILOGUE

And I open them in the real world.

The hour is late. 4:03 AM. And I stand relieved, rescued from a free fall.

The computer screen is blank on the opposite side of the room. I walk to the machine, and a voice whispers at the back of my mind, "Now you've earned it. Now go ahead. There is time before getting your sleep."

I tap the keyboard, and a search window appears with the cursor waiting in the input field. The temptation continues with its soft appeal, "You held out long, and you feel victorious. Reward your wearied mind and body."

'Feel victorious'? I find this temptation more annoying than appealing. I have no desire to 'feel victorious.' I want to *be victorious*. Embracing sin at this point feels absurd. Does the enemy think me so weak?

Of course he does. Maybe not at this moment. Maybe not today. But maybe in a month or a year from now. Maybe then I will listen. If he tempts me each day, then perhaps I will fall, if only to quiet his incessant noise. He knows that my resolve is only as strong as my love for the Lord, and he is reminding me that he will not stop.

And neither shall I. This battle was a single night of victory in a lifetime of failure. Much remains to be done in order to restore what was lost.

The stronghold's wreckage cannot stay intact. The debris must be ground to dust, and the remnants removed—the tunnels filled with concrete and the scaffolding burnt to ember. However that manifests itself in daily life, so shall my conduct be.

Likewise, the retaken lands cannot lay unguarded. New fortifications of good must be built; new havens of purity must rise. The fighting of the war will shift in the present—from singular assault to a focused defense in addition to the recapturing of more dark valleys. Other invaders must be chased from the kingdom; more fields must be renewed. I must dedicate myself to the reconstruction of righteousness, and I intend to do it as long as the Lord wills.

Scripture must be memorized. Truth must be digested. Help must be sought among the brethren. I must continue to learn from the counsel of others, to ensure that the stronghold is not rebuilt. I must also aid those in need of encouragement and assure them the battle can be won, that the Lord is good and he delivers his children through temptation when they seek his face. I must maintain vigilance in the pursuit of Christ Jesus, and I must do it for his glory, not my own.

Tonight was the beginning, for the war will continue when I awake from sleep tomorrow. By God's grace, I will hold the retaken valley. To The Lamb's glory, I will fight for it always. Through the Spirit's leading, I will be on my guard and assist others in their own battles through their own Solslands. The orchard of the new fields will bring forth a harvest, and this evening will not have been fought in vain.

I shut down the computer and leave the room. My eyes close as I make my way to my bed. As I lay upon it, I feel a great sense of peace. Despite all the days of war to come, I can sleep victorious tonight. Too many others have I laid here lamenting, begging forgiveness and feeling my failure. But not tonight. Tonight I can rest. Truly rest.

My final thought as I drift to sleep: all praise and glory to him who is worthy, for to him is due honor from the first to the last.

Amen.

APPENDICES

APPENDIX 1: ON SALVATION

I would be remiss if I did not disclose the following truth to the reader. While the story of *Stronghold* is fantasy, the love I have for Jesus Christ, personified by The Lamb, is real. As if you could not tell, right? I did my fair share of gushing, after all. But I must do more; otherwise I will have done you a great disservice. You see, I take great joy and pleasure in my relationship with Jesus Christ, and my hope and my desire is for each of you to experience that same fulfillment in and through him.

Perhaps a disclosure is appropriate.

I have wrestled with the inclusion of this appendix. In one hand I had the inherent desire to share the truth of Christ more clearly and fully than this narrative allowed. In the other, I had the code of the artist that demands art speak for itself, that anything in the form of an altar call is creatively repugnant. To be fair, I sympathize with this latter outlook, and up until a few years ago I would have held to it with a certain severity.

Over time, however, I have found it neither harmful nor foolish for artists to be forthcoming about their desires for their audiences; and as such, I have maintained this section in the book for one simple reason: I wish for you to have the same great love and joy of knowing Christ that I do.

If you do not know the truth of Christ's story, allow me to describe it briefly and explain its importance.

Jesus Christ was not merely a good teacher; in fact, his own teaching refuses the assignment of such a label. On the contrary, Christ claimed to be God himself, in the personhood of his son, in human flesh, entering into the narrative of humanity as one of its own, born into frailty and capable of evil, yet enduring the former without being guilty of the latter—the only human ever to accomplish such a feat. As he walked the dusty paths of the ancient world, Christ healed the hurting, encouraged the oppressed, gave hope to the broken, and condemned the hypocritical. Christ showed power over the natural realm as well as the spiritual one—rescuing people from forces of darkness and bringing them news of salvation.

This being his status, as God and man, Christ then gave his life willingly for all mankind, to reconcile them to God and cover over their wrongdoings with his loving righteousness. You see, Christ and those who learned from him knew full well that mankind operates at its core in a way contrary to God's design and desire. Whereas God created the world good, human beings rebelled against him and fell into a legacy of separation from him. Christ knew this, and he knew that men's hearts were evil to such a degree that they needed his divine intervention to be right with God. Thus, Christ underwent one of the most brutal punishments man has devised while also accepting the spiritual punishment man deserves. And he did all of this from love.

But that is not the end of the story, not if we are to believe the testimonies of reliable sources after the fact. Christ lived again—he did not merely survive; rather, he died fully, yet through divine power, he rose and assured his followers that his teachings were right and true. After doing so he returned to heaven, and he abides there until he will come to earth again, not only as Savior but also as king.

This is a powerful story—even more so because it is true. And what truth it is! How it changes everything to know that one is so incredibly in need of a savior and to know that one's creator served as that savior. We should not wonder why so many have died over the years before renouncing such a belief. When we accept and hold to such an anchor, why would we ever let it go?

But people have. People reject this idea all of the time. You may have done so to this point; you may still, but I long for your acceptance of it. Consider for a moment what Christ's story proposes: every man's soul is wounded at its core, but the one who created it has provided the means for its healing, and if you ask him, he will grant it. He offers it to us, and when we receive it and pursue him for the treasure that he is, he fulfills us day after day.

Can you tell that I believe it? Can you tell that it's real? Because it is. It is so real. Christ invites us to know him, to know our Creator and give him headship of our souls.

Perhaps an alternate idea is useful here. Imagine standing before God, pure perfection, when *he alone determines* the standard for what is worthy—not other people, not religious rules—but perfection himself. We cannot compare. We cannot make excuses. We cannot account for our lack of worthiness. But Christ can, and he will if we accept him as our Lord who saves us from our own sinful hearts.

Do you not see the beauty of this transaction? The Gospel is this: while we lived in our sin, almighty perfect God provided himself, through the person of Christ, as the means for us to come before him free from judgment.

Those who come before God humbly, who know their need for his pardon will receive it. They may come with words similar to the following: "I know, Lord, I am guilty before you. I put my faith in the grace of your son, in the one who loved you above all things and loved his neighbor, your creation, thereafter. I am only able to speak to you because you allow it, and all I can say is that I love Christ Jesus. I know I need him, and I know I need his gift of redemption. I surrender to his lordship and defer to him as my defender before you." And Christ will claim all those who are his. Savior. Deliverer. Sovereign and true.

Therefore, I beg you. I plead with you, dear reader. Let not the time spent in this book pass in vain. Consider your life; consider who Christ is and what he said. Accept your need for deliverance. In him you will find it. Believe on him, and true belief will yield repentance, repentance will lead to life-altering behavior, and life-altering behavior will lead to fruitful and eternal significance before a Holy Lord. This is your hope. Truly, it is the hope of all mankind.

But do not simply take my word for it. Read Christ's story for yourself in the Holy Bible. I recommend reading John 1:1-18, Luke 1:5-2:52, the book of Mark through Chapter 16:8, and then closing with Matthew 28 and John 21:25. Frankly, I am commending the reading of Mark because it is my favorite of the gospels, and I am bookending it with the other passages for the sake of creating a more dynamic picture than Mark will provide by itself. Any individual read of any gospel is excellent, but the full story of Christ is seen when they are taken in conjunction. Also, once finished with these passages, I invite you to look at Colossians 2:15-21, wherein the Apostle Paul, who God called to ministry following Christ's resurrection, provides a brief commentary on Christ's significance. If you do not have a Bible, numerous versions are available online, and any local church that you visit to request one should oblige you (if they don't, let me know).

I write these things because I want to spend eternity worshipping the Lord with each of you. If you have read this book, you have seen into my soul, and you can surmise I am the last person "worthy" of salvation, but that is the beauty of who Christ is and all that he can do for the wretched. I hope to see you in his heavenly kingdom.

APPENDIX 2 : ON ADDICTION

Stronghold is not true—not in the sense that I wish it were. The vanquishing of lust is an empowering concept, but it is not the truth of addiction. I have never been so naïve to think that one evening of imaginative, heart-exploring self-expression could undo sixteen years of adulterous habits. The power of addiction is greater than that.

I would not want anyone reading this book to assume my struggle ended the night this story first developed. Yes, I went through an imaginative process by which I chose to fight sin rather than embrace it, but the evening was taxing, and the hour was late. The very next morning I had to make a conscious choice to leave the computer shut down when I woke, for I knew my diminished sleep would make me vulnerable to temptation. The Christ-exalting quest of the prior evening was another step on a long and difficult road of recovery, not the finish line at the end of a race. The memory of that victory is a wonderful gift of the

Lord, but it did not end the journey of repair. In some ways it was only the turning of a corner.

Therefore, I accept that this area of my life requires vigilance. The power of lust is not always at the same strength, and the temptation of pornography is no longer a daily occurrence for me, but the devil is cunning and aware of my weakness, and I believe he will use that knowledge against me. This is my reality, and I want to share it with you.

Addiction is a strange thing. It is the essence of doing what one does not want to do and not doing the things that one wants to do (Romans 7). Had someone asked me several years ago to describe my relationship to pornography, I would have probably answered like this: "I do not want to fall but I cannot stop myself. I want to be disciplined, but I cannot find the strength. I set controls in place but I circumvent them and add a new dimension of thrill seeking to the habit. I trick myself into thinking the best release from my tension is the very behavior that I know is causing it." Isn't that the worst part of it all? I embraced my addiction, and for a moment felt free though I knew I was falling further into bondage.

I know that's how it is for some of you. It's your reality, like it was mine.

What do we do now? How do we fight? How do we walk on the long, narrow road when we feel that restraint is the burden and sin is salvation? Well, I have a few ideas and a handful of practices that have worked in my life and may work in yours also.

That being said, I want to start the discussion by inviting you to look at your own life. Are you at a place wherein you cannot imagine a day without a given indulgent behavior? Do you ever notice that the thought of said behavior occupies a great deal more of your mind than you want it to? Have you ever tried to stop the behavior and found you could not?

The following is a good litmus test: if you have attempted to stop a behavior but have been unable, you can consider it a habit. If you have attempted to cease this practice more than once, specifically because it has unfavorable outcomes, yet each time you return to it, then you can consider it an addiction, especially if it meets a perceived need that you have developed. All manner of behavior can become addictive, and those unhealthy behaviors we want to stop but cannot are addictions that one could also picture as strongholds in the soul.

What does one do if they identify an addiction? To those readers who do not believe in Jesus Christ as their source of salvation, I can offer you little help. Truly, my heart breaks in saying such a thing, for I wish I could be of more immediate assistance to anyone who wants to fight this battle. Unfortunately, I cannot separate the process from Christ. I believe that every human being on this planet is born with a desperate need for a Savior; without him, all hope for complete deliverance is lost.

This does not mean many valuable programs do not exist. A great variety of substance abuse and addiction recovery methods have proven successful in overcoming and altering behavior for thousands of people. I do not intend to denigrate the usefulness of those programs or methods, in the least. They are wonderful resources that may be an essential component of recovery for some individuals.

But my process has been wholly dependent on my faith and relationship with Jesus Christ. I do not know how to fight this war without him. Any attempts I made to overcome apart from him were unsuccessful. And even so, as a believer who has recognized his sin and repented of it, I engage in a difficult journey still—the day-to-day task of choosing Christ above all, including the sin that has driven me to him. This is an insurmountable job for my human will, and I would never tell anyone that I believed I did this without the grace of Christ and manifestation of his Holy Spirit.

Yet even in Christ, we may fall from time to time. We may return to habitual behavior (I know I have in the past), but to love Christ is to pursue righteousness and holiness. Thus, we must renew our cause again each day. This will be an ongoing process and, as such, will require patience. You will need to plan accordingly to wage this war. These are methods of recovery that I know to have worked (and, in my case, continue to):

1. *You must have good, Christian friends of the same gender to whom you can be accountable for your addiction.* These individuals must be trustworthy and must keep your confidence without gossiping. They must be willing to walk with you in both dialogue and prayer—the latter of which is an integral part of recovery, for it returns the focus to Christ and enables you to re-assess your temptation in light of his glory, not merely your perceived need. These individuals will be your 'true-to-life forty-nine,' who will fight alongside you for your deliverance. Given the degree of your addiction, they may recommend resources and programs, and you should take their counsel seriously. Whereas your perception of your own issue may be skewed, they can be more objective and recognize the severity of your struggle in ways you cannot.

2. *Commit to contacting these individuals if you find yourself tempted to embrace your sin.* You may text them or leave them

a message, but you must express that you are being tempted and *own* that reality. For example, you might call and say "I want to commit 'x,' and I am afraid I will. Please pray for me." It is that simple. Depending on your relationship with the person, he or she may go to the Lord on your behalf immediately with you on the phone or may ask you to get together. Because your partners want to aid you, you should be mindful of their requests in regard to actions and next steps, even if you do not want to do them.

3. *Contact your accountability partner after the temptation has passed or if you failed to call them earlier and have fallen.* You may feel that you are a bother, but if your accountability partner loves you as a Christian sibling, they will not see you as a nuisance at all. Rather, they will be joyous with you in your victories and heartbroken with you in your defeats, and they will want to know of both. Trust them in this, and maintain honest communication.

4. *Take the offensive through prayer, reflection, study, and Scripture memorization.* In battling addiction, the default setting for most individuals tends to be defensive. I find this unhelpful after a certain point. The realization that you are an addict or engaged in habitual sinful behavior can lead to an initial amount of healthy fear in regard to your environment, but this fear should not be your final emotional connection to your sin. Christians are sealed with God himself in the form of the Holy Spirit, and we have mighty power in that—power far greater than we can imagine. Furthermore, God assures us that he will not allow us to be tempted beyond what we can bear. In time, you must come to know that your identity is not "addicted" but "redeemed," and you can thrive with the reasonable expectation that you will be victorious in this

fight. Pause and reflect on that thought. Read texts that will encourage you in that truth and provide additional tools to combat your sin. Memorize Scripture to recall in times of trouble. For me, one of the most powerful passages is 2 Corinthians 10:3-4, which was recommended by my own accountability partner and reads as follows:

> For though we walk in the flesh, we do not war according to the flesh. For the weapons of our warfare *are* not carnal but mighty in God for pulling down strongholds,

Scriptures such as this one can be brandished as a spiritual sword versus the evil one and his minions. They fear God, and they loathe hearing his word.

In addition to studying Scripture, pray for deliverance and be willing to break down during said prayers. I have been to the point of weeping and tearing my shirt from my body, beating my chest, begging for God to deliver me, and in those hours, he did so. In fact, I cannot recall a time wherein my prayers of desperate brokenness did not end in beautiful victory. This is not a guarantee that if you say, "God, I don't want to do it," you will be delivered; however, when you come before the Throne of Grace in eager need and longing for help, God does not turn his children away wanting.

One can also avoid temptation before it begins by evading situations that lead you to sin. This proactive step against my addiction has taken the following forms: planning a get-together with others to ensure I would not be alone, performing a fitness routine to deplete me of the time and energy to embrace my addiction, undertaking a significant activity that focuses my attention and distracts from temptation (reading a novel or watching a film, etc.). Boredom usually leads the mind to wander, and boredom can be fought in various ways.

5. *Finally, consider the long term in your fight.* What will it mean five years from now when you have not given into your addiction? Consider the testimony you will have. Consider how your relationships will deepen. Consider how you will feel about not only yourself but also Christ Jesus who delivered you. Embrace those distant rewards and long for them. Crave them. In time, you will come to want them more than the fleeting pleasure of your addiction, and you will come to be overjoyed with righteousness.

The Spirit blesses you with these attitudes, and once he does, be willing to serve others and help them in their struggle. Perhaps it will be different than yours; perhaps it will be similar. Regardless, your journey of seeking Christ and denying yourself will be the testimony another needs to hear. One of the most beautiful facets of the Christian family is that we are all at different points in our walks with God. As he deepens the faith of one member, he calls another to begin believing. We need to seek one another and find each other, that we may grow the kingdom of God together.

Be strong and of good courage, dear reader. The life of recovery is not only one of vigilance but also one of assurance in Christ, for he shows himself vividly and clearly and consistently to those who pursue him and seek his deliverance.

APPENDIX 3 : ETYMOLOGY OF SPIRIT BEINGS

THE FORTY-NINE**
(Alphabetical by Class)

ARAYIL (Ah-rye-eel) – OFFENSIVE WARRIORS
From the Hebrew, 'ayil (ah'-yll), meaning "strong man"
1. Adofo (Ah-dough-foe)
2. Armand (Ar-mahnd)*
3. Bowen (Bow-in)*
4. Gavrill (Gahv-reel)
5. Klahan (Klah-hahn)
6. Prewitt (Proo-it)*
7. Rylie (Rye-lee)*

CHAR-RASHA (Car-ra-shah) – SMITHS

From the Hebrew, charash (khaw-rawsh'), meaning "artisan" or "craftsman"

1. Arif (Ah-reef)
2. Boone (Boon)*
3. Cutler (Kuht-ler)
4. Emmett (Eh-mit)
5. Fabrizio (Fah-breeze-ee-oh)*
6. Ferris (Fair-ihs)
7. Nirav (Knee-Rahv)*

DIAKONAE (Dee-ahk-own-eye) – SCOUTS

From the Greek, diakonos (dee-ak'-on-os), meaning "servant," "waiter," or "deacon"

1. Abdalla (Ahb-doll-uh)
2. Dashawn (Dah-Sean)
3. Elkan (El-Kahn)*
4. Ivan (Eye-vun)
5. Laszlo (Laz-low)
6. Makaio (Mahk-eye-oh)
7. Toby (Toe-bee)

EXHARTS (Ehx-Harts) – TRAINERS

Combination of the English, "exhort" and "heart"

1. Cais (Kay)*
2. Chimelu (She-may-low)*
3. Deron (Der-ahn)
4. Illias (Ee-lie-us)*
5. Mateo (Muh-tay-oh)*
6. Saku (Sah-koo)
7. Thane (Thain)

RAHFAAD (Raw-fahd) – MEDICS

From the Hebrew, rapha' (raw-faw'), meaning "to heal"

1. Avidan (Ah-vee-dahn)*
2. Clement (Kleh-ment)
3. Evan (Ehv-uhn)
4. Gakuto (Gah-koo-tow)
5. Jadon (Sha-don)
6. Lazzaro (La-zah-row)*
7. Vashon (Vah-shown)*

ZAQUENAN (Zaw-kweh-non) – ELDERS

From the Hebrew, zaqen (zaw-kane'), meaning "elder"

1. Agyei (Ahg-jay-ee)
2. Alden (All-den)
3. Cato (Kay-tow)
4. Gyan (Juhn)
5. Manuel (Mah-nwel)
6. Si (See)
7. Viho (Vee-Hoe)

AMUNAMAI (A-moo-nahm-eye) – GUARDIANS

From the Greek, amunomai (am-oo'-nam-ahee), meaning, "to ward off" or "to defend"

1. Alexavier (Al-ex-ayv-ee-ur)
2. Alastair (Ah-lus-stair)
3. Argus (Are-gus)*
4. Edmund (Ed-mund)
5. Ganit (Gah-neat)*
6. Greer (Greer)*
7. Tarak (Tah-rock)

*Unnamed in text.

** Each angel's name was chosen specifically for its meaning as well as its ethnic origins in order to create a diverse host of heaven. While I would have liked to include these particulars, all efforts to reach the copyright holders of said information were unsuccessful.

THE DEMONIC HORDES

(In order of first appearance or mention, by location)

CHAPTER 1: THE CELLAR

MOKMAH (Moke-mah) – Demon of Temptation

A combination of two words, moichos (moy-khos'), from the Greek, meaning "an adulterer," and machmad (mahk-mawd'), from the Hebrew, meaning "desire"

RA'SHROG (Ruh – shrog) – Demon foot soldier

Amalgamation finding roots in the English word "ogre" and Hebrew nouns ro'sh (roshe), meaning "gall" or "venom," and resha' (reh'-shah), meaning "wickedness" or "guilt," as well as the Hebrew adjective ra' (rah'), meaning "bad"

CHAPTER 2: THE PLAINS OF SOLSLAND (Members of the Armored Patrol)

SYCOMA (Sik-oh-mah) – Demonic probe

From the Greek word omma (om'-mah), meaning "an eye," with the phonetic sound similar to "sick" affixed to its front

CRON (Krohn) – Demon scout

This term simply sounded appropriate for a smaller devil or evil creature similar to "goblin" or "orc"

BAQOSH (Bahk-ohsh) - Mechanical suit driver *

From the Hebrew verb baqash (baw-kash'), meaning "to seek" or "to find"

NEFQAHAN (Nehf-kah-hahn) – Giant demon sentry
Amalgamation of the Hebrew nouns for "giant," naphiyl (nef-eel'), and "spear," qayin (kah'-yin)

CHAPTER 6: THE DISTANT EASTERN VALLEY
AGRA (ah-grah) – Loitering demon
From the Greek verb argeo (arg-eh'-o), meaning "to linger"
GEHOOND (geh-hund) – Demon ruffian
From the Hebrew noun gaduwd (ghed-ood'), meaning "marauding band"
AWTHOOMGAW (Awe-thuhm-gau) – The Demon of Lust
From the Greek epithumia (ep-ee-thoo-mee'-ah), which can mean "lust," "longing for the forbidden," or "craving," as well as the Hebrew agabah (ag-aw-baw'), meaning "lustfulness"

CHAPTER 7: OUTSIDE THE TABERNACLE
YAOSH (Ya-ohsh) – Demon of Despair
From the Hebrew phrase ya'ash (yaw-ash'), meaning, "It is hopeless"
EXPOREX (Ex-pour-ex) – The poisonous worm
From the Greek verb exaporeomai (ex-ap-or-eh'-om-ahee), meaning "to renounce all hope"

CHAPTER 10: THE MOUNTAIN
STRADAIN (Strah-dane) – Flying demon warrior
From the Greek noun daimonion (dahee-mon'ee-on), meaning "evil spirits" and "ministers of the devil," as well as the Greek verb strateunomai (strat-yoo'-om-ahee), meaning "to do military duty, service, or make war"
VHULRAK (Vhool-rock) – Flying demon scout
From the Hebrew term racham (raw-khawm'), meaning "carrion vulture," and the English term, "vulture"

CHAPTER 12: THE HALLS OF MYKMUN

ZATEARK (Zah-t-airk) – Demon clerk *

From the Greek verb zateo (zay-the'-o), meaning "to seek in order to find"

SYOLENSE (See-oh-lenz) – Demon sharpshooter *

Phonetic re-tooling of the English word, "silence"

CHAPTER 13: THE PLAINS FROM MYKMUN TO THE FORTRESS

NOFAYN (No-fah-een) – Demon of the Wandering Eye

Combination of the Hebrew noun 'ayin (ah'-yin), meaning "eye," and the Hebrew verb na'aph (naw-af'), meaning "to commit adultery"

MOICUON (Moy-ku-on) – Demon Guardian of Nofayn *

From the Greek word moicheuo (moy-khoo'-o), meaning "to commit adultery"

CHAPTER 14: THE STRONGHOLD: MOAT

RABPONRAH (Ra-pohn-rah) – Demon of the waste *

From the Greek adjective poneros (pon-ay-ros), meaning "evil," and the Hebrew verb ra'eb (raw-abe'), meaning "to be voracious"

TOLRAPONS – Demonic worms in the moat *

From the Greek adjective poneros (pon-ay-ros), meaning "evil," and the Hebrew noun for "worm," towla' (to-law')

CHAPTER 17: THE STRONGHOLD: COURTYARD

NEFCOVEK (Nehf-koh-vehk) – Demon giant who covets (felled by forces at the citadel wall)*

NEFCOLLT (Nehf-kolt) - Demon giant who collects (killed by The Believer in courtyard)*

Both names influenced by the Hebrew word for giant, "nephiyl (nef-eel')." Suffixes "covek" and "collt" used for phonetic similarity to the words from which they are taken: "covet" and "collect," respectively

GEBELAYAL (geh-beh-lie-ull) – Demon royal guards to Awthoomgaw
Taken from the two Hebrew words, beliya'al (bel-e-yah'-al), meaning "wicked" and geber (gheh'-ber), meaning "warrior"

CHAPTER 18: ON AWTHOOMGAW

MEORAB (May-or-awb) – "The Bitter Archer," Demon archer in Awthoomgaw's left hand *
From the Hebrew nouns merorah (mer-o-raw'), meaning "bitter thing," and rab (rab), meaning "archer"
MEORACH (May-or-awk) – "The Bitter Spear," Demon sentry at Awthoomgaw's chest *
From the Hebrew nouns merorah (mer-o-raw'), meaning "bitter thing," and romach (ro'makh), meaning "lance"

*Unnamed in the text.

AFTERWORD

All the characters and situations within the story of *Stronghold* are representations stemming from my own creative choices; they are neither meant to express the true reality of the spiritual realm nor serve as a text on theology. I commend to the reader the Holy Bible and discussion within his or her local church body for more insight into the ideas presented in this text.

That being said, I hope that this narrative was valuable to you. My goal in writing it has always been that you are drawn closer to loving God and valuing Christ as your most trustworthy deliverer, not only in spiritual temptation but in all things.

Thanks for reading,
C.J.

19559368R00165

Made in the USA
Charleston, SC
31 May 2013